PRAISE FOR THE FIRST NOVEL IN
THE JEWELL COVE SERIES

The House on Blackberry Hill

"Wonderful, witty, and memorable . . . A heartwarming, delightful debut to an engaging new series. Readers will love discovering the richly layered stories and enticing secrets residing in Jewell Cove."

—*New York Times* bestselling author Shirley Jump

"A wonderful story with plenty of sizzle and the perfect hint of mystery. Donna Alward writes with emotion and heart."

—RaeAnne Thayne, *New York Times* bestselling author of *Willowleaf Lane*

"Donna Alward writes warm, memorable characters who spring to life on the page. Brimming with old family history, small-town secrets, and newfound passion, you'll want to pack up and move to Jewell Cove, Maine!"

—Lily Everett

Treasure on
Lilac Lane

DONNA ALWARD

St. Martin's Paperbacks

This is a work of fiction. All of the characters, organizations, and events portrayed in this novel are either products of the author's imagination or are used fictitiously.

TREASURE ON LILAC LANE

Copyright © 2014 by Donna Alward.
Excerpt from *Summer on Lovers' Island* copyright © 2014 by Donna Alward.

For information address St. Martin's Press, 175 Fifth Avenue, New York, NY 10010.

ISBN: 978-1-250-04517-1

Printed in the United States of America

St. Martin's Paperbacks edition / November 2014

St. Martin's Paperbacks are published by St. Martin's Press, 175 Fifth Avenue, New York, NY 10010.

10 9 8 7 6 5 4 3 2 1

ACKNOWLEDGMENTS

With many thanks to my brilliant and very patient editor, Lizzie, for having the vision to see the forest for the trees and for knowing exactly what to do to make this story shine. You're absolutely right: Teamwork does make the dream work. You rock.

Special thanks to my family for persevering while Wife and Mom worked on this book during summer break. Thank you for taking on the onerous chore of enjoying the pool on my behalf, keeping the sunscreen industry in business, and for putting up with barbecued hot dogs more than you should have. I love you guys.

For Barb, Fiona, Wendy, Julia, Abbi, Jenna, and Jenn— my writing buddies who kick my butt and hold my hand and write alongside me, all in equal measure. You're the best.

CHAPTER 1

Jess Collins hated funerals.

She avoided attending when she could, though in a close-knit town the size of Jewell Cove, that wasn't easy. When she found herself in these types of situations, she often offered condolences and got away as fast as she could.

Funerals brought back too many painful memories. Too many reminders of a time when life started to unravel. As a teenager, losing her father had been the worst thing she'd ever experienced. How she'd handled her grief, however, had led to something far more traumatic. Something she could never forget no matter how hard she tried.

The crisp breeze blew a strand of her hair into her lip gloss, and she tucked it back behind her ear. Today was about more than neighborly politeness. Rick Sullivan was a close friend of the family, and as much as she was annoyed with him, she owed it to him—and to his mother—to stay for Roberta's funeral and interment at the Jewell Cove Cemetery.

Maybe Rick had gone off the rails lately. Maybe she didn't approve of his choices. But once upon a time they'd been close. He'd been at her house more often than at his own, it seemed, hanging with her big brother, Josh, and her cousins Bryce and Tom. Rick had been one of the family. And one moonlit night on the beach he'd very nearly been more.

Rick had also served in the Marines, and bore the scars to prove that service to his country was no cakewalk. She couldn't help but notice his prosthetic hand beneath the cuff of his dark gray suit, both the appendage and the clothing looking out of place on a rough-around-the-edges man like Rick . . .

And so here she was, standing with her sister and brother and cousins, part of a united show of support, while the autumn wind buffeted her navy skirt and the scent of funeral flowers mingled with the unique, musty aroma of fallen leaves and late September sunshine.

Roberta Sullivan's fight with cancer had been very different from the accident that had claimed Jess's dad, Frank, who'd been lost at sea when his fishing boat capsized in a storm. Jess's family hadn't had any time to prepare, just numbing shock and then the terrible weight of dealing with a funeral without a body. Suddenly Jess's whole world had been turned upside down. She'd lost much more than a parent, she'd lost her greatest confidant and best friend.

Pushing away her own memories of grief, Jess looked at Rick, noticing the haggard lines around his eyes, the strained tightness of his cheeks, and knew what he was going through. Yes, he was a grown man and not a child as she'd been when she'd lost her father. And maybe Roberta had had a little time to say good-bye. But losing a parent was losing a parent. It was painful no matter the circumstances, and the cancer had been aggressive. It had only been a few months between her diagnosis and her death. Jess still had the blessing of her family around her. Rick had no one now.

Her heart ached at the thought. Still, knowing Rick, he'd handle his grief by heading to The Rusty Fern right after the burial, in a pathetic attempt to forget his troubles by drowning them with whatever his favorite drink happened to be. She didn't imagine he was too choosy.

With a sigh Jess turned her attention back to the gravesite in front of her. No matter how much she sympathized with Rick, his drinking was something she didn't want anything to do with. And so she stared at the casket, feeling a heavy grief for things that couldn't be changed, and sad that the laughing boy she'd once known no longer existed.

And neither did the carefree girl.

She came.

Rick stole a glance at Jess Collins and tried to ignore the pain that squeezed his heart and made it hard to breathe, the constant feeling like the very last thing holding him together had just been snatched away, leaving him defenseless and alone. His mom had been the only reason he'd come back home to Maine at all, and now she was gone. He was alone. Completely and utterly.

But Jess was here, her black curls tumbling over her shoulders, her sharp gaze softened now with compassion, her plump lips unsmiling. His best friend's sister, and even though her deep blue eyes were currently filled with pity, he knew that under normal circumstances, she would be spitting nails just being in the same room with him. Jess didn't even try to hide her disapproval or disdain these days.

Half of Jewell Cove had been at the service, but now only a handful surrounded the gravesite, dark skirts and somber ties ruffling in the stiff autumn breeze. Other than himself and the minister, he considered the assembled group the closest thing he had to family: Meggie Collins; Pete and Barb Arseneault, and their collective children; Bryce and Mary; Tom and Abby; Josh; Sarah and her husband, Mark; . . . and Jess.

Despite Jess's apparent opinion of him, he wasn't surprised to see her here. Jess had loved his mother, too, and the Collinses were like his second family. What he hadn't expected was for her to look at him with such compassion. Even if she did stay as far away from him as she could. Jess was good at that. Almost as if she didn't want any of him to rub off on her.

He wished he didn't care one way or the other.

The taste of regret was bitter in his mouth. So much regret. He knew he'd disappointed Jess. Disappointed so many people . . .

He swallowed past the lump in his throat and tried to focus on the spray of roses and calla lilies blanketing the top of the casket. He knew the one he'd disappointed most was his mom. The one person who'd never given up on him since he came back from Afghanistan, less of a man than when he left. She'd never given up faith or hope that things would get better. His mom, the optimist. Even when she'd been fighting for her life, she never gave up on him.

She'd been braver than he ever hoped to be.

Rick choked back the grief inside of him. He couldn't imagine life without his mom's warm smile and constant support. Hell, he'd give anything just to have her nag him about his bachelor lifestyle one more time. But instead he was standing here in the chilly wind, willing himself to hold on.

Even standing with the Collinses and the Arseneaults he felt alone. Rick had known he was adopted since he was seven years old, though he'd never shared that knowledge with a single soul. At the time he'd had questions, but soon after that his father had left them and all Rick and Roberta had was each other. Over the years she'd always let him know that if he wanted to find his biological family, she'd help him. She'd especially pushed it when she'd received her diagnosis, insisting that he shouldn't be alone, but he'd merely kissed her cheek and repeated the same thing he'd told her his whole life. That she was his one and only mother. He'd never meant anything more in his life.

The casket was lowered into the ground, the sound jarring against the peaceful backdrop of leaves rustling and birds chirping from the nearby rosebushes, which had long ago lost their blooms and now held clusters of reddish-pink rose hips. God, he could use a drink. Just a shot or two of rye to steady him out. Shit. His hand started shaking just thinking about it. The sharp fire of it on his tongue, the soft, smooth glide of it down his throat, the warmth of it spreading through his belly.

Tears stung his eyes and he blinked them away. His mom had made him promise one last thing before she died, and though he wished she'd asked anything else of him, he wouldn't let her down. Not this time. It had been days since his last drink. All through the time she'd been in the hospice, and for the last few days as arrangements had been made. Josh and Tom had taken turns checking on him as if they didn't trust him. They knew what Rick knew: promising his mother that he'd stay off the bottle was an impossible promise to keep. But damn if he wouldn't do the impossible for her this one last time.

"Richard?"

The mellifluous voice of the minister reached Rick and he lifted his head, confused. Reverend Price was holding out a spade; it was time for the ceremonial shovelful of dirt on the casket.

He could really use that drink.

He took a step forward, then another, took the spade in his right hand as he approached the hole in the earth. Teeth clenched, he anchored his prosthetic hand on the top of the shovel handle.

Goddammit to hell.

Scooped up a bit of dirt and dropped it, the sound a hollow rattle on the top of the box, meaning nothing.

Goodbye, Mom . . .

He handed the shovel back to Reverend Price, but he couldn't go back to his spot. Couldn't wait for the ceremony to end, couldn't bear to shake everyone's hand or see their long faces or hear the sympathetic words. He turned around and kept walking, through the maze of headstones, over the soft grass to the dirt lane that wound through the small cemetery on the hill. And he didn't stop until he reached his beat-up old truck.

He couldn't think right now. Couldn't imagine anything beyond the excruciating pain of knowing that he was finally, absolutely alone.

He was stuck with no one but the man in the mirror. And that man was not someone Rick cared to spend much time with.

CHAPTER 2

Jess sat behind the cash register, her hands busy with knitting needles and a ball of super-soft pale yellow yarn. Foot traffic was slow this morning at her store, and it gave her time to work on the blanket she'd started knitting way back in June.

Summer in Jewell Cove was always busy—a frenetic crush of tourists descending on the pretty seaside town for whale boat tours, sea kayaking, and lying on the beach. The waterfront was generally crowded on sunny days—kids begging for an ice-cream cone from Sally's Dairy Shack, families taking over the picnic tables on the grassy fringes with platters of fish and chips or lobster rolls from the Battered Up canteen. On Thursday nights in August, a local drama group put on Shakespeare in the Park at Memorial Square, in the shadow of the statue of Edward Jewell, the town's founder.

It was Jess's most lucrative time of year, too, and for the most part she loved it. Her store, Treasures, was always bustling with people looking for handmade local items. She enjoyed meeting them, listening to different accents, learning where they were from. She enjoyed the long days of sunshine, the way the sun sparkled off the water of the bay, and the crazy riot of blooms that happened up and down Main Street. Window boxes and planters were always a profusion of petunias, geraniums, impatiens, and trailing lobelia.

But she loved this time of year, too—late September, right before the leaves turned into a glorious kaleidoscope of color. It was like a brief oasis of calm between the busy seasons of summer and autumn. The air cooled, and the front stoops were decorated with the more hardy potted mums. The gardens let go of their brazen summer hues and settled into the more sedate colors of asters and goldenrod.

The fall lineup of workshops she held at the back of the store would start in another week or so. Then there was the quilting club at the church, where she coordinated different projects for the quilt show in the spring, which in turn made a fair bit of money for the women's group and attracted visitors from all along the midcoast. When winter arrived, Jess could really focus on her first love—creating many of the items that graced her store shelves. Beaded jewelry, soaps, scented candles, felted articles. But for now, she was enjoying the time to herself before all the leaf watchers descended en masse to admire the fall colors in Jewell Cove.

Her first project was to finish the soft blanket she'd begun when she'd found out her sister, Sarah, was pregnant, then put aside when Sarah miscarried. It felt wrong to have those stitches sitting on the needles, incomplete.

Jess planned to finish it and pack it away. When the time was right, she'd pass it on to someone. She figured she'd know when. And who. Life was funny that way.

Besides, maybe she could save it for her almost cousin-in-law, Abby. Abby Foster had inherited the legendary Foster mansion up on Blackberry Hill and in a few short months had managed to steal the heart of the town's most eligible bachelor, Jess's cousin Tom. Jess was particularly happy for them. Both of them had had their share of heartbreak, but Abby was perfect for Tom. Abby had fit right in with their family and felt like another sister. It was hard to believe she hadn't always lived in Jewell Cove. Jess figured they might not wait too long to start a family of their own.

The door to the shop opened, bringing with it a gust of sea air. *Speak of the devil,* Jess thought with a smile.

"Morning, Jess." Abby smiled brightly. As of course she would. Her wedding to Tom was only a few weeks away.

"Hi, Abs. What brings you by this morning? Say muffins. Please."

Abby lifted a bag of muffins. "Straight from the bakery. Raspberry cream cheese."

Bingo. "You're a mind reader. I'll put on some tea."

In the summer months they'd gone through this routine occasionally, only with iced tea or lemonade and in between customers. Jess slipped to the back room and switched on the kettle. "How're wedding plans going?" she called out.

"That's what I came to talk to you about," Abby called back. "I have a favor to ask."

Jess heated the pot, added the tea bags, and then poured in the boiling water. She took a small tray and added two mugs and a little carton of milk from her bar fridge and carried them to the front. "Favor? I'm intrigued. Because you *never* ask me for favors." She raised an eyebrow, teasing.

Abby grinned at the deliberate sarcasm and Jess chuckled. Abby was always asking for favors and Jess was happy to help. First it was to recommend a seamstress to do the alterations on Abby's wedding dress, a lovely vintage gown that had belonged to Abby's great-grandmother, Edith. Then it was to ask for advice about flowers and colors. And to Jess's surprise, Abby had asked her to be her maid of honor—and sole attendant.

"You've been very patient," Abby commented as she grabbed the spare chair, pulled it up to the desk, and helped herself to the first muffin. "I know I'm probably turning into a Bridezilla."

Jess laughed and poured the tea. "No, you're not. You're happy and excited. And that's just as it should be."

"Well, you and Sarah are the closest thing to sisters I've got." Abby's face shadowed a bit. "How is she, Jess?"

Jess frowned, added a bit of milk to Abby's cup, and handed it over. "She's getting there. The miscarriage really hit her hard, but she and Mark have come through lots. They'll come through this, too."

Jess turned her attention to the muffin, biting down with a satisfied sigh. "You are a lifesaver," she said, washing it down with a sip of tea.

"Well, I still haven't told you the favor." Abby grinned at her, her blue eyes sparkling. "I wondered if you'd make me my wedding jewelry."

"You're sure? You could find something lovely at a store in Portland." Jess loved making jewelry, but it was a lot of pressure creating something for someone's wedding. It was an important day. One that would never be duplicated. A day when everything should be absolutely perfect.

Not that she'd know. Or probably ever know. She'd have to actually start dating again to ever have a chance at a proposal. Jess figured she'd be relegated to the role of Fun Aunt. It wasn't necessarily a bad thing . . . but it didn't sound as thrilling as it once had.

"I looked, and I couldn't find anything I liked. I'd like something vintage-y feeling, but not too heavy, you know?"

Jess couldn't help it. She was already formulating a picture in her mind of something that would suit Abby's dress. "What color?"

"What about ruby? The dark red would look fabulous with the ivory satin, don't you think?" She reached into her handbag and took out a photo in a frame. "Since I'm wearing her dress, I wondered about replicating my great-grandmother's necklace."

Jess looked at the photo, examining the piece carefully. The necklace was stunning, a simple yet elegant circlet of dark red stones. "Where's the original?"

Abby shrugged. "I honestly don't know. I have a box of a bunch of Edith's finer jewelry, but the necklace wasn't in it."

That was too bad. If it belonged to Edith Foster, it

had most likely been genuine gems and expensive. "Hang on a minute." Jess went back into the workroom, pulled a drawer out of a plastic organizing box, grabbed a few more items, and returned to the desk. Once there she moved her tea and muffin aside to clear a spot and began lining up garnets and wire.

"It would need detailing, and the stones would need to be set in something special to imitate the foil backing, but I can see this with your dress. They're not real rubies, of course, but . . ."

She looked up at Abby hopefully.

Abby's eyes lit up. "I knew you'd know exactly what I'd like. How do you do that, Jess? You've got such a talent and a wonderful eye."

The words sent a pang through Jess's heart. She knew she was talented, but sometimes she let her own insecurities get the better of her. For a while her creativity, the deepest part of herself, had been stifled. More than stifled, she ruefully thought as she started packing away the beads. It'd been completely silenced by a man who had been charming on the outside and a monster in private. This life, this business, was her victory over an ugly past.

"You like it, then?"

"It's perfect. That design would complement your dress, too. Can you make two?"

"I could make a smaller one in dark blue for me. If you want."

Abby nodded. "That sounds wonderful. I can't wait to see your dress when it's back from the seamstress."

Neither could Jess. It was the prettiest thing she'd ever put on. They'd found it in one of the chests at Abby's along with lots of other vintage clothes. Most of the items Abby had graciously donated to the Historical Society. But some she'd held onto, including the deep blue gown that they'd guessed to be post World War One. The filmy fabric, beading, and drop waist suited Jess's slightly bohemian style perfectly.

"Only a few more weeks now." The wedding was scheduled for mid-October and would take place at the church with the reception at the Foster House garden, weather permitting. After a brief honeymoon—rumor had it they were going to Paris for a week—Abby and Tom would be living in the grand house together. Tom was already looking at turning the old garage into a woodworking shop and they were planning on renting out his cottage at Fiddler's Rock.

Changes. Good ones. Sometimes Jess felt a little left behind. Which was silly because she had everything she wanted right here.

"I can't believe I'm getting married," Abby said quietly, a soft smile touching her lips. "It seems so impossible, and yet . . . not. Your cousin is pretty special, Jess."

Jess raised an eyebrow. Tom *was* special. He'd supported her dream to open Treasures when others had discouraged it. He was also a pain in the butt, but as a member of the family, that was part of his job description. "I'll never confirm that. It'll get back to him and go straight to his head."

Abby looked down at her mug and turned it around in her fingers. "I should probably tell you that he finally decided on a best man."

Something in her tone made Jess's heart beat out a

warning. "Is it Bryce?" It made sense Tom would ask his brother to stand up with him.

There was a moment of silence in which Jess had a feeling she wasn't going to like the answer.

"No, not Bryce. Rick."

Something strange swirled in Jess's stomach, a weird flutter of nerves that she credited to her recent aversion to Rick Sullivan. "Really? But what about Bryce? They're brothers and . . ."

"He offered it to Bryce first, but you know Bryce. For such a burly, alpha male, he really hates being anywhere near the center of attention. It was all Tom could do to convince him to be emcee at the reception. I wonder how he even made it through his own wedding."

Jess forced a chuckle. "I think Tom had to drug him."

The two women shared a smile. "Jess, tell me honestly, will Rick being the best man be a problem? I know you don't get along, but he's Tom's closest friend."

Jess frowned. To say how she truly felt would sound awful and small-minded. And she of anyone should know that people deserved second chances; that challenges and trials could take a lot out of a person, and Rick had had his share of both. Still. Rick was unpredictable with a substance abuse problem. And he'd be paired up with her for the entirety of the wedding day.

"I don't know, Abby. I mean it's your day. It's just . . ." Jess sighed. She remembered the boy he'd been before joining the Marines. Always good for a joke and laughing, getting into his share of trouble with the boys, but nothing serious. Once, when he was fourteen and she

was twelve, he'd kissed her in the equipment room at
school while they were putting the basketballs away
after lunchtime intramurals. It had been her first kiss,
and she'd looked at him with stars in her eyes until he'd
pulled some prank with Josh and Tom that had her
steaming at the ears.

But the truth of the matter was, their relationship had
always been fraught with ups and downs that went beyond childish pranks. When she was eighteen, they'd
almost started something at her graduation party. Instead he'd cooled his jets without any explanation, leaving her behind a dune wondering what on earth she'd
done wrong. These days all he thought about was feeling sorry for himself.

With another sigh and a shrug, Jess conceded defeat.

"Rick and I can manage to be civil for a day, I'm
sure," she assured Abby. She would not cause wedding
trouble. It was Abby and Tom's day and they should
have it the way they wanted without bridesmaid drama.
She just hoped Rick would stay sober throughout the
day and not make an ass of himself.

Abby reached over and took Jess's hand. "I know you
have worries. Rick's a bit of a loose cannon. But he's
been so much better since his mom took sick. And now
she's gone. Tom and I thought it would give him something positive, you know? He needs that."

Jess couldn't argue. And at least Rick had finally gotten a job. Granted, he'd been working for one of the
whale boat charters, and like her own business, that was
slowing down for the season. What would Rick do with
all the extra time on his hands?

Hand, she reminded herself, and immediately felt guilty for her negativity. He *had* lost his hand in combat, after all.

"He does need that. I haven't been a very good friend. It's just that . . ."

She hesitated. She never talked about her past. Never talked about Mike, or the year and a half they'd spent together. It was something she'd rather forget and knew she never would. Some scars ran too deep.

"Just that what?" Abby asked, her face wreathed in concern. "Jess, are you okay?"

No, she wasn't okay. Rick's drinking had shaken her more than she liked to admit, bringing up painful memories of a history she'd worked hard to move beyond.

"I'm fine," she said, putting on a smile and reaching for a second muffin. "It'll be great, Abby. Your wedding is going to be perfect."

Rick put the key in the lock and let the door swing open with a long, lonely squeak. He stood on the threshold, not entering the cozy white-and-green Cape Cod he'd once called home. It seemed wrong. Wrong that his mother wouldn't be there to say hello in her warm, welcoming voice. She wouldn't give him shit for never coming over or having a decent meal. She'd never make his favorite clam chowder again, or the blueberry cake with the cinnamon crumb topping that he liked so well, or hang clothes out on the clothesline to dance in the breeze.

It felt . . . final. That once he stepped off the porch and into the kitchen, it would really be real. She was never coming back.

He swallowed, trying to screw up his courage. All his life his mom had been his lighthouse. Even when he'd been far away, she'd been there, a light in the darkness to bring him home safely again, especially after she and Rick's father had divorced when he was eight and it had just been the two of them. She'd driven him to Little League, gone to every parent-teacher conference, and once bailed him out of jail when he'd been picked up for underage drinking when he was seventeen.

The disappointment in her eyes was worse than being arrested. Worse than the punishment she'd doled out, which had been walking the highway ditches three Saturdays in a row picking up garbage wearing an orange jumpsuit just like inmates wore.

He stood, looking in at the empty kitchen, and felt his anger build. It was damned unfair. Unfair that she'd taken sick just when he'd come back for good. Unfair that she'd had to suffer, that she'd had to die. Unfair that she hadn't said anything about the recurring pain until the truth couldn't be ignored. Now he was left all alone. No family. Not one relative he knew of that cared if he lived or died.

He'd needed her. He'd pushed her away more than he ought to. And now he wouldn't have a chance to make it right. One thing he knew for sure. He didn't give a good damn whether he'd been adopted or not. Roberta Sullivan had given him far too much for him to push her memory aside just because she'd died. She was, and always would be, his mother. He'd loved her as a son and he mourned her the same way.

A hornet buzzed by his head, reminding him that he was standing with the door open. He stepped inside and closed it, the catch clicking loudly in the silence. He felt a grief so intense he hardly knew what to do with it.

He'd seen horrible things, gruesome things, some of the worst parts of humanity, and he'd come through all right. Well, mostly. So why couldn't he handle this without feeling like he was going to fall apart?

The house was too quiet. His footsteps echoed off the hardwood as he walked farther into the kitchen and threw the package his mom's lawyer had given him that afternoon onto the worn table. Inside were his mom's final papers, bank statements, and a safe deposit box key. God only knew what his mom had placed in the thing. Probably more papers and his childhood treasures. All of which he was definitely not up to going through at the moment. Instead, he walked over to the sink and turned on the radio on the kitchen counter. It was set to a country station out of Portland, so he turned the dial to the classic rock station instead. The familiar guitar licks of Angus Young and AC/DC filled the air and he let out a breath.

This was his house now. It was where he'd grown up. He shouldn't feel so weird about the possibility of moving back in. But it was like trying to put on shoes that were a size too small. The shape was familiar but didn't quite fit. The man he'd become bore little resemblance to that long-ago kid. He'd thought he'd had it so rough, but those had been the easy years. It really was true what they said: you couldn't go back.

He turned on the tap and poured himself a glass of water. He could always sell the house, he supposed, looking around the room. A thin film of dust covered the surfaces. No one had lived here for several weeks. But he knew that under the dust was a place that his mom had taken great pride in—especially considering she'd shouldered all the financial responsibility after his dad took off. It would be stupid to sell when he was scrambling to pay rent for a run-down bachelor apartment on the northwest side of town.

If Jewell Cove had a "bad" area, that was it. It wasn't the picturesque rainbow-colored buildings of Main Street with their fancy window boxes and stained-glass windows. It was people struggling to make ends meet and keep their heads above water. It had suited him just fine, because people minded their own damn business.

He went from the kitchen into the living room, past her favorite chair and the silent television and the video cabinet that held her chick-flick DVDs. Beyond that was the back porch, where a few pieces of wicker furniture made a nice spot to sit in the sun. Rick frowned, realizing that this porch would be the perfect spot to work on his painting. Lots of natural light and space that wasn't taken up with anything important. Cabinets along one end, below the windows, where he could store his paints and brushes . . . and privacy, so no one need know what he got up to in his spare time. Not that anyone would believe it if they saw it. He wouldn't have believed it either, but he could honestly say that his new hobby had been the one thing that had kept him sane since leaving the hot, dusty hell where he'd been deployed.

Was he really considering doing it? Moving back home?

He went up the stairs to the master bedroom, looked in on the abandoned bed and floral duvet, stared at the closed closet doors, and ventured into the bathroom where the scent of her lavender soap still mysteriously clung to the air even though she hadn't lived at home for over a month.

He couldn't do this. Couldn't go through her things like they didn't matter, like they belonged to someone else.

But he had to. He was the only one. He didn't want a bunch of women from the church coming in and pawing through his mom's stuff like a flock of crows. He took a moment and inhaled, and then exhaled slowly, dropping an intentional barrier over his emotions, deadening himself to the grief and sentimentality that had overtaken him so often lately. He knew how to do it. To block out the darkness and guilt and simply do the job at hand. God knows he'd managed it while overseas, any time Kyle's name was mentioned. Dead inside. Yeah, that was it.

Jaw set, he went back out to his truck and retrieved the bundle of boxes and packing tape he'd brought along. Methodically he made up the boxes, adjusting to the awkward task using his prosthetic. Then he went through his mother's clothing and personal effects, boxing them up for Goodwill. It was what she would have wanted. He had no use for her clothing, the shelves of old romance novels, face creams and makeup and hair rollers. Someone else might as well get good use out of them.

Lifting the boxes into his arms was awkward, but once he had the weight balanced it was no problem to carry them downstairs and into the back of his truck. Box after box of shirts, jeans, dresses, shoes. It was okay as long as he didn't stop to think too much about them belonging to his mom. Detached. Unemotional. He could do this.

When her bedroom and bathroom were done, he ventured into the third bedroom, the "spare" room as she'd always called it, and the closet there. It contained very little: a few heavy winter coats that were out of season and a handful of banking boxes tucked in behind the clothes. Rick took one out, lifted the lid, and saw a row of coiled spines—photo albums.

His stomach clenched.

He put the lid back on. There were some things he simply couldn't tackle today. One of them was a trip down memory lane.

"Rick?"

He jumped as a deep voice called up the stairs. Tom, if he could venture a guess. Part of his every-other-day check-in. Rick wanted to be annoyed, but the truth was he'd started to look forward to the short visits from Tom and Josh. Not that the two of them ever showed up together. Things weren't that easy between the cousins yet. After falling in love with the same woman, Tom and Josh hadn't spoken for years. But after Erin's death, they'd both agreed to put the past behind them. Plus, Tom had Abby now. "Up here," he called back.

Boots sounded on the stairs and Tom's dark head peered around the corner. "Hey, buddy."

Rick shut the closet door. "Hey."

"I went by your place and your truck was gone. Asked Jack if you were working today and he said you were off. Figured I might find you here."

"Detective Tom. I thought your brother was the one for police work."

Tom grinned. "Law enforcement is so not for me. Bryce can have it," he replied. His face sobered. "Packing up your mom's things?"

"Some. Clothes and personal stuff. I don't know what to do with the rest."

Tom nodded. "You thinking of moving in? The furniture would come in handy."

Rick shoved his hands in his pockets, looked around the room. It was so familiar, with the same dresser and curtains and bedspread that had been there for a good twenty years. His bedroom was the same, too—a boy's room with white walls filled with thumbtack holes from old Red Sox and Bruins posters, a pine bed, and dark blue spread. Baseball trophies lined a shelf. His mom hadn't changed it even after he'd joined the Corps and left home. Like she'd expected him to come back the same Rick he'd been when he left.

"I don't know. It's definitely nicer than my current situation, but . . ."

"But there are a lot of memories here. And it's still feeling very fresh."

Rick met Tom's even gaze. "Yeah," he agreed. "That."

"I bet Josh felt the same way when Erin died. Having

to live in their house, you know? You should talk to him."

Rick chuckled, a dry sound. "I'm not going to be the one to bring up Erin with Josh. You . . . you've got Abby now. Josh isn't in a good place like you. He'll tell me to shut the hell up and go pound sand."

Tom smiled. "Probably. Listen, you need a hand with anything?"

Rick's throat tightened. Tom had never judged, not even when Rick had messed up. He'd bailed Rick out of trouble more than once since he'd come home to stay and had been the one to convince Jack Skillin to give him a job. Rick was an only child, and Tom and Josh were the closest thing to brothers he'd ever had.

And Jess and Sarah and Bryce, too. That whole clan had accepted him. But when push came to shove, they weren't blood. "I think I've done all I'm going to today."

"Then let's get some lunch. Crab cakes are today's special at Breezes."

Breezes, Rick thought dryly. Not The Rusty Fern, where they normally would have gone for a bite. But at the Fern there'd be the temptation of ordering a beer with lunch, and there was no alcohol served at the café. Not that Tom needed to worry. Rick understood his friends' concerns, but he'd made his mom a promise. Plus, it wasn't like it was *that* bad. Sure, he'd made a fuss a few times, but he wasn't dependent on booze. He thought of Jess's disapproving looks and something in his gut clenched.

"Hey, where'd you go? You in for lunch or what?"

Rick looked around him and felt the walls closing

in. "Yeah, I'm in. I can drop that stuff off later. I've done enough for today, I think."

"Sounds good."

Rick followed Tom to Main Street and parked on a side street a block from the restaurant. When they entered, the noise was deafening and the smells fantastic. Bright light beamed through the walls of windows and he could see the bay below, the blue of the water particularly intense as it could only be in autumn. Tom was right. It was a good idea. Paul Finnigan's little fishing boat came chugging into the harbor, probably with a good-sized catch of haddock aboard. Jack had mentioned that the fishing was still good past Widow's Point, and Paul would get in as much time as he could before putting his boat to dock for the winter.

As Rick watched the wake from the boat form a *V*, he thought he might like to paint it on the new pane of glass he'd found last week, maybe with a beveled edge so that it could be hung in a window, letting the light shine through the colors. Of course it would mean another trip to Portland for supplies, but that was okay. There wasn't much work with Jack now and he was bound to get his layoff notice any day.

"Hey, I found us a table," Tom said, giving Rick's arm a nudge. "Come on before we lose it."

They sat at a table in the corner, waited while a young girl Rick didn't recognize cleared the mess from the previous diners and then reached for menus. "No need." Tom smiled. "We'll both have the crab cakes and home fries."

Rick nodded. "And make sure there's a piece of Linda's chocolate cake left, huh?" He smiled at her, noticed her staring at his hand, and discreetly tucked it beneath the table.

She recovered quickly and smiled. "Sure thing. Won't be long."

Tom frowned at Rick. "That happen a lot?"

Rick wasn't sure why the question made a thread of anxiety spiral through him. He should be used to it by now. "All the time. People don't expect to see this." He held up his hand, stared at the synthetic material that looked real at first, . . . but was clearly not on closer examination. And as much as he could use it for a lot of tasks, he would never achieve the same dexterity again.

But it wasn't really about the hand. It never had been. He just let people think that because it was better than facing the truth.

"You can't let it hold you back, you know." Tom reached for his ice water. "Any ideas what you're going to do now that business at Jack's is slowing down?"

Rick considered saying the word *paint* and then laughed to himself. He could just imagine what the fine people of Jewell Cove would say if they knew tough, booze-loving, ex-Marine Rick Sullivan had taken up painting birds and flowers. They'd think it was a joke.

"Not so much. I think Jack'll give me a good recommendation, though."

"There must be something in town somewhere. Even part time. Just to get you out of the house, you know?"

A female voice sounded behind him. "I'm sure there is. If he can stay sober long enough, that is."

Rick's hackles rose at the condemning tone, but he turned in his chair and regarded Jess Collins blandly.

"Always nice to see *you*, Jessica," he said. And it was. She was the most beautiful woman he'd ever known.

And also the most judgmental. Which was probably best for all involved. Because Jess deserved a much better man than him.

It just pissed him off that they both knew it.

CHAPTER 3

Jess had thought to stop in, grab a chicken salad crois-
sant for her lunch, and dart back to the shop. She hated
having to put up the CLOSED sign, but Cindy White,
who'd been working for her part time, had been offered
an assistant job at the school and Jess's high school girl,
Tessa, only worked after school two days a week and
Saturdays during the school year.

If Jess wanted to skip out at all, it meant closing the
store. She paused, though, after placing her lunch order.
She hadn't expected to see Tom here, especially with
Rick. She considered walking back out without acknowledging either one of them. But she'd been meaning to
talk to Tom anyway, about building some extra wall
shelves in her workroom. Now that her classes were really taking off, she needed the room without sacrificing
work space.

With the workload and the wedding plans, she might
not get another chance for a while.

She got to the table just in time to hear Rick say something about his job situation. Tom replied, "There must be something in town somewhere. Even part time. Just to get you out of the house, you know?"

Indeed. Work was there if someone was inclined to actually look for it. Which hadn't seemed much of a priority for Rick. At least not until this past summer. He'd been far too busy running up a tab at The Rusty Fern.

"I'm sure there is," she said, her voice tight. "If he can stay sober long enough, that is."

"Always nice to see you, Jessica," Rick replied. His tone said otherwise.

She looked at Tom. "Mind if I pick your brain for a second? I'm waiting for my order and I wanted to ask you about some shelving."

She watched as Tom looked at Rick, who picked up his napkin and unrolled it, revealing his cutlery. She watched as he placed it on the table precisely using his prosthetic. She swallowed. She knew she should cut Rick some slack. So why wasn't she able to? Why did she always feel so angry when he was around?

"Don't mind me," Rick said. "Pick his brain all you want."

She pulled out a spare chair and focused on her cousin. "I was thinking of adding some wall shelves to the workroom. Do you think you'd have time for that, and can you give me an estimate?"

"You're running out of space already?"

She smiled. "Business is good. And rather than stack things on the floor, having it on shelves makes it easier to find and access. Plus I can organize it so that everything for certain classes is in one spot. I probably should have had you do it from the start, but the store shelving was more important."

"You need it right away? I'm tied up for the next few weeks, and then it's our honeymoon . . ."

"Do you think you could do it before Thanksgiving? With all the Christmas materials arriving, I can really use the extra space."

"That should be doable." Tom nodded. "I'll come over and measure and stuff first, and when I get a free day or two, I'll bring one of the guys and we'll do it up right."

She smiled. Tom always came through. Despite tension between the two sides of the family over the last few years, he'd been on her side through it all. Tom had stepped in and built her display counters and shelves, added on a back deck and pergola. He'd believed in her, and she wouldn't forget that.

"You know, Jess," Tom mused. "Maybe Rick could put in your shelves. Jack's not going to have much more work for you, is he, buddy?"

Rick looked startled at the suggestion and Jess's stomach clenched. She could kill Tom for putting them both on the spot like that. What was she supposed to say?

She looked over at Rick. Tom had helped him get the job with Jack Skillin, too. She felt a little guilty that she didn't have the faith in Rick that Tom seemed to have.

"He hasn't given me a pink slip yet," Rick stated, avoiding her eyes. "Besides, I appreciated the reference before but I don't need a pity job. Thanks anyway."

"It wouldn't be like that. You'd be helping me out," Tom insisted. "My schedule's pretty tight."

Rick met Tom's gaze. "Sure. That's it exactly." He reached for his water. "Thanks, but no thanks."

Jess let out a slow breath. Rick didn't want to work at her place, either.

"But you're going to need . . ."

"How are you making out, Rick?" She interrupted Tom's persistent voice and softened her own, removing the little bit of condemnation that usually found its way there. He had just lost his mother, after all. And he'd refused the job. Maybe she should give him a break.

He looked up. "Fine. Right as rain."

Tom butted in. "We were at his mom's place, taking out boxes."

Her heart did a strange beat. "Oh. That must be a hard job. Sorry." She met Rick's gaze, surprised to see pain and defiance in the brown depths. "Is anyone helping you go through it? That's not something you should have to do alone." Indeed, now that the shelving issue was off the table, she was feeling quite generous. She could probably spare an hour to help. She owed it to Roberta if nothing else.

He was surprised at her offer, she could tell, but he dropped his gaze to his hands. "No, thanks. It's something I have to do myself. But thanks for asking."

Tom jumped in again. "He's got clothes for Goodwill in his truck."

Jess frowned. It was good that Rick was donating to charity, but it was so soon. Too soon? Plus there was a problem. The clothing bank drop-off was only open two days a week. She knew because she volunteered there one Saturday a month. And today was not one of those days.

"You know the drop-off's closed today, right?"

Rick's scowl deepened, creating a wrinkle between his eyebrows. "It is? Damn. I guess I'll have to unload them again. I don't want to leave them uncovered in the truck overnight."

She imagined how taxing it must have been, lugging boxes with only one good hand. Now he'd have to take them out and put them back again . . .

"Jess?" The waitress interrupted. "Your sandwich is up." She held out a Styrofoam takeout container. "And yours will be here soon, boys," she said to Tom and Rick.

Jess took the box. "Thanks, Elaine." She looked over at Rick. "You know, there's a women's shelter that could probably use your things. I could give them a call, and you could drop them off this afternoon."

"I think my mom would like that."

She felt her heart turn over. No matter Rick's mistakes, he'd just lost his mom, a woman he'd clearly loved. "Roberta was always helping out with our charity efforts," Jess said softly. "I think she'd like that, too, Rick. Do you want me to call them?"

"That'd be nice of you, Jess."

He met her gaze. Her stomach did a little flip-flop. No matter the changes in their lives, Rick was still the dark-haired rascal who'd kissed her on the beach in the moonlight . . .

She pushed the memory aside. "I'll arrange it. Do you have a cell? I can call you with the details."

Details, heck. She knew exactly what to do and where to go. Because for a few days many years ago she'd slept at the shelter, eaten there, been frightened there. She'd been a quiet supporter of the organization ever since.

He wrote the number on his napkin and slid it over just as Elaine returned with two plates of crab cakes.

"I should get back to the store. I had to close while I grabbed lunch." Jess stood and grinned down at the pair of them, knowing they were dying to cut into the cakes. "Now my chicken salad isn't looking so tasty." She put a hand on Tom's shoulder. "Thanks, Tom. And Rick, I'll call you in a bit."

"Thanks, Jess."

She took her boxed sandwich and made her way to the door, her heart clubbing a strange beat. That exchange had been almost civil. Certainly without the biting rancor that generally characterized their conversations.

Outside the fall air was crisp and golden and she took a deep inhale, returning to her senses. Rick was the guy who'd come to the Memorial Day picnic at her sister Sarah's with a flask tucked in his pocket, who'd gotten Josh drunk at his welcome home party, and who'd been kicked out of the pub more times than she could count for having one too many. She'd heard he'd gotten three sheets to the wind the night his mom had gone into palliative care, though at least he'd been sober for the funeral.

She wasn't stupid. Some people could handle their liquor. She wasn't opposed to a few glasses of wine with the girls now and again, or a cold beer on a hot summer's day. But some people couldn't. And she wasn't dumb enough to put herself in the middle of that sort of situation again. Not when it had cost her so much.

She hurried back to the shop and ate her sandwich while searching for her phone book, then took a moment to make the call. Two minutes later she took out the napkin with Rick's number on it and dialed.

"Hello?"

The sound of the café filtered through the phone. "It's Jess. You're still at lunch?"

"Just finishing up."

"I've got directions for you. You ready?"

He hesitated.

"Rick?"

"Um, yeah, about that. Look, I was wondering . . . are you free to go with me?"

She blinked. "Go with you?"

"Yeah. I feel kind of awkward going there by myself."

"Because . . ." she prompted. Surely he wasn't prejudiced. No one ever intended to get in a position that they'd need a shelter.

"Maybe the women there don't appreciate a man being around. I don't know," he answered, sounding flustered. "I've never done this before."

"You intimidated, Rick?" She smiled into the receiver. "It's just a drop-off."

"Never mind, then," he answered sharply. "Give me the damn directions."

She sighed, suddenly feeling guilty for breaking the tentative truce between the two of them. What would it hurt, spending an hour at most with him? For charity.

"I can't just leave, that's all. My after-school help doesn't get here until three thirty."

There was a pause. "I could wait and go then."

He was making a concession. An effort. And he was doing a good thing, so why was she fighting it so hard?

"Swing by and pick me up at quarter to four," she said heavily.

"Forget it."

She pinched the bridge of her nose. "Rick, let's not make this into an argument. You want me to go and I'm going. Let's just leave it, okay?"

There was a long silence. The clacking of dishes and cutlery was gone and she assumed he'd gone outside.

"Fine. I'll see you later," he muttered, and then clicked off without saying good-bye.

She would not let him get to her.

At precisely 3:45, Jess hooked her handbag on her shoulder and waved to Tessa as she left the store. When she got down the boarded walkway that Tom had built for her, she discovered Rick in his truck parked along the street, tapping his fingers impatiently against the steering wheel.

She hopped in and pasted on a smile, determined to start the drive on the right foot. "Hi. Again."

His fingers stopped tapping. "Hey."

He pulled away from the curb and at the next intersection, turned left onto Main and continued until they hit the exit to the highway, all without saying a word. If traffic stayed light, they'd reach the shelter in thirty, thirty-five minutes tops.

Over an hour when all was said and done. It would

be the longest she'd spent with him since high school and even then they'd rarely been alone. Considering his apparent lack of conversational skills, an hour was going to feel like a lifetime.

"So," she began uneasily. "You went through some of Roberta's things."

"I'm thinking of moving in." He stared straight ahead. "No sense putting it off, really. Going through her clothes, I mean."

"People grieve in their own time. I don't think anyone should be held to certain rules, you know? If you felt like doing it, then it was clearly the right time."

His shoulders relaxed a little. "At first I thought about putting the house up for sale."

Jess considered the cute two-story house. Situated on one of Jewell Cove's side streets, it had a splendid birch tree out front and a profusion of perennials—forsythia in spring, rhododendrons and lilacs, cosmos and phlox. She'd always thought Roberta's house looked like something out of a magazine or book. "I'm assuming your mom kept it in primo shape," she mused. "I bet it wouldn't be on the market long." In fact it would be perfect for a family. She could easily imagine a swing set in the backyard. A dog to fetch sticks or a tennis ball. A perfect family life for a perfect family.

"She did, until the last year or so when she started feeling tired and then was diagnosed." Rick's voice was tight, as if talking about it physically hurt. "But it won't take long to fix up what fell behind."

Jess studied his profile. His dark hair was a bit longer now that the jarhead look was gone, and curled slightly at his T-shirt collar. His eyes were dark brown, and his face was angular . . . at times it seemed harsh and unrelenting, especially when he had a shadow of stubble on it. Like now, when he clenched his jaw. His words were easily spoken but his face told the truth. He was hurting, and hurting badly.

"I'm so sorry, Rick. I didn't mean to be insensitive." She paused, and then carefully asked, "What about your dad? Have you contacted him? I mean, now that your mom is gone . . ."

He shook his head quickly. "You weren't being insensitive," he assured her. "And as far as my dad . . ." He hesitated, then let out a breath. "I haven't spoken to him in years. And I don't plan to either."

The harsh tone was startling and she stared at him. "But . . . he's your father. I mean, I know he left you and your mom, but so much time has passed. Surely it wouldn't hurt to get in touch."

Rick's eyes blazed as he looked over at her. "He left and hasn't bothered to stay in touch, ask about me, even pay any child support to my mom. I don't owe him *anything*."

She understood his anger, but family was important. Particularly since Rick no longer had any. Perhaps if they could make amends . . .

"Maybe not. Or maybe he just doesn't know what to say after all this time. If you just—"

"Look, Jess," he interrupted sharply. "The truth is, I've known since second grade that I'm adopted. A year after that Graham left. So you see, he wasn't my father in *any* sense of the word. So what's the point in calling him up now?"

"Adopted?" Shock rippled through her as her mouth

dropped open. Granted, Rick had never really looked much like Roberta, but that didn't really mean anything. "You've known all these years and never told anyone?"

"Marian Foster arranged it. I was the last baby she helped place."

Nothing he could have said would have surprised her more than this. If there wasn't even biology connecting him to his dad, she understood his hostility better. "I don't know what to say."

"There's nothing to say. It's not like it makes any difference. My mom was my mom, and nothing will ever change that." He looked sideways at her, then turned his attention back to the road.

There was a beat of silence in which Jess saw Rick differently. He was clearly grieving for Roberta, and the way he spoke of her proved that he'd loved her very much. "What about your birth parents, Rick? You might have family out there somewhere."

"That's not really on my radar at the moment. Maybe down the road I'll reconsider, but I doubt it." He stopped at a stop sign, and looked over at her again. "Being in the Marines taught me to look at things by taking them down to the lowest denominator. To keep things clear and straightforward. And the truth is that she was my mother. No one else. And that's all there is to it."

And his declaration drove home the point that he was now all alone. She kept quiet, knowing the last thing he'd want was her pity.

"Well, no decision has to be made right away. It's probably better not to rush this sort of thing. Make rash decisions and all that."

He paused, and then blew out a big breath, relieving

some of the tension that had marked their conversation. He winked at her. "Hey, haven't you heard? Rash decisions are what I'm good at."

Jess blushed and looked away, staring out the window. It was no secret that Rick had enlisted out of the blue on his twenty-first birthday, surprising the heck out of everyone. Roberta especially had been distressed as he was her only child. But she'd been proud, too. Proud of him for serving his country. As they all were. He'd come home on leave, dressed in his uniform, looking heroic and strong and invincible.

And then he'd come back after being discharged and rented a place, which wasn't much more than a dump, instead of moving in with his mom. And proceeded to spend the majority of his disability pay at The Rusty Fern.

This was the closest she'd been to Rick since before he'd enlisted. She swallowed. The cab of the truck suddenly felt much smaller as Jess stole glances at Rick's strong profile out of the corner of her eye. His jawline was firmer now, more masculine, and he'd grown into his features.

Jess's gaze lingered on his lips. That feature, however, had remained the same. It had been graduation night. She'd been eighteen and had gone to a party at Fiddler's Beach, just down the bay from where her cousin Tom's cottage now sat. Rick had been there, two and a half years older, wearing jeans and a white T-shirt and looking dangerous. She'd met his gaze over the flickering light of the fire and something in her had stirred. That same stirring was happening now, only she was looking at the man he'd become. He was harder, tougher, and if possible, more handsome now than he'd been back then.

"Oh, let's just call it part of your charm," she replied. He'd deftly changed the subject, and she got the message that he was both done talking about himself and determined to lighten the mood.

"Of course, you never make rash decisions, do you, Jess?" He raised an eyebrow.

Her cheeks heated as she blushed. Thank God he couldn't tell what she'd just been thinking. "Me? Well, I try not to."

"That's right. I can see that Treasures was a well-thought-out, smart business decision guaranteed to succeed. You're very, very careful, aren't you? My goodness, you're just about perfect." A dimple threatened to pop in his cheek.

"Hey," she corrected him. "Starting up any business is a gamble, Rick. Besides, I never said I was perfect." She was far from it.

"Oh, come on." He chuckled as he began a laundry list of her attributes. "You can't do any wrong in the Cove. Successful businesswoman, church committee member, volunteer for everything, can make crafts out of bottle caps and wire. Friend to all, a real go-to girl. You really should be in line for sainthood."

She looked over and saw his lips twitch. Damn him for being so deliberately provoking and sexy as hell at the same time. "Hey, everyone has a skill," she returned. He grinned at her and her breath caught. They weren't . . . flirting, were they? How sad was it that she was so out of practice she couldn't tell?

"I'm not so sure about that," he said. "I sometimes think my only skill is screwing up."

"I'm pretty sure you didn't mean to get . . . um . . . wounded," she answered.

"Doesn't mean I didn't screw up just because it was unintentional."

Lordy, how right he was. Jess had made her share of mistakes. And they'd been doozies. No wonder she was extra cautious now. Her slew of errors had begun when she'd fallen for the wrong man, who'd turned her life into a place of addiction and violence, while showing a sweet-as-apple-pie face to the world. It hadn't ended until a few years later . . . when she'd walked into the shelter looking for help.

"Take the next right," she said quietly, pointing at a road sign.

"Did I say something wrong?" he asked, sparing her a glance. "You got real quiet all of a sudden."

"Not at all," she lied. But Rick could take a hint, too. They'd both halted conversation when the subject hit a little too close for comfort.

For the next few minutes she gave him directions to the shelter. The radio played softly in the background. There was so much about him she didn't approve of, so it made very little sense that looking at him, being this close to him, was still enough to make her pulse speed up a little bit. Their chat today shouldn't have changed anything—and yet somehow it did.

They were turning into the parking lot next to the shelter when Jess finally asked the question she'd wanted to ask for close to ten years. "Rick, why did you leave and join the Marines? What was so bad that you had to get out of Jewell Cove, leave your mom all alone?"

He considered his answer. "It wasn't about getting out of town. We all know someone who was touched by nine-eleven. We all remember where we were that morning and the scenes from the news. You don't forget something like that."

Rick looked over at her. "I knew I wanted to do something important, though I wasn't sure what. I wanted to serve my country, Jess. To stand up for what was right. The Marines allowed me to do that. It's just that simple."

He'd served. And paid a high price for that service. The knowledge hung between them, unspoken, as Rick parked, turned off the ignition, and got out of the truck.

She got out, too, and shut the door, suddenly feeling a little ashamed of herself. She'd never considered Rick's service as anything but another example of him running away from responsibility, but he was right. The conversation was pretty heavy for an afternoon drive, so she tried to lighten the mood again. "Hey, if you'd hung around, maybe we would have . . . you know. I thought we were sort of heading that way." She gave a light laugh.

There was a long moment where Rick stared at her, like he had words sitting on the tip of his tongue but wouldn't speak them. Finally he shrugged. "Naw, I doubt it. We were kids. Anyway, by the time I had my first leave, you'd hooked up with Mike Greer. What ever happened to good old Mike, anyway?"

His words slashed open old wounds that lately never seemed to heal. Wasn't it ironic that Rick, with his alcohol issues, was the first person to bring up Mike in years? Particularly since it was Rick's actions that had made Jess think of Mike so often in the last few months.

"We broke up and he left town," she said hoarsely. It wasn't quite the truth, but it wasn't exactly a lie, either. There was just a whole lot more to the story he didn't know. That he'd never know. Josh was the only one who knew the truth behind Mike's rapid departure from Jewell Cove. As far as Jess knew her brother had never breathed a word of what had happened that last night to anyone, and Mike had known better than to press charges against Josh. There'd been proof of Mike's crimes all over her body.

Rick seemed distracted as he moved to the back of the truck, struggling to untie the tarp covering the truck bed. His prosthetic hand kept slipping on the cord. Cursing under his breath, Rick tried to secure the line while untying the knot. "What? Did he not manage to measure up to Saint Jess's standards?" he asked in a snarky tone, a direct contrast to the lighter mood they'd established.

Jess reeled back in confusion. She couldn't keep up with his mercurial mood changes. What he'd said before in jest, now hit her like a punch in the gut. "For goodness' sake, Rick," she snapped. "What is with you? When you asked me to come along today, I thought we were past all this juvenile sniping at each other." In fact, there'd been moments in the truck she'd actually felt closer to him than she'd been in years. And then he came out with something that cut her to the quick.

"Me, too." He shook his head, abandoned the tarp, and stepped closer, close enough that her heart started banging against her ribs and her breath came in shorter gasps. "God, I don't know. I'm sorry. I was out of line. I just . . . I shouldn't have said that. I was annoyed and frustrated and hate this damn hand. And I guess sometimes being around you . . . it reminds me what a screwup I am." He sighed, softly saying, "I've never been good enough for you, huh?"

Did he even *want* to be good enough for her? She didn't dare ask the question; she didn't want to know the answer. The opportunity passed, too, as the shelter coordinator came out the side door and Jess and Rick stepped apart. Jess had known Catherine Jenkins for years. She smiled at Jess now, and offered a hand to Rick. "Thank you for coming, Mr. Sullivan. We appreciate your donation."

Jess concentrated on slowing her breathing, unsure if the rapid rise of her pulse was the result of her irritation or something very different. Something unexpected. She hid her face as she moved to untie the tarp Rick had abandoned.

"Where should I put the boxes?" Rick asked. Jess cursed him in her head for having the ability to sound so normal when her emotions were still swinging wildly.

"I'm going to open our garage, and you can stack them there. We'll go through them later."

"Yes, ma'am."

Jess stepped forward, determined to act like nothing had happened. "I'll help. Many hands make light work."

Rick sent her a pointed stare . . . of course she'd said "hands," plural. Funny how everyday sayings took on an extra meaning . . .

Catherine smiled. "Me, too. Why don't I get in the back and move the boxes forward for you?"

With an agility unexpected of a woman of her age, Catherine climbed over the tailgate and dusted off her hands.

Rick let down the tailgate and reached for the first box. Jess grabbed one, too—she was used to hauling around supplies and inventory for the shop, so the weight was nothing at all. For a few minutes they worked, stacking the boxes in the spotless garage that housed Catherine's car and the yard-care equipment. With a grinding sound of dust on cardboard, Catherine slid the last box over the bed of the truck into Rick's waiting arms. He went off to the garage, leaving Catherine to hop down and Jess to wait.

"What's his deal?" Catherine asked quietly.

"His mom just died."

"And the hand?"

"You noticed," Jess acknowledged quietly. "Courtesy of a firefight, from what I gather. Not that he talks about it."

Catherine nodded. "He's troubled, isn't he?"

Jess's heart clubbed. "Yeah, he is. And I should want to help him. Except he makes me angry and very, very defensive."

"Oh, Jess." Catherine smiled at her warmly. "You've been very cautious and smart since you were here." She put her hand on Jess's arm. "Maybe a little too careful? He can't take his eyes off you." Her gaze followed Rick as he put the box down on the concrete floor of the garage.

"Me? And Rick?" Jess laughed, though the idea of Rick not taking his eyes off her did funny, delicious things to her insides. "Not in a million years. He's too unstable. We fight too much. I know that he'd never lay a hand on me." She knew in her heart he wouldn't. That wasn't the problem. "But he's got too many issues, Cath. I'd be crazy to take that on." She didn't mention the alcohol. Catherine sensed a troubled soul, but Jess refused to gossip.

"Well, you could be a good friend, then. He looks like he needs one."

Rick came back, brushing his hand on his jeans. Jess knew she wasn't being fair to him. As she'd told Catherine, intellectually she knew Rick was nothing at all like Mike, no matter how much he drank. But that didn't matter, she couldn't be around him. Not without worrying and wondering. Soon Rick would have more time on his hands when he was laid off for the winter. How was he going to fill his days?

"That about does it," he said with a smile. The physical labor had seemed to help get rid of some of his frustration. His facial muscles were much more relaxed, and his voice had lost its hostile edge.

"Thanks so much," Catherine said. "It'll be like Christmas here later. Some of the women show up with only the clothes on their backs."

Rick nodded soberly. "You're doing a good thing," he confirmed. "If I find more, are you interested?"

"Just call in advance so I can make sure I'm here to receive it. We do try to protect our residents' privacy."

"Of course."

Catherine lifted a hand. "Jess, always a pleasure to see you."

Jess nodded. "Call when you have your next fundraiser. I'll lend a hand or donate items, whatever."

"You bet."

Jess and Rick got back in the truck, cocooned by silence once more.

CHAPTER 4

The drive back to Jewell Cove was quiet. Rick kept his hands on the wheel and Jess stared out the window. She wasn't sure what to think. This afternoon with Rick was not what she'd call quiet or even restful, but even though their conversation had been serious, there'd been a moment where she'd seen a lighter side to him that she hadn't seen in a long time. And what he'd said about never being good enough for her had her brain buzzing. She'd had a schoolgirl crush on him years ago. She hadn't truly thought it had gone both ways.

She sighed. It didn't change anything, though, did it? The Rick who was sitting beside her on the bench seat of his pickup wasn't the same guy she'd known back then. He was harder, angrier . . . he tried to brush it off but it was clear he had demons.

And so did she.

He finally broke the silence. "You ready for this big wedding in a few weeks?"

Right. They'd been paired up, hadn't they? Sole attendants to the bride and groom. "I guess. Abby's got things well in hand. She's very good at organization. Comes from working so long with five- and six-year-olds I suppose. Must be a bit like herding cats."

His lips tipped up a little.

"Rick . . . I can be honest with you, right?"

"Haven't you always? Seems to me you don't worry too much about self-editing."

She remembered her curt statement about him finding a job and knew what she was about to say would probably fire off his temper. Still, she felt it needed to be said. It had been weighing on her mind ever since Abby had told her Rick was to be Tom's best man.

"I just . . . I don't know how else to say this, so I'm going to come right out and say it."

"That's usually the best way."

Dammit. "The thing is . . . this is their wedding day. I'm hoping you'll, well, leave off the drinking. The last thing they need is a scene."

The smile slid from his lips. "You're worried I'll come drunk? Jesus, Jess. When have I ever shown up to something like that three sheets to the wind? Give me a little credit."

"You showed up to Josh's homecoming with a flask and proceeded to empty it. You weren't exactly walking straight when you headed home."

"If you'll remember, it was Josh and Tom who got in the fight that night, not me."

"Except Josh had been drinking—with you."

"Sucks to drink alone."

"Then there was this summer at The Rusty Fern when you got kicked out . . . again. Bryce had to haul you out of there in cuffs."

His cheeks flushed. "Hell," he said, his voice raw. "I'd just put my mom in the hospital. Give a man a break, Jess."

"What about the time Tom found you passed out on your picnic table in the backyard because you couldn't find your keys to let yourself into your apartment?"

He angled her an insolent look. "You calling me a drunk, Saint Jess?"

Her stomach shifted, unsettled by the whole tone of the conversation but feeling it needed to be brought out into the open. "I'm saying there are better uses of your time, that's all. And that at Tom and Abby's wedding, it might be good to stay off the bottle."

"My, my. I'm surprised a paragon like yourself is willing to drive in a vehicle with such a degenerate. You must fear for your very safety. What a high opinion you have of me."

"Don't be like that. You know I have good reason to bring it up."

"Of course. Judging me is just one of the perks, right?"

"I'm not judging you."

"Really? Sure looks like it from where I'm sitting." He frowned. "If it makes you feel better, I promise not to knock over the wedding cake or throw up on the minister's shoes."

"Now you're being an ass."

"Which is exactly what you expect from me, right? Always happy to please."

He was impossible. Laughing one minute and defensive and angry the next. And perhaps a little bit right, but was there any good way to broach the topic that wouldn't be offensive? Especially since Rick didn't even acknowledge that he had a problem. The teasing atmosphere they'd achieved during the drive to the shelter was completely obliterated.

They were nearing town now and Jess could hardly wait for the drive to be over. She closed her eyes and wondered why Rick always managed to goad her into an argument.

"I'm sorry," she finally said softly. "You asked me to go along today for moral support and all I ended up doing was picking a fight. I shouldn't have done that."

His breath came out on a whoosh. "Arguing with you takes my mind off other things, so don't worry about it."

"Things like what?"

He shrugged.

They started down the hill to Main Street. The ride was almost over and nothing felt settled or on solid ground. "Things like what?" she repeated.

"Like my mom's empty house," he answered. "Like having to go through her things knowing she'll never touch them again. Like knowing she is my only family in the world and she's gone."

Jess recognized his tone for what it was—pain.

"Look, I know I'm not perfect. I have issues. I'm a huge disappointment. I'm angry. I'm angry all the time and I don't know where to put it. But I'm trying. Maybe it doesn't look like it, but I am. And I do that one day at a time."

She was about to respond when he finished with, "So it would be great if you could just back off."

He turned off of Main onto Lilac Lane, pulling up to the curb outside the shop.

Jess gathered her handbag and opened the door.

"Thanks for coming with me," he said, but there was a distinct lack of warmth in the words.

"You're welcome."

She was about to shut the door when he stopped her. "Jess?"

She looked up. It was so hard to read his face. He'd made stonewall expressions an art form. But there was something in his eyes, something a bit softer than the hard line of his jaw, as he nodded. "I promise I won't make any problems at the wedding. You can count on me to be the soul of propriety."

It was hard enough to imagine Rick saying the word *propriety* let alone being the epitome of it. But he was trying. He'd been honest. More honest than he'd been since his arrival home, at least. Even if they'd argued, there had been moments of truth. She should be glad for that.

"I'll hold you to that," she replied, looking up at him.

"And I'd appreciate, if you kept the adoption thing to yourself."

"I promise," she replied solemnly, meaning it. It struck her now that she was the first person he'd ever shared that information with and she'd rewarded his confidence by picking a fight. "I won't say anything."

Then she slammed the door and scooted across the street to the shop, feeling his gaze on her back, wondering what he was going to do now.

Rick Sullivan would only cause her trouble. She should really stop spending so much time thinking about him and worry more about her own life.

Rick's layoff notice finally came, one day before the end of the month. Rent was due in forty-eight hours and his truck was nearly out of gas. It made no sense to pay rent for a tiny dump when a perfectly good house with no mortgage and up-to-date taxes was sitting vacant, so he put in his notice and moved home.

Tom had repeated his job offer of installing Jess's shelving, but Rick hadn't given him an answer yet. It felt weird, accepting a paycheck from his best friend. Besides, Jess would never agree. He knew exactly what she thought. They were old friends and she felt sorry for him. To a point. But she hadn't exactly jumped at the idea at the café the other day. He still remembered the look of relief that had passed over her face when he'd refused.

So . . . first things first. He began with unpacking his painting supplies. Panes of glass, vinegar, rags, paints, brushes, and his sketchbook where he worked out his designs. He put them out in the porch, where all the natural light would flood through when the blinds were opened.

Painting had gotten him through some rough times over the last few months, providing not only something to occupy his hands but his mind, too, when the memories and images wouldn't leave him alone. He took out the wrapped piece of glass, only five by seven, that he'd been working on. Paul Finnigan's white boat, bobbing at the Jewell Cove dock in the sunset. It was his favorite so far, a simple scene depicting something he truly enjoyed. Sure, he'd been happy for the job in the boat shack, but he'd longed to be out on the water, too. Anywhere that he didn't feel boxed in . . . but Jack hadn't needed him on the boat, and Rick had taken whatever job was offered.

He sighed. He'd sail the bay another time, maybe with Josh on his new twenty-footer. First he was going to go upstairs and put his clothes away. And then go somewhere for dinner until he could put some groceries in the house.

He worked for an hour or so, settling back in, trying to ignore the memories that crowded around him. No sense in dwelling on the past, because nothing could be changed and you could never go back in time. It was just too bad then that even when he tried to keep occupied during the day, he couldn't control what he saw when he went to sleep. His dreams usually fell into the categories of mistakes and regrets.

The house was too quiet and his stomach rumbled in the silence, so he headed downtown to Breezes Café for something to eat, avoiding The Rusty Fern because today was one of those days he wasn't overly confident in his willpower to stay off the rum.

It was growing dark as he made his way to the waterfront, and beams from the streetlights bobbed with the waves on the water. On a Thursday at the end of September, most of the shops closed at six and the traffic was mainly local, making for a quiet, soft evening. There was a back-to-school display still up at Eulalie Harris's bookstore, Cover to Cover, and Halloween candy was already stocked in the pharmacy storefront for the trick-or-treaters who'd make their way through town in costume in a month's time. His gaze drifted up the hill toward Jess's shop on Lilac Lane. Had she closed for the night? Was she holding any of her classes in the back room? He could imagine her shining in that element, surrounded by friends and doing what she loved, her eyes sparkling. Her heavy curls would be pulled back in a ponytail and there would probably be paint splatters on her work shirt as she laughed at something someone said. She had a great laugh, soft and husky. The kind that made a man sit up and take notice.

She never laughed when she was with him. Except for the other day, when he'd been teasing her. When she gave that low, sexy laugh, something inside of him eased.

Frowning, he pulled open the door to the café and stepped inside. As he expected, most of the clientele was local, with some strange faces, probably from the few bed-and-breakfasts scattered around town. Rick went to the counter rather than take a table. It would feel too conspicuous to sit all alone. Pathetic.

"Rick Sullivan. Twice in a week. To what do we owe the pleasure? The Fern must be missing your business."

Rick tried not to wince. He really had damaged his reputation, hadn't he? The words were said lightly in simple teasing, but the truth of them cut a little. He forced a smile. "Well, Linda, it's either Gus's roast chicken or your apple pie. Maybe a little of each."

Linda's face softened. "Aw, hon, you know I'm just teasin'. How're you making out, anyway? Heard you were moving back into your mom's house."

He raised an eyebrow. "I just moved out of my apartment this morning."

"Nothing is secret in this town." She flashed him a grin. "You really want the chicken dinner, or do you want a menu?"

"The chicken's fine. And don't be stingy on the gravy. Ice cream on the pie, too, please."

"You got it."

She bustled away, leaving Rick nothing to do but sit and wait.

He'd folded a paper napkin into a tulip when someone sat on the stool next to him. "Well, look what the cat dragged in," Bryce Arseneault said jovially.

Rick looked over at the police chief. Once the two of them had nearly gotten caught drinking Pete Arseneault's Wild Turkey and smoking behind the school. It had been Bryce who had shown Rick how to jimmy the lock to the auditorium. They'd waited there until the coast was clear. Rick always found it ironic and more than a bit amusing that Bryce was now the head of law enforcement for the town.

Rick picked up his ice water and took a sip. "Maybe you should sit somewhere else. You might tarnish my good reputation."

Bryce chuckled. "Right back atcha. How're you making out? Heard you moved back home."

Rick shook his head. "Grapevine's alive and well, I see. Yes, I'm back at my mom's house." His house now. He wondered if he'd ever see it that way.

Linda came back with Rick's dinner and nodded at Bryce. "What can I get you, Chief?"

"Piece of whatever pie you've got back there and a coffee. Thanks, Linda."

She disappeared and Bryce rested his elbows on the counter. "Seriously, Rick . . . how're you doing?"

"Trying to keep it so you don't have to haul my ass to the drunk tank."

Bryce nodded, his face sober. "That's good. That's real good. You've had a lot to deal with. Shit happens. You do the best you can."

That was one thing he liked about Bryce. He might be the chief but he never judged. He was probably the fairest person Rick had ever met. Unlike some people, who seemed to judge first and get details later.

Dammit. He'd almost managed to go without thinking about Jess for . . . what, twenty minutes?

He dipped into his chicken dinner. God, it was good to have home cooking. Gus had been cooking here at Breezes as long as Rick could remember. Not that Rick starved, but he never made something like this for himself. There never seemed to be much point.

Linda came back with Bryce's pie and coffee and they relaxed, eating and catching up on what was going on in the Collins family. Tom was ecstatic to be getting married; Bryce's wife, Mary, was feeling better now that her morning sickness had passed; Josh was enjoying the new medical practice. According to Mary, Jess had put on a new quilt at the shop and it was going to be gorgeous.

Somewhere along the line Linda had gone on break and Summer Arnold came by and cleared away Rick's plate, delivered his pie, and topped up Bryce's coffee. "So," he started conversationally, "I hear you're emceeing the wedding."

Bryce nodded. "Yeah. And you're best man. Looks like you get to wear the monkey suit." Bryce's wide grin made Rick chuckle.

"You don't think I can pull it off? Listen, it's way better I wear that than my dress uniform. The chicks wouldn't be able to resist me."

"You don't have to tell me about uniforms." Bryce nodded. "It drives my wife crazy. There's a reason we've got another kid on the way." He winked at Rick and they both laughed.

Rick told himself he didn't feel the least bit envious of his pals, who seemed to be dropping like flies at the mercy of marital fever. "Better you than me," he replied.

They were quiet for a few moments and then Bryce looked at him, all traces of teasing gone from his face. "You need any help, Rick?" He spoke in a low voice, like he didn't want to be overheard.

"Help with what?" Rick frowned. Why did everyone look at him like he was going to fall apart at any moment?

"Listen, I'm not trying to tell you what to do, but if you're having a hard time . . . with dealing with your mom's death . . ."

"I'm fine," he insisted, but that nervous churning in his stomach hit again.

"Okay. I just know that a lot of guys come home from deployment and have trouble making sense of stuff. They don't always handle it the right way."

"This is about my drinking," Rick guessed, gritting his teeth.

"Hey, you said you've been doing better. That's great. I just want you to get help if you need it, brother. Give me a call if that happens. I can help." Bryce put his hand on Rick's arm. On his prosthetic arm.

Sharp words sat on Rick's tongue, but he remembered feeling badly about snapping at Jess and knew, deep down, that his friend was just trying to help. "I'm dealing with it, don't worry," he assured Bryce with a smile. It felt slightly forced. "But thanks for the concern."

Bryce finished his coffee and took out a ten, tucked it under his plate. "You bet. I gotta go, but I'm just a phone call away. Got that?"

"I appreciate it."

Bryce laid a hand on his shoulder. "You hang tough. It'll get better." He gave Rick's shoulder a reassuring thump and then left the café.

It'll get better. Maybe, if people would stop reminding him how bad it was. He took a bite of pie and wished he wasn't longing for a stiff shot of rum.

Rick put his hand on the doorknob and hesitated. He'd finally given in to Tom—and his shrinking bank account—and agreed to work on Jess's shelves. But now he was an hour and a half late showing up, feeling rough around the edges and not prepared to face Jess right now.

The choice was taken out of his hands when the door to the shop swung open. "Are you going to stand out here all day?"

Nice beginning. Not even a chance to figure out what he was going to say to her to smooth any ruffled feathers. Perfect.

"Morning," he offered gruffly, sliding past her into the store. He halted, unprepared for the kaleidoscope of color that made up her shop. There were racks of quilts, fabric, a rainbow of yarn shoved in cubbies, racks with sparkly jewelry, candles of every color and size, and shelves of jams and jellies. She'd built quite an enterprise here, and Rick found himself incredibly proud of all she'd accomplished. Particularly since she'd done it on her own. Not that he felt compelled to point that out right at this moment. She was hardly in a receptive frame of mind. One look at the hard line of her eyebrows and the thin slash of her lips and he'd felt like the tardy kid in Ms. Robertson's second-grade class.

When Jess shut the door firmly behind him, he knew he'd better keep moving and made his way to her workroom in the back. It was huge. The perimeter was comprised of floor-to-waist cupboards and countertops. There were boxes and plastic storage containers with supplies lined up along the counters, vying for space with the stove, fridge, several bar stools, and a line of hot plates. In one corner was a quilting frame, the material stretched taut across it.

"What's all this for?" he asked, stopping in the middle of the room. The lighting was fantastic, considering there were fewer windows here than in the showroom. She'd been smart with her choices.

"My classes. The hot plates are for candles. We work at the counters a lot, but some of the classes need different seating. Like when I do a beading class. I have folding tables and chairs in the closet over there. I find it easier to show everyone something at once and put the beads in organizers along the middle of the tables. Knitting is like that, too. If the group's small enough, sometimes we take the knitting up to the loft. It's cozier."

"And the fridge and stove?"

"I use the stove for my candles. The fridge has supplies, and we often have snacks after classes. It's social, too."

He thought that perhaps the questions had soothed those ruffled feathers until she added, "Did you come to chat all day or are you going to get to work?"

"Sorry I'm late."

She walked up to him, surprising him by cupping his chin in her fingers and staring him in the eyes. Disapproval showed on every feature. "I'm sure you are," she replied, letting go and turning away.

"Jess, I overslept. That's all. I didn't hear the alarm."

She laughed, but it was a hard, dry laugh. "Sure, Rick. Whatever. I've got work to do. Tom left you the supplies on the back landing and said to call if you needed anything else for tools."

Frustration burned inside him. She was making assumptions again. It was as plain as the nose on his face. "Don't dismiss me like that, like you're all high and mighty. Don't you dare, Jessica Collins."

She spun back. "What am I supposed to do when you show up nearly two hours late, with bloodshot eyes and looking like you were dragged out of bed? Well, if nothing else, Rick, you're consistent."

Rick was tired. He'd had a rough night last night. He couldn't sleep—scenes with Kyle kept revolving in his head, making his mind whirr and his body tense. He'd kept thinking about what he might have done differently. If it would have changed the outcome. Naturally, he'd felt the urge to drink and drink a lot, just to make the whole cycle stop. It was ironic, wasn't it? That the thing Jess was accusing him of was the one thing he'd worked hardest to avoid?

"You automatically think I was drinking," he ground out. His temper was short today, he realized. He needed something physical, an activity to take up some of this energy pounding through him. He clenched his fingers into a fist and released them again.

"Weren't you?" One eyebrow went up this time. He had the unholy urge to kiss the condemning expression off her face. Plant one big one on her and wipe that smug, disdainful look clean away. That would fix her wagon . . .

Who was he kidding? Kissing Jess would be about like puckering up to a viper, the mood she was in.

"If I said I wasn't drinking, would you even believe me?" She opened her mouth but he held up a hand. "Enough, Jess. I'm late, I'm sorry you're angry, let's both just get to work and stay out of each other's way."

She stood there, hands on hips, glaring at him.

"Look," he challenged again, fed up with her passing judgment all the time. "Do you want these shelves or not? If you don't, I'll take off right now, and you can call Tom and explain why you need someone from his crew to fit you into their schedule."

Ah. She looked slightly uncomfortable at that notion. And he supposed he could tell her the truth—that he'd stayed up late working on a project to keep himself from breaking a promise. But he shouldn't have to. Especially when his painting was something he guarded carefully. It was his and his alone.

Besides, Jess might laugh at him. And he'd rather take her anger and judgment than mockery.

"Well?" he asked, none too kindly.

She flounced her hair over her shoulder. "Fine. I'll be in the front working on consignment statements."

Jess was gone in a cloud of scent that reminded him both of his mother's garden and sugar cookies. He sighed and wiped his hand over his face. Thank God Tom had sent over the dimensions for the shelves a couple of days ago. Otherwise Rick might have needed to ask Jess for input and he'd rather deal with an angry badger than tangle with her at the moment.

He spent the next hour lugging in the materials, taking longer than normal since he could have used two arms at 100 percent. Still, he managed, including a large tote that held all the tools he'd need for the job as well as a spare battery and charger for the cordless drill.

It helped that the shelves were pre-cut and only needed to be installed. Once Rick made sense of the lengths and where they'd go, he sorted through the hardware and organized brackets and screws into neat piles. He measured, then marked everything with the level, and it was all going smoothly until he went to screw the first bracket into place. He was holding the metal piece with his prosthetic, and the screw clung to the magnetic tip of the drill bit, but he didn't get it set quite right and the moment he pulled the trigger, it spun off the tip and went careening away, tap-tapping on the floor as it fell.

Rick sighed.

"Do you need help?"

Jess's voice was soft, coming from the doorway. He looked up, irritated. Her expression had softened and she'd lost that condemning look she'd had when he'd first arrived. Just looking at her made his body react in ways he wished it wouldn't. It made things damned uncomfortable. How could he possibly be attracted to someone who made him so angry?

"I'm fine." He retrieved the screw from the floor, then marked the spot, gave it a tap to set the tip, put the bracket back in place, and pressed the drill bit firmly against the top of the screw. To his relief it went perfectly into place.

"Rick, I'm sorry I was so angry."

For some reason her apology made him nearly as mad as the accusation. Maybe he should do the gracious thing and accept it. He didn't feel like it. Maybe Jess needed to learn to think before she spoke . . . and that words were more than just words.

"Okay," he answered. He picked up another screw. This one was easier now that the first screw held the bracket in place. The drill whined through the silence.

"You're mad at me," she said, and he looked up. Sure enough, her eyes were asking for forgiveness. He should give it. He knew that. But because Jess made him feel weak, he held back.

"I'm busy here, Jess. You want your job done or not?"

She turned on her heel and disappeared again.

When she was gone Rick dropped his head and let out a breath. This wasn't good. His feelings for Jess weren't exactly friendly. They were more, much more, and she was convinced that he was nothing more than a disappointment.

The old Rick would have shaken that off, put on the charm, and proved her wrong. The problem was, he wasn't convinced she was wrong. And until he was, he had no business messing around with the likes of Jess Collins.

CHAPTER 5

Jess had just rolled the quilt and was now immersed in making tiny, even stitches. She loved the feel of the needle and thimble, the slight popping sound as the needle poked through the taut fabric, the bubbled texture of the previously quilted spots under her fingertips. Summer Arnold, one of the regulars from Jess's craft classes, sat beside her looking like the last person to be spending an afternoon with a needle and thread.

Summer's hair had a pink streak down one side, a silver nose ring looped through one nostril, and her jeans had tears at the knees and thighs. Her youthful face had a healthy glow, though, and she seemed to blend an edgy rebel look with a natural, earthy vibe.

It was a relief for Jess to spend time with Summer, one of the few friends she had who was unmarried. It seemed lately that every time she turned around she was faced with her family and friends and their perfect husbands, perfect families, perfect lives. Sometimes it put Jess's life in stark relief. It seemed like everyone was married or in love these days. And Jess was alone.

Which was her choice. She'd rather be alone than settle just because she was lonely, but sometimes—not that she'd admit it to another soul—that choice sucked.

She focused on the pieced blocks that made up waves and a sailboat. Summer tied off her thread and grabbed the spool for more. "Hey Jess, I heard you and Rick took some donations to the shelter. How's he doing?"

Jess started at the mention of Rick's name. The last few days she'd had to endure his presence in her workroom, and he barely said two words to her. He was still angry at her accusations that first morning. But she'd taken one look at his bloodshot eyes and tousled hair and had known. She wished she had better control over her reactions. It didn't seem to matter what she knew intellectually—certain things still triggered an automatic response, like a muscle memory to a threat. One of those things was the way a man looked after a binge. In her experience they were irritable at best, and a hair trigger at worst.

Once she'd had time to process things, she'd calmed down. And felt a little foolish for being so snappish.

"Oh, you know," she said as lightly as she could manage. "Okay, considering."

"I saw him the other night. He was with Bryce."

Great. Rick plus the police chief. "What trouble did he get himself into this time?"

"Trouble?" Summer's brows pulled together in confusion. "No trouble. He was having some dinner at Breezes and I was on shift that night. He's moved back into his mom's house, you know."

Jess hadn't known. She'd tried to keep her nose firmly out of Rick's business. It was too complicated and all they usually ended up doing was arguing anyway. "That's good," she said, concentrating on a line of stitches. "It's got to be better than where he was."

"Sure, but I bet it's hard, too. Bryce said Rick really seems to be making an effort to get his act together. Shame he's laid off. It would probably be easier if he were working."

Keeping busy was always a good idea, Jess knew firsthand. It was a rare thing for her to sit idle. It gave her too much time to think. Like think about how Rick's mouth had quirked up when he was teasing her in the car, or how the muscles had rippled his shirt when he lifted boxes. Now she felt smaller than ever, because Rick had really needed this job and she hadn't made it easy for him.

"Anything else new?" she asked, wanting to change the subject.

Summer shrugged. "Remember Karen Greer? I heard she and her husband just moved back to Jewell Cove. Apparently, she has cancer and isn't doing so well, so Brian moved them back to town. Says she wants to be by the ocean." Summer paused to shake her head sadly. "Word is, Brian called the kids and asked them to come home. I guess they don't want to wait until Christmas. It might be too late by then." Her words were quiet, in deference to the sad subject.

Jess's body went suddenly cold and her hand stopped midstitch.

"Didn't I hear that you went out with Mike Greer back in the day?" Summer's voice perked up as she knotted a new thread. "I think Bryce mentioned that."

Summer had continued on as if the mentioning of Mike Greer's name was simple gossipy conversation. Her stitches were smooth and even; she was utterly unaware of how Jess had frozen in her chair.

Mike Greer. Just the name was enough to make her tremble. Josh had made him promise to never come back to Jewell Cove and to her knowledge he never had. Of course, Josh had also promised Mike that if he did return, he'd never walk again. And he'd meant it. The quilt in Jess's hands faded as she struggled to breathe, trapped in her memories. Josh had been the one to tend her cuts and bruises. He'd been staying at their mom's place, home on leave, when he'd stopped by the little house she and Mike had rented from his parents. She had been so young back then, so determined to have her own way by moving out, unwilling to admit that her boyfriend would never change. But when she saw Josh's reaction to her injuries, she'd known enough was enough.

Jess's fingers tightened on the scrap of cloth in front of her. That night she'd left Mike, but no matter what Josh said, Jess had felt so stupid. She'd refused to let anyone else see just what her life had become. Instead, Josh drove her to the shelter and held her hand as she'd called their mother and explained that she and Mike had broken up and she was visiting friends for a while to clear her head. He'd made sure that Mike was really gone, and once the visual evidence of that night was gone from her face, she'd returned home. Started getting on with her life.

Sort of.

"Jess, are you okay?" Summer's voice came from beside her, deep with concern. "You've gone really pale."

Breathe. In, out. In, out. Jess forced a smile and slipped the thimble from her finger. "Sorry. I've got a bit of a headache. I felt a little woozy there for a minute."

"We can stop for today. Maybe you need to lie down? Or maybe it's the fine detail of the stitches bothering your eyes. Do you want to take something for it?"

Bless her, Summer was in mothering mode and it was hard for Jess to say no. Mike had no power over her now. Never would again. She'd repeat it to herself until she believed it, just as she'd done in the years since she'd left him. And it would be okay.

"I'll be fine. I just need to make some tea or something."

Summer popped up from her chair. "You need to relax. Let's leave this for now and go up to your loft. You can chill out and I'll make the tea."

What Jess really wanted was to be alone, but she could hardly throw Summer out. Truth be told, she was tired. The foot traffic was picking up again and she had added extra evening classes. During the day she'd been working on replenishing her stock—something she didn't have much time to do over the summer months. Yesterday she'd spent the whole day on candles, which sold briskly when the autumn set in. There were still the necklaces for the wedding to make, too . . .

They climbed the stairs to Jess's loft—her living space above the store and workroom. It was a huge area, the entire second floor divided into a single bedroom, bathroom, and common-area living room and kitchen.

She'd kept the colors deliberately light and restful—creamy white and pale aqua with the smallest splashes of taupe and apricot in the decoration. The floor was natural maple hardwood, adding to the impression of light and space. An array of Jess's candles and seashells were arranged atop a glass-topped coffee table. The same wall of windows faced the harbor, with white roman blinds pulled open now but ready to drape down for privacy as needed.

Jess preferred to keep them open as much as possible.

Just being here brought her stress levels down. Summer instantly went to fill the kettle sitting on the stove and told Jess to sit.

Jess obeyed, sinking into the soft cushions of her sofa. From there she directed Summer to the cups and tea bags, leaned back, and gratefully closed her eyes. It made sense if Summer thought she had a headache, but truthfully she was just trying to calm down and not have a panic attack. She'd already felt her head go light, her leg muscles tighten up, the telltale tingling of her scalp. It didn't happen often, not anymore. The mention of Mike Greer was enough to set it off.

"You like milk, Jess?"

"Just a little, yes, please." She opened her eyes, feeling slightly more in control. "Thanks, Summer. I don't know what came over me." *Liar*, a voice in her head accused, but she ignored it. She'd learned how to cover a long time ago.

"Please," Summer chided, bringing over a steaming mug. "You're always taking care of everyone else, Jess. Sometimes you need looking after, too. How's the head?"

"A little better, thanks." She sipped at the hot tea . . . delicious. More of the tension drained away. Summer, for all her quirky appearances, was a nurturing soul.

"I really love it up here, Jess. It's like having the beach right in your apartment."

"That was the general idea." She smiled faintly. "Thanks for this. I think I needed the sit-down."

"Tessa's got the store and you're right here if she needs anything. You should have a nap. You've got that burning the candle at both ends look about you."

"I might do that."

"In that case I'll let you go. I want to stop by the soap shop on the way home. I'm out of lavender oil."

Summer took her mug to the kitchen and came back, giving Jess's hand a squeeze. "Take some time for yourself, sweetie. You deserve it as much as anyone else. See you later."

When she was gone Jess sighed and put her mug on the coffee table and slid down on the sofa, pulling a cream-colored throw over her. Maybe just a short nap. Just for a few minutes . . .

Darkness filtered through the windows as Jess jerked awake from a nightmare, sitting up abruptly. Her breath came hard and fast; sweat trickled down her temples and she pulled her knees into her chest while she tried to get her bearings.

God, it had been so real. Like he was right there, back in the Greer summer cottage where they'd moved in together. Sheltered by the woods on three sides and with wide open water on the other, the property was secluded and private. More like isolated. A prison. Over the years, Jess had learned a lot about abusive relationships, about the emotional and psychological damage that came with living with someone like Mike. But at night, she just remembered the sight of his face twisted with ugly anger, the sound of his hand hitting her cheek echoing through the air the millisecond before the numbing pain struck.

Jess smoothed her hands over her face, trying to shut the memories out and focus on the present, but in the dim light of her living room, she could still feel Mike's hands circling her neck until she saw black and gray blotches. Not long enough for her to lose consciousness. Only long enough to keep the fear pounding through her veins, just the way he wanted it.

She trembled all over and couldn't stop. Tears streaked down her cheeks as she fought to banish the images from her mind. She was in her home. She was safe, and Mike Greer was long out of the picture. But his family had just moved home, and his mom was sick. There was no way one promise made years ago was going to keep him away for good.

Shoving her damp hair back from her face, she rose unsteadily, went to the kitchen, and poured herself a glass of water. Then she picked up the phone and dialed.

"This is Josh."

"Hey, brother." Her voice came out slightly shaky. Damn.

"Jess. What's wrong? You sound funny."

"I'm okay. Just a bad dream."

"Aw, honey. You want to come over?"

Josh lived in a house just down the street from Sarah and Mark. But Jess didn't want to risk seeing anyone else, not in her state. "No, it's okay. I just . . . it's the reason for the nightmare that I wanted to talk to you about."

"Yeah?"

"I heard today that the Greers moved back. Karen has cancer. And Brian has asked the kids to come home."

Josh let out a long breath. It sounded like a whistle in Jess's ear and she closed her eyes. After their dad had died, she'd relied on Josh. He was so much like their father. Caring but tough. Reliable. Just talking to him helped immensely.

"You worried about him coming near you?"

There was a long pause, and then she whispered, "Just hearing his name made me melt down, Josh."

Josh cursed under his breath. "We should have had him arrested back then. Do you want to tell Bryce? I doubt there's anything he can do about it, but it wouldn't hurt to have him know."

"No!" Jess tried to temper her voice and not panic. "You're the only one who knows what happened that night. And I want to keep it that way. Please, Josh."

"Jess . . ."

"I just . . . I don't know what I want. To give you the heads-up, I guess. To . . . to tell someone rather than keep it inside. This way if I show up on your doorstep, you'll know why."

"You can come stay here," he suggested. "I doubt he'll be in town for long if he shows up at all. I could always use a roommate."

She thought of Josh's hours, and his dislike for

housekeeping and cooking. "Thanks, but no thanks. At least not for now. Talking to you has helped." Besides, she'd fought hard for her independence, moving out, taking night courses in business, and opening the shop. She wasn't about to give that up at the first sign of trouble.

"If he causes any grief—and I mean any at all, I want you to promise me that you'll talk to Bryce about it."

"I'd rather keep it quiet."

"Promise me, Jess. Mike Greer is a manipulative asshole who thinks he can have whatever he wants. I convinced him otherwise once, but I don't trust him and neither should you."

"Don't worry, I don't. Not for a second."

"So promise me."

"I promise. You're a good brother, Josh."

"Of course I am. And remember—you're not in this alone. You never were. And I can guaran-damn-tee you that you've got backup in me, and Tom, and Bryce, and even Rick if it comes to that. The slightest whiff of trouble and you go to any one of us, okay? We've got your back one hundred percent."

Her throat closed over a wad of tears. "Okay," she whispered into the receiver.

"Love you," he said, making her even more weepy.

"Love you, too," she said.

After she hung up the phone, she went to the bathroom and ran a hot shower, scrubbing away the sweat and the lingering dregs of the nightmare. Too bad she couldn't scrub away the memories of the past, too. But they were there to stay. She ran the puff over the puckered scar on her belly and swallowed the tears that clogged in her throat, refusing to let them out.

He'd marked her for life.

As maid of honor, it was Jess's duty to hold a bridal shower for Abby, and she hosted it on the Saturday night one week before the wedding. She closed the store at five, and at seven thirty about a dozen women would descend on her apartment for an evening of food, wine, and silly shower games. She was also aware that the boys were having their stag night tonight.

Jess put out a few wine bottles and glasses, and then a punch bowl for those who chose not to drink. Her mind automatically drifted to Rick like it seemed to quite frequently these days. She wondered how he was doing in his mother's house all by himself. And then whether he'd be any trouble at the bachelor party tonight. For Tom's sake, she hoped not. She was glad that tonight's party was low-key—just a poker night for four at Josh's house with pizza and beer. Maybe Rick would be sensible for once.

And maybe she should spend the time getting ready instead of thinking about Rick so much.

She mixed the punch in a large juice container and put it in the fridge—she'd add the soda when it was time to serve, and the berries she'd frozen, too. All around the room she'd put jars of her homemade candles, the scent she called "Wedding Cake" which was a yummy blend of almond, white cake, and vanilla scents. Each jar was tied with navy-and-white ribbons—Abby's wedding colors—with a small silk sprig of lily of the

valley. She'd made miniature jars, too, as favors for all
the guests, and had popped into the flower shop for a
bouquet to help dress up the apartment. Knowing Abby's
preference for warm fall colors, she brought home an
enormous arrangement of miniature sunflowers, red
gerbera daisies, orange circus roses, lilies, and wheat.
She'd deliberately steered away from the paper stream-
ers and wedding bells, though she'd be sure to keep
the bows from the presents and make Abby one heck
of a "bouquet." Every bride deserved that sort of silly
memento.

At seven twenty people began arriving. Jess poured
the punch, uncorked wine, deposited presents on the
glass-topped table, and put her scallops wrapped in
bacon under the broiler. Cindy White arrived and brought
tortilla chips with salsa and a huge bowl of fresh guacamole. Then came Gloria Henderson, church organist
and head of the Historical Society, carrying her Tupperware container of ambrosia salad. Summer swept in,
the tips of her hair dyed a new shade of pinkish red and
carrying a tray of veggies and dip. Mary and Sarah arrived and added grapes and a variety of cheeses to the
feast. Lisa Goodwin, who was one of the last babies to
be born at Foster House when it was a home for unwed
mothers, came in quietly, a bit shyer than the others.
She put her present on the table and then asked Jess for
a plate for her crackers and if she had room to heat up
her crab dip a little.

The noise in the apartment was rising, ringing with
laughter, as everyone filled Abby in on some of Tom's
more embarrassing moments growing up in Jewell Cove.
Jess laughed as Sarah started in on the time Tom, Josh,

and Rick decided to search for the fabled treasure out at Fiddler's Rock. Jess had tried to tag along until Rick had implemented a no-girls rule.

Rick. Jess stiffened as the image of the man he was today popped into her head. She should be relaxed and enjoying herself, so why was it she couldn't stop thinking about Rick and wondering what he was doing tonight? Was Rick laughing with the guys at these same memories? He hadn't been by the shop for a few days. Why on earth did she keep wishing to spend time with him again? Like in the cab of his truck, maybe? Driving to nowhere in particular?

The thought didn't sit well, so Jess busied herself in the kitchen. Someone had been gracious enough to take her scallops out of the oven when the timer went off; they were arranged on a shell-shaped platter and put with the other food along with the warm crab dip. Jess grabbed a plate since she'd missed dinner and filled it with goodies, then poured a cup of punch and took it to a stool by the breakfast nook. Abby came over and put her hand on Jess's shoulder just as she was scooping some guacamole onto a curled chip.

"Jess, this looks lovely. The candles are gorgeous. Flowers, too. You didn't have to go to all this trouble."

"It was my pleasure. I was young and living at home when Sarah got married. I never got the chance to throw her a shower; our mom did that. I'm more than happy to do it for you. So, this is your last week as a single woman. How does it feel?"

Abby's smile blossomed. "Awesome."

"Well, grab something to eat, and we'll get some presents going before long."

"Thank you, Jess. For everything." Abby leaned over and kissed Jess's cheek, the gesture so sweet and uncommon that Jess's eyes misted over for just a moment. On impulse Jess reached out and took Abby's hand. Their eyes met and Jess felt an odd, strange community with Abby. Like the other woman could see past her barriers.

"My great-grandmother would have liked you," Abby said. The comment struck Jess as a bit strange, seeing as Abby had never met Edith Foster. "You're stronger than you think, Jess."

Before Jess could even react to the odd words, Abby dropped her hand and moved away to the kitchen table, where the buffet was spread. What did Abby know? Was it possible Josh had said something to Tom since her call the other night? It was the only explanation she could think of. On one hand the idea made her furious. It wasn't Josh's secret to tell. On the other . . . it was good to know she wasn't alone if Mike did show up in town again.

You're stronger than you think.

She certainly hoped so. Because the idea of facing Mike Greer alone scared her to death.

CHAPTER 6

On a cloudy Monday morning, Rick finally got up the nerve to go through the spare room closet.

He'd been thinking about it ever since closing the bank box lid over the photo albums. He hadn't even known they were there . . . boys didn't pay attention to that sort of thing growing up. Sure, he'd posed for a few sports photos but for the most part a mom with a camera was a nuisance.

Now he wasn't sure if he was happy to still have the memories or not.

With a stainless steel mug filled with coffee, he dug the boxes out of the closet and sat on the bed, sipping and looking through pictures.

The ones on top were the most recent, but ended several years before, when he'd officially become a Marine. There he was, a few pounds lighter, tall, and in the best shape of his life in his uniform, standing with his arm around his mom. She looked so happy and proud, and it sent another pang of regret slicing through him that he hadn't given her many reasons to be proud in the last while. He stared at the face looking back at him. It was so young, so energized . . . that young man had thought he was ready to face whatever the world would throw at him.

He missed that guy.

That guy—that *boy*—had been slowly worn down by the unrelenting monotony of sand and sun, by miles of roads littered with IEDs, by the bodies of the enemy, and worse, the bodies of comrades. The man he'd become had seen the ugliness of war and it had taken its toll.

Long, hot days, the isolation, the constant stress. And one ambush that changed everything.

He was so sick of people saying he was lucky it was only his hand. They had no idea what he'd lost over there. None. His friend. His self-respect.

He flipped backward through the photo album. Basic training, summers at home, his skin tanned and healthy, his arm strung around Josh after a day on the water. Graduation . . . Jess standing in the background with her family. In his baseball uniform and a team picture from high school at the state championships. He'd been a junior, Josh and Tom seniors. Looking like they had the world by the tail . . .

His coffee was long gone by the time he'd flipped through two more albums, each one going back in time to earlier years, complete with cowlicks and T-shirts sporting the logos of his favorite teams. At ten years old, standing on skates and a hockey stick in his hand. At six, riding a two-wheeler. His chest constricted as he saw a picture of his dad, smiling, standing behind the bike as if he'd just let go of the seat, pushing Rick to go forward on his own.

The preschool years, complete with curly hair and pudgy cheeks. First steps. First birthday. And the very first picture in the album.

The plain-painted walls and trim were rather utilitarian, like a hospital, though he couldn't be quite sure. His mom, looking impossibly young and happy, a blue bundle in her arms, and his dad, standing behind her, a huge grin on his face. And someone else—a young-looking Marian Foster.

Rick peeled back the now-brittle plastic on the album and took out the picture for a closer look. It was her all right, though clearly much younger than she'd been when he'd last seen her. There was no mistaking that dark hair and the big brown eyes that always seemed to be hinting at humor. He'd always liked Marian. She'd never had kids of her own, but whenever there was a town function she was there helping and she talked to the kids like they were human beings, not stupid or babies. He turned the picture over. The pen on the back was faded, partly worn away by the semi-sticky surface of the album page. But he could make out the blue ink. *Meeting our new baby son, June 11th, Camden.*

Rick touched the writing with his fingertip. June 11th—he'd been exactly one week old.

He read the words again. *Meeting our new baby son . . .*

He put the photo back in the album, smoothing the plastic sheet back. A wrinkle creased down the middle of the page and didn't want to smooth out. Over the years the plastic had dried out and yellowed slightly. Still, he couldn't take his eyes off the picture. There he was, bundled in a tiny blue blanket, only a week old, while the words "meeting our new son" ran through his head. That was the moment, then, that he'd become Rick Sullivan. His heart constricted as he stared at his mom, so young and obviously happy. He didn't know the circumstances surrounding his birth parents, but he was in no doubt that he'd been wanted and loved.

God, how he missed her.

He put the album back in the box and returned it to the closet.

"Rick?"

The sound of his voice being called from downstairs made him jump.

"Rick, are you up there?"

It was Jess. Shit. Hurriedly he tucked the top on the box. "I'll be right down," he called, wondering what the hell she was doing here. He shut the closet door and his stomach suddenly clenched. He'd left the porch door open . . . and he'd been working on a new project— sunflowers on a four-pane window he'd found out in the back of the shed.

She couldn't see it. Couldn't see what he did with his days . . . and sometimes nights, if the nightmares kept him awake. Quick steps took him to the stairs and then down. "Hang on, be right with you!" he called, hoping she'd stayed in the kitchen.

But he smelled the soft scent of her perfume the moment he hit the bottom step. Damn. "Jess?" he called, hoping she answered behind him.

"In here."

His stomach seemed to drop to his feet. In the porch. Where his easel was set up, the window propped on it, the frame sanded until it was soft and the glass cleaned and prepped for painting. He'd finished one pane already, with three sunflower blooms surrounded by dark green leaves and a smattering of miniature daisies. Dread rolled through his stomach . . . he hadn't wanted anyone to find out, not here in Jewell Cove. There was a reason why he took his finished pieces to Portland and sold them to a shop there. He could remain anonymous.

Jaw clenched, he stepped to the door of the porch. She was standing in front of his easel, her eyes wide as she examined the work. Lord above, she was beautiful. He never tired of seeing that black tumble of curls, just begging to be tamed by a man's strong hand, or the curves that were only hinted at beneath her loose, casual clothing. Today it was a soft white tunic shirt and a pair of tan linen trousers. Her skin was still tanned from the summer and he could see a light dusting of freckles on either side of her nose, making her look younger than she was.

She was life and beauty and vitality. She was beach glass, made smooth and vibrant from the water while he was driftwood washed upon the shore.

And now she knew his secret.

Jess looked up and saw him there. He looked angry, annoyed, and if she was any judge of facial expressions at all—guilty.

She couldn't believe what she was seeing. The long,

narrow room had been transformed into an artist's studio, complete with easel, rags, tubes and bottles of paint,
brushes, sponges . . . it was the real deal. In Rick's house.
She couldn't be more surprised if he'd announced he
was the Dalai Lama and was petitioning for world
peace.

"You did this? These?" She swept her hand out, the
gesture encompassing the half-dozen paintings he'd
finished, which were placed along the wall beneath the
windows. Glass and frames of various sizes, with images of flowers, trees, birds, the ocean. Spectacular.

He didn't answer, just stared at her. Jess doubted
anyone in Jewell Cove knew what Rick did in his spare
time.

He'd been a Marine, for God's sake. All-star first
baseman in his senior year and Jewell Cove hell-
raiser before that. It was hard trying to reconcile that
testosterone-fueled image to one of him as a painter. As
an artist, she corrected mentally. There was no doubt
about it. He was incredibly talented.

"They're beautiful, Rick. Really stunning."

"Was there something you wanted, Jess?"

She was taken aback by the sharp question. Did he
really think she'd ignore what she'd walked into? He'd
barked the words with more than a hint of accusation;
he might as well have said *get out*.

"Well, yes. But it can wait a few minutes. How long
have you been doing this? And why glass? What are
you doing with the paintings?"

"Let's just try to forget you saw them, okay?" He
turned away from her, taking a step back inside the main
part of the house. Was he hoping she'd follow?

"Forget? Not likely. I really like this one."

He turned back. She stood in front of a long pane, again in an old window frame. He'd painted the frame an antique white and then distressed it to make it look old. Then on the back side he'd painted a winding profusion of hollyhocks climbing a cedar log fence with an oak tree in the background. The colors were vivid and yet soft on the clear medium. It was absolutely gorgeous. And worth money, she was sure of it. A lot of it. He should be selling these things, she thought.

"Jess . . ."

She went over to him then, took his hand, and pulled him into the porch. "Why are you trying to hide it? My God, Rick, this work is gorgeous. I had no idea . . ."

"And you wouldn't have, either," he said, pulling his hand away, "if you'd bothered to knock."

Her brows pulled together. "I did knock and you didn't answer. Your truck was out front and the door was unlocked. Anyway, it's nothing to be ashamed of. Don't be so touchy."

"I'm not ashamed. I just didn't want to have to explain. It's private."

Her heart caught a little. This was a side of Rick she never knew existed. "It is for most artists," she explained. "What they create . . . it's a part of them. It's like revealing yourself to the world. But Rick, this shouldn't be hidden away. You've got a real talent. When did you start painting?"

"Just leave it alone," he answered impatiently.

She frowned. "No."

He shrugged, then sighed, as if he realized he might as well speak since she wasn't giving up.

"Fine. When I was in the hospital, I guess. Sometimes I don't sleep that great."

"Most people count sheep."

"God, you're persistent."

She smiled. "Well, duh. This can't be the first time you've realized that."

Rick's mouth curled up in a half smile that caused a strange pang near Jess's heart. His eyes looked clearer today, his face cleanly shaven. The air around them relaxed as the argument dissipated, leaving intimacy in its wake. Their eyes met and something zinged between them. Attraction? Maybe. Recognition? Definitely. They had history whether they wanted to admit it or not. They'd been friends a long time.

"Yeah, it's not the first time." He gave a low, grudging chuckle. "You're a wicked pain in my ass, Saint Jess."

When he smiled like that, when he teased her, it was hard to remember the reasons why she was so determined to keep her distance. "I try," she answered. "So. You started painting when you were laid up . . ." She led him with a new question.

"It wasn't painting at first," he explained. "I started doodling in the hospital. I was bored, and I started scribbling pictures of things I remembered from home. It wasn't just my hand that I lost. I'd been poked with a few more holes and had to stay in the hospital longer than I would have liked. The doodling turned to sketching. I enjoyed it, and thought maybe the sketches weren't too bad. I got a new pad, a few different pencils. After I got stateside I went to rehab at a clinic and they had this neat painting. It was the ocean but it was on glass and with the light behind it, it almost looked like the waves were moving. I did a little online research into how to do it and gave it a try."

"How long ago?"

"A year? Maybe a year and a half."

She shook her head. "Remarkable."

"Not really. It's just something I do. Besides, the first ones were horrible." He shrugged again.

He was determined to minimize it. To make it no big deal when the truth was seeing his paintings gave her goose bumps. She was good with her hands. She was creative. But she knew her limitations, too. What Rick had was special.

"I could never do this, not in a million years. There's something about them, something so alive and yet soft and romantic." She grinned up at him, impressed and proud. "Who knew, right?"

"Yeah, well, can you just imagine what would happen if I admitted to the population of Jewell Cove that I fiddled around with paints? First of all, they'd never believe it. And second . . . well, it'd be a big joke."

"Who cares what people think? Shoot, they already think you're . . ." She paused.

"Think I'm a what, Jess? A nuisance? A has-been? A drunk?"

She felt her cheeks heat. "Rick . . ."

"That's what you were going to say, right?"

She looked away, ashamed. "It's possible I've been a little judgmental in that regard. I've also heard you've been doing much better . . . despite having to deal with your mom's passing."

"How generous of you."

She looked up quickly. Her gaze locked with his and an unfamiliar breathless feeling took over as his dark eyes held hers steadily. They were clear and endless, without the red lids and fuzzy focus she'd seen in him in the past.

But was he really cleaned up or was she just looking and hoping for the best?

She took a mental step back. "Forget about all that for a moment. What are you doing with your paintings?"

He scooted past her. The room was narrow and there wasn't much space to pass by her, but he managed to do it without touching her at all. Her gaze followed him as he made his way to the easel, touched the frame with a fingertip.

"I've been selling them to a shop in Portland. He buys what I have, calls when his stock is getting low. The summer was good for business, plus I had less time to paint once I started working for Jack. He probably won't need as much now, with the tourist season dropping off."

"Still . . . it's Portland. Bigger population base, and the holidays are coming up. Besides, if it's a bit slower it'll give you a chance to stockpile some for next year, when the tourist traffic is high again." Personally she was thrilled that Rick had taken them somewhere—that he'd seen the value in them. Even though he'd deliberately chosen someplace out of Jewell Cove. She looked at the finished work against the wall. There was no real signature. Just a small "RS" in one corner, marking the artist. Protecting his identity all the way.

"I suppose."

She went up to him, made a point of looking at what

he was looking at—the golden yellow sunflowers on the glass. "What if you had an alternate market for them?"

"What do you mean?" He lifted his chin and looked over at her. She was trying hard not to imagine him sketching in a hospital bed after leaving a war zone but it was difficult. He didn't have to say it for her to know this was his outlet. The same way that she knit and melted wax for candles and designed jewelry and pieced quilts . . . this was Rick's way of shutting out the painful part of his world. Well, one of his strategies, anyway. At least this was a way of dealing with his troubles that she wholeheartedly supported.

She marveled at the simple beauty of flowers on glass. After what he'd been through, she would have expected to see something more dark and ugly and, frankly, cathartic. But Rick didn't paint the world he'd seen. He painted the world he *wanted* to see. It was remarkable.

If it wouldn't have been incredibly awkward and potentially misconstrued, she might have hugged him.

"I mean, what if I sold some of them for you? We could do it on consignment like I do with my other clients. If you want to keep your privacy you can. But why take them all the way to Portland if you can sell them here? Besides, you'll get a better return from me. You'll make a better percentage than if you sold to me outright and then I did markup. With the boat season ending, that should be good news."

He was frowning. "Well, except with him I get paid up front, and with you I'd have to wait for them to sell, so I'd never know when the money was coming. I'd probably be better off going to The Three Fishermen."

Damn, he had a good point. The local art gallery was a perfect place for them. But on a personal level she wanted a crack at them first.

"They'll sell. No question. And I review the consignment books every month. Besides, I'll guarantee your anonymity. Paul at the gallery wouldn't."

"If I tell you I'll think about it, will you finally tell me why you really came over here?"

Distracted, Jess waved in agreement. It was more than she'd actually expected for a response. Rick was a stubborn cuss when he wanted to be. But he was honest to a fault and if he said he was thinking about it, he was thinking about it and not just putting her off. She'd have to reorganize the shop floor to make room and in a spot where the light was sure to set the colors off to best advantage . . .

She was still trying to wrap her head around the discovery.

"Want a coffee? I put a pot on earlier."

"Sure." Following him into the kitchen, Jess couldn't help but examine her surroundings. Despite being a guy and living alone, Rick kept the place up pretty well. Maybe there was a little dust in the corners, but the dishes were done and everything put away neatly. She'd seen worse. Like at her sister's, after a day playing outside with the kids. Sarah's kitchen often looked like a plague of locusts had gone through, razing everything in sight.

"How was the bachelor party?" she asked. She'd heard, actually, from Josh, but figured it was a good way to make conversation. According to Josh it had been fairly uneventful, though Bryce had fleeced them all at poker.

"It was good. Just a night with the boys and some cards."

Funny he omitted the beer portion, as if he knew it would set her off. Though Josh—her inside source for everything these days—did mention that Rick had stuck with cola all night, much to everyone's surprise. "I heard Bryce made out fine."

Rick chuckled as he took mugs out of the cupboard. "He's a shark. Good thing the stakes were low. I might have lost my inheritance."

She laughed. "Abby's shower was good, too. Presents, food, punch . . . we made Abby wear a wedding gown made from toilet paper and gave her a bouquet made from the bows from her gifts."

He turned around and leaned back against the counter, folding his arms. "Cluck cluck. Sounds like quite a hen fest."

She grinned back. "To be honest . . . it was good, but I think cards and pizza would have been just as fun."

"You'll have to come some night when we're playing." He raised an eyebrow. "Then again, maybe not. Pretty girls are big distractions at the poker table."

Pretty girls. Despite all their animosity, he'd just called her pretty. And she should not be flattered by it but she was. Rick Sullivan still had the power to be charming.

"Right," she said, clearing her throat. "Anyway, the real reason for my visit. I've been working on a surprise for Tom and Abby, but I need your help."

"My help? You're asking for my help with a wedding?" He looked around himself curiously. "Did I fall into an alternate universe?"

"Smart ass," she answered.

He put a steaming mug in front of her. "You want cream?"

"And sugar if you've got it."

He got a spoon, sugar bowl, and a carton of milk. "Sorry. I guess I just have milk."

"That's fine." She worked on stirring the sugar into her coffee while he poured his own cup and left it black. "Anyway, a friend of mine around Auburn has agreed to lend me his car to chauffeur Tom and Abby around for the day. It's a very special car. The kind of car I'm not sure I'm comfortable driving."

He sat across from her and raised his eyebrows. "What kind of car is it?"

"A 1966 Mustang convertible. Mint."

She watched his eyes light up. Men were so predictable. A little testosterone, a vintage muscle car—and boom! Game over.

"Where do I come in?"

"I want you to drive it. I've talked to Glen and he said it was okay with him."

"Glen? And how exactly do you know this Glen and his awesome car?"

She couldn't help but smile. Was that a proprietary note in his voice? At least it wasn't the insolent sarcasm he so often reverted to with her. He had a tendency to get defensive. Like he had on the porch this morning. And in the truck after the drive to the shelter. He was fine as long as they were strictly polite. But when she got too close, up went the walls. Not that she was interested in knocking them down . . .

"Glen is into woodworking and his wife does tole painting. I carry some of their things in the store—finished and unfinished."

"Oh."

He took a drink of his coffee.

"Well? What do you say? Will you drive it? We'd have to go up early Saturday morning to pick it up, because I have to be back for hair and makeup with Abby. But . . . I was thinking you could pick us up at the house and drive us to the church. And then after pictures, back to the house for the reception. Glen said we can return the car on Sunday."

"You're sure he's okay with me at the wheel? I wouldn't let just anyone drive my car—especially one that valuable." He gave her an assessing look. "Are you sure *you* trust me with it?" He didn't need to explain why. It was a dig at her for her accusation when he'd shown up at her shop that first morning.

She ignored the insinuation. "I gave him my guarantee that you'd treat it with kid gloves. It's just . . . I mean, Abby's car is okay, and so is Tom's truck. I asked them about renting a limo but Abby said it's not her style—too big and flashy. So what about smaller and a little bit flashy? Who can say no to a 'stang? I just think . . ."

She paused and stared into her cup, feeling suddenly shy.

"You think what?" When she didn't answer, he leaned forward a little. "Jess?"

His voice was softer now. She really had a hard time when he spoke to her that way. He hadn't in so long . . .

his voice often held that undertone of agitation and impatience. But not right now. Right now he was more like the Rick she remembered from years past. A little dark, a little dangerous, but gentle. Trustworthy. Helpful. Oh, Lord.

She looked into his eyes. "I just think it should be a really special day for them. They've both been through so much. Maybe they don't want a stretch limo but this would be a fun ride to the church in style."

"And you don't want to drive it?"

She shook her head. "I've never driven a stick, and I don't think Abby's wedding is the time to learn. We'd probably never make it to the church. So as best man, the duty falls into your capable, manly hands."

He was watching her with an amused expression on his face. "In case you haven't noticed . . ." He lifted his arm, revealing his prosthetic.

Jess was shocked. "Oh, God. I'm so sorry. I'd never even thought . . . I mean you do so much, and I never considered you might have a challenge with . . ." Jess broke off, flushed. "*Can* you drive it?"

He shrugged. "Probably. My truck's an automatic. I haven't tried a stick since I got this thing."

"Oh." She took her first sip of coffee and felt her eyes go wide with surprise. Damn, Rick Sullivan made a good cup. Nice and full without being too strong.

"Look, most of the time I drive with both hands on the wheel. Once I'm in gear, I'm good to go. I can always try it. My dexterity's limited with that hand, but I can probably manage steering. It shouldn't be too bad, since I'm shifting with my dominant hand."

Rick took another drink of coffee, his forehead

creased in concentration. Jess stared, fascinated at the wrinkles around his eyes. For the first time, she really looked at him, not as the broken, alcohol-dependent man she'd come to see and resent since he returned from the military, but at the man who painted beautiful pictures in secret and was willing to help a friend. And while looking at him, Jess realized just how different the two sides of him were. One would be very easy to fall for. But the other Rick was too high maintenance for her. She wasn't equipped to deal with someone else's baggage in addition to her own. Suddenly, she felt guilty for being so hostile toward him since he came home.

"I'm sorry," Jess blurted out.

"Sorry for what? Jeez, Jess, trying to follow you is like trying to follow the weather forecast. It changes every ten minutes."

Her chest felt cramped and her cheeks hot. "You know, for being so . . . harsh when you came home. I just, I don't know. I reacted poorly and was critical when I knew you needed a friend and not judgment." She paused. "I guess what I'm trying to say is, truce? I realize I've been a bit . . ."

"Judgmental?" Rick offered up lightly, causing the soft blush on Jess's cheeks to deepen.

"Yeah. That. It's just . . . it was frustrating seeing you so angry. You have so much potential, Rick! I mean, just look at these paintings, for example, yet you waste it all on booze."

He cupped his hands around his mug. "It's my decision, Jess. When a person goes through something like I did, they need to get over it in their own time." Rick paused, staring into his cup before continuing. "When you lose a part of yourself, there's grief. Not even for what you physically lost, but grief over losing a dream, and knowing that nothing is going to turn out the way you planned. It's having that choice taken out of your hands. The last thing I needed was someone telling me how I was supposed to feel about it or how I should handle it."

She'd done that, and they both knew it. Jess felt torn. On one side, she realized Rick had to work through his issues in his own way, and yet she knew there were better ways he could have dealt with things instead of drinking and picking bar fights and passing out in the square. But sitting with him now, drinking coffee in his sunny little kitchen, she could be honest enough with herself to acknowledge that Rick's drinking was not the same as Mike's. That Rick was not Mike. Staring at his clear eyes, she almost wanted to tell him. Tell him about Mike's alcoholism and what it had cost her. Maybe then he'd understand why she was so against his way of *dealing* with his problems.

But telling him was opening a Pandora's box of issues she didn't want to discuss—with anyone. She'd worked hard to overcome them. She'd worked hard to make something successful of herself.

It was easy enough to imagine the horrified look on Rick's face if she told him everything that had gone on in her relationship with Mike. And once she opened that door there was no closing it. No matter what the counseling sessions or self-help books said, she still couldn't shake the feeling that what happened with Mike was somehow her own fault. She should have been stronger. She should have left earlier.

"Let's just forget about it, okay?" he suggested.

She left her own justifications out of it and was relieved to change the subject. "Consider it forgotten." Jess paused uncertainly. "I'd like to be friends. For Abby and Tom's sake. Clean slate and all that." At Rick's slow nod, she continued. "I guess I should be going, then. I've kept you long enough." She stood, leaving her nearly empty coffee cup on the table.

He stood, too, and walked her to the door. She offered a weak smile as she went out and onto the step.

"Jess?"

She turned around to see him standing in the doorway, looking crazy sexy in faded jeans and an old T-shirt stretched out at the neck, his hair tousled and a day's growth on his jaw.

"Don't say anything about . . . about the painting, okay?"

"Of course not. Not if you don't want."

"I don't."

"Then your secret is safe with me."

She wished he hadn't asked. His work was so beautiful it should be shared and he should get credit for it. But that was his call to make, not hers. And she could be very good at keeping secrets.

Now she was holding two of his in her hands. She wasn't sure what she'd done to garner his trust, and she wasn't sure she even wanted it.

CHAPTER 7

The day of the wedding dawned crystal clear and cool, a perfect fall day. Jess stretched and slid out of the warm covers—no time to dillydally. She had to pick Rick up at eight thirty so they could get the car and make it back in time for her hair appointment. She showered and shaved her legs and put on her favorite lotion before wrapping herself in a robe and heading to the kitchen for her first cup of tea.

Today one of her best friends was getting married to one of her favorite cousins. Abby and Tom were so happy, even though it had been rough going in the beginning. The most important thing was that Abby had opened up her heart to Tom and they'd healed each other. To be honest, it gave Jess a sliver of hope. Maybe someday she'd find someone who would render the past impotent. She couldn't quite imagine it, but for now, she'd enjoy seeing two happy people pledge their lives to each other.

Jess added a little milk to her tea and took a few minutes to sip it, looking out the window. A teenager on a bike went down the quiet street, throwing newspapers at each walkway. A few seagulls dipped and then caught the draft of the wind, their wings buffeted by the breeze as they soared, looking for any tasty morsel that might come their way. And one solitary boat pulled away from the dock, sliding effortlessly through the still cove, headed out to the bay and beyond for a day of fishing before it got too cold to do so enjoyably.

Jess couldn't stand gazing forever. She had to get a move on or else she'd be late. She tossed the rest of her tea down the sink and checked her watch. Rick would be expecting her any minute.

He was up and waiting for her when she arrived, and he hopped in her car with a huge mug of coffee to keep him company. The radio filled the morning silence as she drove to Glen's place, and as she turned off the interstate into Auburn's town limits, Jess snuck a glance at Rick out of the corner of her eye. Sitting there in the morning light, he looked relaxed, calm. With a start, Jess realized she was seeing Rick completely unguarded for the first time since he'd come home. For once, there had been no fighting, no awkward pauses. It had been strangely comfortable—she hadn't felt the need to make small talk. What was more, Jess felt safe. Content. Who would have guessed she'd ever feel that way with Rick Sullivan? She was glad now that they'd made the truce. It would make everything so much easier.

Glen's driveway came up on the left, a wide, gravel road that wound its way to his cabin. In a matter of moments Jess and Rick were out of the car, had exchanged greetings, received the keys to the Mustang, and Jess was back in her vehicle, heading to Jewell Cove, driving behind the gorgeous vintage car.

Rick was ahead of her the whole way, and Jess was pleased he appeared to be doing just fine managing the manual shift. She blew out a breath in relief. Sometimes it amazed her how much Rick could do with his prosthetic. Even things like tying shoes were nearly impossible with one hand. It had to be a huge adjustment.

They split ways at the first stop sign in Jewell Cove; Rick went on to his house while Jess checked her watch and realized she had ten whole minutes before she was due at Shear Bliss for hair and nails. For the first time since Abby had asked her to be her maid of honor, Jess was excited and nervous for the day ahead. She'd be primped and polished and she'd walk down the aisle on Rick's arm . . .

Today was going to be perfect.

Just before two thirty, Rick drove up the lane to Foster House and parked the car next to a catering van and a few other vehicles he assumed belonged to the staff working the reception in the garden. Driving the vintage Mustang was fun. Cars just weren't made this way anymore. There was a substance to it that no amount of flashy accessories or convenience could replace, and as much as Rick would like to really open it up out on the highway, he was being extra careful. It was someone else's baby he was borrowing.

He was less comfortable, however, about the tux. The collar felt too tight and he hadn't managed to fasten the cuff of one shirt sleeve, but otherwise he'd gotten into the damn thing just fine. Rick pulled into the designated parking at the side of the house and got out of the Mustang, shutting the door with a heavy *thunk,* before making his way up the walk to the steps leading to the front door. With a snort, he thanked the stars Tom had insisted on a regular tuxedo and not something out of the Foster House attic like the girls were wearing. He could only imagine the look on Josh's face if he'd been forced into some vintage monkey suit. The jokes would go on for years.

Abby had really poured some of the Foster cash into restoring the mansion, though Rick was pretty sure Tom had given her a good bargain on the renovations when all was said and done. The pillars and railings were perfectly white, the trim on the new windows freshly painted. All the shrubbery had been neatly trimmed— all in all it looked like a new place.

He knocked on the door using the heavy brass knocker, and it was opened shortly after by the bride herself. Rick had to admit his best friend was certainly marrying up. The floor-length dress fell in delicate swaths of ivory satin and lace, and the hairdresser had done something to Abby's hair, making it soft and pretty around her face. It was all framed by a simple but long veil.

"You," he said, "look beautiful."

A smile blossomed on her face. "Thank you, kind sir." She stepped aside. "We're nearly ready. Come on in for a minute."

"We don't want to be late getting you to the church," Rick said, stepping into the huge foyer and closing the door behind him. "I saw Tom earlier. He's so nervous you need to show up and put him out of his misery before he ties himself in knots."

He'd never seen his friend so keyed up. Rick had left Tom at his parents' place, having a rose pinned to his lapel while he tapped his foot repeatedly.

"Nearly there. Jess is just putting on her shoes." As she said it, Rick heard the *tap tap* of high heels going across the upstairs hall.

He swallowed, feeling suddenly nervous and self-conscious in the black tuxedo. Before he could think better of it, he swept his hand over his hair, smoothing it and hoping nothing was out of place.

Footsteps started down the stairs to his right. Her shoes appeared first, navy shoes with a little strap over the top of her foot and feminine hourglass heels. Then the hem of her skirt that swished with each step. Finally the rest of her came into view as she descended the last eight steps. A delicate, pale hand on the bannister, and Jess, stunning in navy satin embellished with antique lace, the shape of the dress making her look willowy and somehow both sophisticated and impossibly young. He ran a finger beneath his shirt collar, which suddenly felt very tight. Her normally natural makeup was amplified for the occasion. The heavier shadow and liner made her deep blue eyes even bluer, and her lips were shiny and begging to be kissed.

Rick blinked as his gaze clashed with hers. As if she'd ever let him close enough for him to kiss her. Though that really wasn't the point, was it? The point was he actually wanted to. Badly. Wanted to pull her into his arms and find out if she tasted as sweet as she looked.

"What do you think?" she asked softly, turning in a circle at the bottom of the stairs. "Not bad for something stored in an attic for fifty years, huh?"

He nodded and swallowed again . . . why did his throat feel so tight? "You look great, Jess. You, uh, deserve a better escort than a rough old soldier."

She frowned. "Don't sell yourself short. After all, someone needed to drive the car."

Talk about puffing him up and taking the wind out of his sails in one brief sentence. Rick smiled. Jess Collins might have a soft nature, but she wasn't one to wallow in sentiment, and he liked that about her.

She came up to him, a sparkle in her eyes. "Your tie isn't quite right," she said quietly, and before he could react she lifted her hands and her fingers were right there, an inch away from his throat, straightening the black bow tie while the scent of her surrounded him, soft and sweet.

"It's fine," he said, his voice gravelly. He cleared it. "We should get going."

"We just need our flowers. I'll be two seconds."

She disappeared into the dining room where two waxy-white boxes waited, holding the bouquets. Rick looked over at Abby, who was watching him with an amused expression. "So it's like that," she observed in an undertone, her eyes twinkling.

"What's like what?" He played dumb, hoping that the heat crawling up his neck didn't manifest in a blush. Had he been that obvious?

"You and Jess. You looked like you swallowed a frog when she fixed your bow tie."

He shook his head. "It's not like that at all. I've known Jess since we were kids."

Abby laughed. "If you say so."

"You're getting married," he replied. "You just think everyone should be as happy as you are today."

She came over to him and put her hand on his arm. "Everyone *should* be as happy as I am. Everyone. Even you, Rick."

She noticed his unfastened cuff and, with gentle fingers, did it up for him. He looked down at her, feeling an unfamiliar flood of affection. "Tom's a lucky man, Abby. You're a good woman. A good friend."

"Why, thank you." She gave his lapels one last brush and stood back. Jess came out of the dining room and handed Abby a bouquet of autumn-hued flowers.

"And now we're ready."

Jess followed Abby out the door with Rick bringing up the rear. "Do you want this locked?" he asked, pulling the door shut.

"No, the catering people are in the garden setting up, and guests will be back here before we are. It's fine left open."

He caught up to them at the bottom of the stairs and went to the Mustang, opening the back door for Abby to get in. Jess slid in beside her, both girls holding their bouquets in their laps. He started the engine and gave the gas a little rev just for fun. When they laughed something stirred inside him. Had he been so far out of the social sphere that he forgot what it was like to hear someone laugh, to do something silly? He knew he'd hidden himself away, but until now he hadn't realized how much.

He drove slowly into town, knowing they had a few extra minutes and letting them enjoy the drive. Neither seemed to mind that the top was down on the convertible and the breeze ruffled their hair. As they proceeded through a stop sign he took them down along Main Street on a whim—and proceeded to honk the horn at passersby as they crawled along to the church.

Jess leaned forward and tapped his shoulder. "Good idea," she said behind him. "Can't believe you thought of it."

"It's a nice day and an extra two or three minutes won't hurt."

"You're full of surprises, Rick."

Rick smiled at her over his shoulder, liking her praise far more than he wanted to admit to himself.

At exactly three minutes to two, the Mustang pulled up in front of the small, white church—right on time. Rick eased the car in front of the steps and cut the engine. He got out and pocketed the keys and then opened the door and offered his right hand. There was a pause while Jess hesitated, and then she put her fingers in his.

His calloused thumb pressed down on top of her fingers, as he stepped back a bit to help her out of the car. Jess met his gaze briefly, their hands still connected, and he almost jumped at the spark of attraction he felt. He wanted to hold on longer, but instead forced himself to turn away and let go. Out of the corner of his eye he watched her nervously smooth her skirt as he helped Abby from the car.

"You ready?" he asked, turning back to Jess as Abby arranged the hem of her dress.

"Yeah. You go ahead and meet Tom at the front of the church. I've got it from here."

He turned to leave but her voice called him back. "Rick?"

Jess was waiting just to the side, her flowers in her hand. God, she was beautiful. A soft smile lit up her whole face. "Thanks for the lift," she said. "And for the drive down Main."

"Yes, ma'am," he said, giving her a salute.

Then he jogged off to the back door of the church, where his friend waited.

Jess halted at the church door and took one last look at Abby behind her. Radiant, happy, jubilant. So very certain that she was doing the right thing. So in love, so secure.

The music started—her cue to begin her walk down the aisle. With one last smile, she turned from Abby and straightened her shoulders, made sure her bouquet was centered at her waist, not too high . . . she stepped onto the carpet as Gloria Henderson played the organ.

The small church was full. Jess felt every eye on her and focused on putting one foot in front of the other. She looked up toward the altar and there stood Tom, looking tall and rugged and handsome in a tuxedo. And beside him, Rick, his face unsmiling, but a heat in his gaze that made her stomach flip like it was full of butterflies. It was the same feeling she'd gotten when she'd put her fingers in his outside, and earlier when they'd driven down to Auburn together.

Rick Sullivan was an attractive man, but Jess had assumed her libido would know better. She should run, not walk. Very far away and very fast. She was not equipped to take on a fixer-upper, no matter how she admired his sense of dry humor, his fantastic art, and his chiseled jawline. There was no way it would work.

Yet she couldn't bring herself to look away. Not until she got to the front and moved to the left and the music changed. Then all eyes were on the bride as Abby stepped to the door, angelic in her great-grandmother's dress.

For a moment Jess's vision blurred. She blinked a few times to clear it, and discovered she wasn't the only one getting emotional.

Her gaze fell on her mom, Meggie, sitting with Matt and Susan and Mark and Sarah on the other side. Jess smiled when Sarah threw her a discreet wink. Looking around the church, it felt like the whole town had showed up for Abby's special day. Jess's gaze skipped happily over the familiar faces of family and friends when one face in the crowd caused her entire body to freeze. Karen Greer looked thin and gray and wore a scarf on her head because of the chemo. The rumors about her illness all appeared to be true.

Jess felt terrible as she looked at Karen's drawn face, but she wished the Greers had never come back to Jewell Cove. She knew it wasn't Karen's fault but just seeing her today brought back a rush of memories Jess would rather remain buried. When Abby reached the altar and took Tom's hand, Jess turned back around. But not before she saw Rick's concerned expression.

He'd been watching her. She wasn't sure if she was flattered or unsettled by that knowledge.

She forced her face to relax and focused on the minister's words and not on the Greers. She shouldn't be surprised they were here; Tom's mother, Barb, and Karen Greer were old friends.

Before long Abby gave Jess her bouquet and put both her hands in Tom's to exchange vows. Their voices rang out clearly in the sanctuary and Jess watched as Rick reached into his pocket and withdrew the wedding ring, placing it on the minister's bible. Jess slid Tom's ring off her thumb and gave it to Abby to put in the crease of the pages, too, and then looked up at Rick.

And couldn't look away.

She tried to remember the way he'd staggered out of Sarah's party last summer. Reminded herself that he'd been cut off at The Rusty Fern more than once, that he was no good for her. Instead she could only think of glass paintings of hollyhocks and fence posts, the touch of his fingers on hers, the dark depths of his eyes. What had he been through? Just what had happened to him over there that he'd gone off the rails completely?

Her heart was beating so hard it felt like it was going to pound its way right through her ribs.

She snapped out of the moment when the music started and she realized it was time to sign the register. Jess sat next to Rick at the table to witness the documents. The photographer was there, forcing them to look up and smile, and then Jess took the pen and signed her name before handing it to Rick.

Before he took the pen from her fingers, he leaned in. "Are you okay, Jess?"

"I'm fine," she whispered back.

"You looked like you saw a ghost there for a while. It's a wedding. You're supposed to smile."

"I'll try to do better." She forced a smile and placed the pen in his hand. "Your turn to sign."

He did, but as they got up, he moved behind her. "I didn't mean you had to do better." His rough whisper caressed the back of her neck. "I just wanted to make sure you were all right."

A tingle went down her spine at his warm words. She would have answered, but the minister called out, introducing the bride and groom and they were off down the aisle again, into the sunny autumn afternoon.

The last thing she needed was Rick being observant. She was entirely too vulnerable right now. The best thing would be to keep her distance. And that was near to impossible tonight, seeing as they still had the reception to get through . . .

And wedding party pictures.

And a dance.

It was going to be a very long day.

CHAPTER 8

When the receiving line finished, the small wedding party made the short drive in the Mustang to Memorial Square for pictures. Abby had hired local photographer Ryan Donovan to do the honors, and the first shots were taken in front of a blazing, red-hued maple tree and then at the small gazebo set in a corner, surrounded by a small garden. The flowering annuals were gone, but the steps of the gazebo held fall mums in a riot of warm colors: red, bronze, yellow, orange—the same colors as were in the bridal bouquets.

The four of them stood together on the narrow gazebo steps. Jess and Rick bookended the happy couple, and then it was time for Abby and Tom's solo shots. "Jess, if you could just move forward out of the frame," Ryan instructed. "Rick, you, too. Perfect!" The click of the camera continued for a few shots. "Now, we're going to try something a little cuter. Rick and Jess, I want you two to stand just outside the image and extend your arms, each of you making half a heart with your hands. I'm going to frame the happy couple inside the heart." Ryan demonstrated with his own hands.

Jess felt Rick's body stiffen up behind her, and she realized that the pose would have him making the heart with his left hand—which meant it would be his prosthetic hand.

"What if we swapped sides?" she asked, raising her eyebrows innocently.

Ryan puckered his brows before shrugging in agreement. As Rick moved to the other side of the shot, his fingers slid over hers in thanks. Jess felt weird making a heart with Rick. For some reason the connection of their hands felt intimate. However, thankfully, a few minutes later it was over.

Ryan packed up his gear and said he'd meet them back at the house for the reception, and a blissfully happy Tom and Abby led the way back to the borrowed car. Jess picked her way across the grass, lifting her hem away from the ground just a little. Rick followed behind, the keys to the Mustang jingling in his hand.

"Hey, thanks for that."

Jess just shrugged. "It's no biggie," she replied before sliding into the front seat of the convertible. She watched curiously as he drove, using his left hand to steer while his right shifted and then quickly joined his left on the wheel. The last few times they'd met she'd gotten a better look at his prosthetic. Science really had come a long way. The color of his prosthetic sleeve was slightly different from the skin on his right hand, but the detail was all there, right down to the fingernails.

"No trouble driving, then?" she asked quietly.

"Nope."

"You've gotten pretty proficient."

"Not always."

Jess stole a look into the backseat. Abby and Tom were curled together, wrapped in their own little world. She turned back to the front and ruefully met Rick's gaze.

"Fun being a third wheel, ain't it?"

She couldn't help but smile. "Maybe a bit awkward."

"They're happy. Hard to begrudge them that."

"It doesn't happen very often."

"No, ma'am, it doesn't."

Did he realize that sometimes he still spoke like a soldier? She wondered if he missed that life. If he missed the camaraderie, the belonging . . . she knew that Josh did at times. It was one of the reasons why he'd hated practicing medicine in Hartford with Erin's dad. He still carried himself like a soldier. Still kept his hair military short. He'd said that while he missed parts of Army life, at least he was back home in Jewell Cove, a place where he belonged. With family.

Only Rick had no family. No career. No wonder he'd lost his way.

"You've gone quiet, Saint Jess."

The name should have made her angry or at least defensive. So why did it sound like an endearment the way Rick said it?

They turned up Blackberry Hill and then on to Foster Lane. Cars lined the long driveway and the side lawn, where Bryce had directed people to park. Music came from the backyard, audible once Rick cut the engine. The afternoon was waning but the October sun was unusually warm, so neither Jess nor Abby needed wraps just yet.

"Hang on a sec," Rick commanded, getting out of the car. Jess waited while he got out and jogged around to her side, then opened her door for her. Her cheeks warmed as she got out and then waited as he opened the door and offered Abby his hand.

They walked to the back of the house, Abby and Tom in the lead. Just before they got to the garden path, he held out his arm. "Shall we?" he murmured.

She tucked her hand through his arm.

Cheers erupted as they entered the garden, which had been transformed into something worthy of a fairy tale. White tents were set up with white linen-covered tables and chairs beneath the canopies. Each tent housed a long row of tables, and chafing dishes with blue flames were precisely lined up, presided over by chefs in spotless white coats and hats. The garden, while devoid of its summer splendor, still held shrubs in various ranges of color, as well as late-blooming mums and asters. A handful of firebushes had turned, the blazing red leaves vibrant and stunning. The colors were repeated in centerpiece arrangements on each table.

"Wow," Rick breathed beside her.

"Abby throws a classy affair," Jess said quietly. "You have to kind of expect it, with the house and all."

"It's not exactly beer and pretzels at the Fern."

"No, it's not."

He looked down at his tux. "I'm not really in my element. I feel like a damned monkey."

She chuckled as they moved farther into the garden,

and she slipped her hand off his arm. "You look fine. Very handsome."

Before Rick could speak, Abby came over, a bright smile on her lips. "Hello, you two. Have I thanked you both for being so amazing today?"

Rick smiled and put a hand in his pants pocket. "No thanks necessary. Now, if you'll excuse me, ladies, I see Josh looking glum in the corner."

Jess watched Rick walk away feeling oddly disappointed to see him go. Today, they'd actually gotten along pretty well. Rick was not a bad guy. He had a lot of good qualities. And she couldn't forget his paintings. It was one heck of a coping strategy. So why did he get under her skin so easily? And that look he'd given her in the church. Man, oh man.

"So, you and Rick . . ." Abby trailed off, wagging her eyebrows at her maid of honor. "He sure does clean up nice."

"Hmm," Jess replied, not wanting to say too much. All she needed was for Abby to go into matchmaking mode.

"Hmm? That's it? Come on, Jess. Rick's got that totally *hot and edgy* thing going on."

He did indeed. And wasn't that the problem?

"Hot, maybe," she conceded, simply because it was stating the obvious. "But my taste doesn't really run to the edgy types."

"You could have fooled me, the way you were looking at each other today," Abby teased.

Jess couldn't help but smile at her friend, who meant well and wasn't being the least bit shy about her intentions. "I get it, Abs. But your groom is looking a little neglected. Don't worry about me. I'm going to get some punch and relax."

"Good." Before she left, Abby folded Jess in a hug. "You really have been the best friend a bride could ask for," she whispered in Jess's ear. "I just want you to be happy, too."

"I am," Jess assured her, giving her a squeeze before standing back. "Now go. Be bridal."

Jess mingled for a while. It wasn't difficult; the guest list was mostly people she'd known for years. Her punch was replenished twice and she caught up with Josh, who had miraculously managed to lose Summer Arnold in the crowd somewhere.

"Lose your date?" Jess teased. She knew Josh wasn't interested in Summer, wasn't interested in dating much at all.

"Hey, we sat together and that's it. We're both attending stag."

"She didn't look like she minded."

He raised an eyebrow. "Don't even."

"Sarah and Mark made it." Indeed, Sarah was looking lovely, if a bit thin, in a deep red dress, and Matt and Susan were in their Sunday best. "She looks better."

"I hope so," Josh said. "Physically she's fine. The rest will come in time."

"And how about you, Josh? How are you doing?"

"You know me," he said easily. "Can't keep me down for long."

"Does it bother you that Tom's so happy?" She'd often wondered if Josh envied Tom the ability to move on and find love.

"Naw. He suffered enough. I might have hated him

but it wasn't really anything he could control. He did his part and stayed away. He didn't encourage Erin's feelings. I know that." He looked down at her, his eyes sad.

"Oh, Josh," Jess said, putting a hand on his arm.

"Well, enough about that. This is a wedding. A time to celebrate, right? Besides, they're calling everyone to dinner. We should find our seats."

Josh was seated with his mom, Meggie, and Sarah's family. Jess made her way to the head table, which was set for just the four of them. Candles had been added to the tables, thick white ones enclosed in glass globes, the flames flickering gently.

Bryce doubled as parking attendant and emcee, and once everyone was seated he went to the front where a microphone had been set up so all could hear, no matter which tent they were in. Waitstaff went around each table, filling goblets with wine or punch. Once each person had a full glass, Bryce stepped up to the mic. "Ladies and gentlemen, may I give you Mr. and Mrs. Tom Arseneault!"

He lifted his glass, and the guests did likewise as they toasted the bride and groom. Jess looked over. Rick was holding an empty glass. She wondered if that was the first glass he'd emptied tonight—or if there'd been more.

The sound of spoons erupting on glassware filled the tents and Jess grinned. Some traditions never changed. When the sound grew to a fever pitch, Abby and Tom stood and kissed, and the glass tinkling faded as everyone cheered and clapped.

The meal was served buffet style—a gorgeous

seasonal feast of pork loin and applesauce, baked haddock and all the trimmings. The sun faded and white
twinkle lights were turned on around the garden. Conversation was spared as everyone ate and then, as dessert was served, speeches were made.

Jess had just dipped into her apple crisp and ice cream
when Bryce called Rick to the podium to give the toast
to the bride.

Jess put down her spoon and watched as he reached
into his pocket for an index card, put it on the podium
in front of him, took a breath, looked up, and smiled.

She swallowed around a lump in her throat. When
Rick smiled, it did something to her. Maybe because
she knew he didn't have a lot to smile about. Maybe
because she knew he was trying. Maybe, most important of all, because she remembered that boyish smile.
And she'd missed it.

"When Tom asked me to be his best man, there was
no way I could say no," Rick began, his crooked smile
charming the socks off the gathered guests. "I've known
Tom for as long as I can remember. We grew up together.
Got into a fair bit of trouble together." There were a few
knowing chuckles in the crowd and he smiled again.
"We went in different directions, but when I came back
to Jewell Cove, Tom was the guy who really went the
extra mile for me. So yeah. Best man—I got your back,
buddy."

Even though he didn't know Abby that well, his next
words about the couple were heartfelt and sweet, talking about how happy she'd made his friend—first by
letting him get his hands on Foster House and then by
giving her her heart. There were damp eyes and big

smiles all around as he closed by saying, "Lift your glasses, everyone . . . To the Bride, Mrs. Abigail Arseneault."

He lifted his glass, which Jess noticed was just plain sparkling water, and she felt a little pang in her chest. This was the Rick she remembered from childhood. As he sipped, his gaze settled on her and his dark eyes seemed to challenge her to change her mind about him.

"To Abigail," the guests intoned, followed by the clinking of glasses.

Jess raised her glass and drank as Rick stepped away from the podium and back to his seat. When he was beside her again, she leaned over. "That was very nice."

"It wasn't that hard, because it was all true."

With the string quartet playing behind them and the scent of flowers and the flickering candles, something clicked between them. Something Jess wasn't ready for. Something she wasn't sure she wanted.

Tom and Abby got up to go cut the wedding cake and together they watched as Tom put his hand over Abby's on the cake knife and they sliced through the bottom layer. Everyone clapped and camera flashes went off like fireflies in the dusky light. Rick leaned over a little and said in an undertone, "Aren't we supposed to dance together later?"

Her throat tightened. "Yes, I think we are."

And heaven help her, she was looking forward to it.

CHAPTER 9

As evening deepened and the temperatures dipped, the guests moved inside for dancing. The chandeliers were dimmed to a soft light, and a small bar was set up in the corner of the dining-room-turned-ballroom room close to the fireplace. A fire burned behind the grate, the light casting flickering shadows on the walls. Jess mingled for a while, visiting with friends and neighbors, until the music started up.

Rick went to the bar and came back with a couple of glasses. He handed one to Jess. "Just soda," he said, hanging back and putting a hand in his pocket.

"Okay," she answered. She took a drink. The house was warmer than she'd anticipated. The fire was nice but it was also throwing extra heat in a house full of people.

"I told you I wouldn't drink tonight," Rick said quietly beside her, his gaze on the fire. "I know you think I'm a drunk, but you can stop inspecting everything I swallow. Besides, if I'm driving Glen's car I have to be on my best behavior."

"You like the 'stang?"

"I do. Not sure I'd want to restore my own, but it was a kick driving it around today."

Bryce picked up the cordless mic and began speaking again. "Ladies and gentlemen, would you please clear the floor for the bride and groom's first dance."

Jess watched with a lump in her throat as Tom took Abby in his arms. He gave Abby such a tender smile that Jess was sure every female heart in the room practically melted, and as the music started and their feet began moving, every eye was transfixed on the happy couple.

"They're great, aren't they?"

She looked over at Rick. "Yes, they are."

"I wasn't sure Tom would ever find someone. But last spring, after Abby showed up . . . he was different."

"Different how?" Jess asked, watching the couple turn on the floor, gazing into each other's eyes.

"He'd been just going from day to day, you know? Running his business, living out at his place, but he was just going through the motions. When Abby showed up, it was like he had a purpose again."

Jess wasn't sure if Rick was describing Tom or himself. "What about you? Do you have a purpose, Rick?"

"I keep looking," he admitted. "At first it was just get through each day. Sometimes it's still like that."

The dance ended, but Bryce called for the maid of honor and best man to join the couple as well as Tom's parents.

"This is us," he said quietly, holding out his hand.

She realized belatedly that he'd held out his left

hand—his prosthetic. She'd never touched it before. She took it and schooled her face while the material felt slightly odd beneath her fingertips. Once on the floor his right arm came around her and her hand was cushioned in the stiff-feeling artificial limb.

"Should I have warned you?" he asked as they started dancing to the slow song.

"About what?" she bluffed.

He chuckled. "Sorry. It doesn't exactly feel like flesh and blood."

She looked into his eyes. "Of course it doesn't." She frowned. She'd never known anyone with an artificial limb before. "How well can you use it?" she asked, curious.

Without breaking her gaze, the pressure on her hand tightened, squeezing, and then released.

"You just squeezed my hand."

"Yup."

"How?"

They kept turning on the floor. "I have a myoelectric hand. It means that electrical signals from my muscles trigger the movement."

"That is so cool." She felt her face heat. "I mean, it's not cool that you lost your hand, Rick. Sorry. But that technology can do that . . ."

"I know what you mean. Fine motor skills aren't so great, but I manage just fine. There are newer, more expensive types that have a lot better dexterity. It's pretty amazing."

"It must have been a big adjustment."

He laughed then, but it was humorless. "The rehab was a pain in the ass. I wasn't a very good patient."

"I can imagine."

"I was pretty bitter. I still am."

"If you ever want to talk about it, I'm here, you know." She bit down on her lip, suddenly wanting him to confide in her. She understood privacy, more so than some, and she didn't make a practice of prying into someone else's business. But she wanted to know Rick's. Since when had that begun to matter?

Ever since she'd walked into his porch and discovered that there was much, much more to him than met the eye.

His arm pulled her closer so that she was nestled against his body. It felt good being close to him. She felt safe. Secure.

Josh might have been right after all. She'd promised that if anything happened in the coming weeks that she'd go to Bryce or Tom or Rick if she needed help. She could smell the slightly spicy scent of Rick's cologne, feel the way he held her close but not too close, and she felt protected. She looked up to see Tom dancing with his new wife, while Bryce held his daughter Alice in his arms. Josh had taken to the floor with their mother.

She wasn't alone.

She wouldn't be alone again.

And for the first time since she'd heard the Greers were back in town, she didn't feel so afraid.

Rick was relieved to finally let her go.

Her innocent questions hadn't bothered him in the least. It was refreshing to have someone just ask rather than look at him sideways or get all embarrassed and blush. What he'd struggled with, though, was having her so close to him. Touching her skin and the silky fabric of her dress, the scent of her light perfume surrounding him, the soft sound of her voice and the sweetness of her smile.

Ten years ago, he'd thought she was pretty. Now she was beautiful. Jess had grown from a striking girl to a stunning woman. When she'd been younger, her eyes had gleamed with a spark of devilment and adventure. The same spark was still there, but it was tempered by wisdom and experience.

Rick didn't know just what had happened to Jess while he'd been gone, but since he'd returned he found himself paying close attention to his best friend's little sister.

He looked across the room. She was talking to her sister and mother and laughing at something they said. It struck him that no matter how often he saw her surrounded by family and friends, she held something back. He couldn't quite put his finger on it. She had a great capacity for compassion, but not in all things. Like when he'd shown up to build her shelves and she'd thought he was hungover. There'd been no compassion or understanding then. Why?

Then his gaze traveled to the bar and he clenched his teeth. He swore he could smell the sharp, pungent scent of alcohol across the room. But he'd made a promise. He would not drink tonight. He could manage to scrape together enough willpower to get through this one last hour. Besides, he'd done so well so far. It had been hell at times. He'd bought himself a bottle of rye only to dump it down the sink before he could drink it.

Been tempted to head over to The Rusty Fern for a beer just to break the silence in the empty house. But he hadn't.

He hadn't.

The bouquet and garter were tossed. Jess hung back, pushed forward into the group of single women but staying on the fringes and he could tell her smile was forced. Summer Arnold caught the bouquet, while Josh caught the garter—funny how the women seemed to lunge forward for the flowers while the men were more content to let the scrap of elasticized lace come to them. Rick laughed at their antics but he was getting drier and drier and in need of either a drink or an exit.

When someone was jostled by his elbow, their cocktail splashed over their glass and landed on his fingers. The sharp scent of gin rose up and instinctively he put his fingers to his lips.

He had to get out of here. Right now. Jess would have to understand.

She was standing by the mantel, laughing at something Art Ellis was saying and the sight of her, carefree and happy, hit him square in the gut.

He found the bride and groom first, and begged their forgiveness in calling it a night. When Tom furrowed his brow, Rick looked up at him and simply said, "Deliver me from temptation, okay?"

"Okay," Tom answered, instantly understanding. Well, mostly understanding, Rick thought. The alcohol wasn't the only temptation he was fighting tonight and both would get him in serious trouble.

He made his way through the crowded room to the fireplace, forced a smile on his lips though the edginess was racing through him now. "Jess, you got a quick sec?"

She put her hand on Art Ellis's arm and excused herself, taking a step away from the older man who'd once been the caretaker for the house when Marian had been alive. "You should hear the stories that guy tells." She laughed; her shoulders relaxed. "I can't tell which ones are true and which are total fabrication. But I enjoy them all."

He hated to burst her bubble. "Listen, Jess, I gotta go. I just wanted to let you know rather than disappearing."

The smile slid from her face. "But it's not even ten o'clock."

"I know. Are you okay to get home? I know you're probably not ready to leave the party. I just . . . I need to get out of here."

Jess's gaze turned sharp. "Why?"

He sighed. "I made you a promise about today and I don't want to break it. And I'm tempted. So it's better if I just leave. There are too many people. Just too . . . much."

He hadn't realized that before. But crowds, close quarters . . . they made his anxiety level spike. And with the anxiety came the need for something to help him relax.

Her eyes softened. "Oh, Rick . . ."

She looked up at him and his heart slammed against his ribs. This was not good.

"I can get Josh or Mom to take me home, don't worry about that."

"Okay."

"What time do you want me to meet you at Glen's tomorrow? You'll need a ride back to Jewell Cove."

Shit. He hadn't thought of that. It was probably better if he didn't get too used to spending time with Jess. Maybe then he wouldn't think of her quite so much. He could just imagine what would happen if he tried putting into action even half of what he'd been thinking lately. Holding her in his arms while they were dancing didn't help matters in the least.

He scrambled to come up with something. "I've got a lift, thanks. You can sleep in and have a lazy day."

"You're sure?"

She almost sounded disappointed. Or maybe that was wishful thinking.

"I'm sure." There was a pause and then he added, "Right. I'd better go."

He didn't kiss her cheek. He didn't dare. He offered a platonic smile instead and excused himself from the group, heading for the front door.

CHAPTER 10

A week went by and Jess neither saw nor heard anything from Rick. Josh had mentioned that he and Rick had taken back the Mustang the morning after the wedding, and then stopped for breakfast at a truck stop. Josh made no mention of Rick being "under the weather," and Jess couldn't help but admire Rick for acknowledging his struggle with the bottle and taking the necessary steps to get through it okay.

And she figured if Rick wanted to talk to her, he'd make an effort to do so. She certainly was in no panic to talk to him. Why would she be? It wasn't like they were really even getting along very well.

Except she couldn't forget the way he'd held her—a little close, but not too close—as they'd danced.

During the time she spent *not* thinking about Rick, Jess kept herself busy manning the shop, holding classes twice a week in the back room, and sneaking in moments to knit on the baby blanket. It was nearly half done, but the lacy pattern meant having to count stitches and was something best done when she was sure not to be interrupted.

Another week passed and the foot traffic was peaking again. She worked long, hard days and in the evenings she threw herself into making items for the fall bazaar at the church—several pairs of earrings, which she hung for display on a three-sided cardboard "Christmas" tree, an assortment of tea candles, bath bombs, and appliquéd holiday ornaments.

That's when she had the perfect idea to keep Rick busy.

Christmas ornaments.

She waited until Tessa was manning the shop on a Wednesday and zipped into the city to pick up clear glass balls. She bought a single box of fourteen to start, and then packed up a selection of candles in holders that she'd already made. And then she headed to Rick's house. If she couldn't get him out of his cave, maybe at least she could prompt him to become active in his community again.

She rang his doorbell, balancing the cardboard box of supplies in her arms.

He came to the door, eyeing her suspiciously as he stood in the entryway. "Jess," he greeted, his voice guarded. "What brings you by?"

His hair was a bit too long, slightly mussed, and a day's worth of stubble shadowed his face. He wore a gray hoodie and faded jeans that had a tear across one knee, and he was in his bare feet.

The look shouldn't have worked, but it did. Ultra-casual Rick was at once both dangerous and cozy, a lethal combination that made Jess unable to speak for a few seconds.

"Jess?" he prompted again, frowning.

"I have a favor to ask," she said, getting a grip. She tried a smile. "Can I come in?"

"I guess."

He stepped aside and let her in.

The change in Rick's house was profound. The last time she'd been here, it had been as neat as a pin. Today dirty dishes were piled in the sink and on the counter, and a laundry basket piled with clothes lay askew on the floor. Three days of newspapers were scattered on the table with coffee cup rings on top. She paused. "Someone fire the maid?"

Rick just kept walking to the back of the house. "Something like that," he said.

She followed him through. The living room to the left looked neglected and unused, a layer of dust on the furniture. Good heavens, when had he last cleaned? Roberta Sullivan would have a canary, seeing her house in such a state.

The porch—Rick's studio—however, was clean and precisely organized. He stopped in front of his current project and picked up his brush. "Whatever you've got to say, say it while I work," he stated. "I'm trying to finish this section and don't want to stop halfway through. The paint needs to be even."

She put the box on top of a supply cupboard, stepped forward, and simply stared at the door where Rick worked his magic.

The door itself was solid wood and stained the rich color of a toasted pecan. A rectangle of glass was set in the center of the door, and she watched as Rick touched his brush to a bit of creamy white paint and expertly shaped a petal on a blackberry blossom. The green climbing stems were already painted, along with some plump, purply blackberries.

"That is beautiful."

"I've been trying to finish it in a hurry. It's the sunporch door to Tom and Abby's place. Tom was going to refinish it and I offered to do it." He stood back and looked at the flower, gave it another small touch with the brush, and nodded. "I figured I'd surprise them with this. In some ways that house will always be the house on Blackberry Hill, you know? So I matched the stain as best I could to the floor, stripped it, refinished it, and I'm trying to get the painting done by Saturday."

"Does this mean you're going public?"

Consternation twisted his lips. "I didn't say that."

"So what are you going to do? Lie? Not take the credit? Jeez, Rick." She didn't know why he was so bent on hiding his talent. Or showing it to the world but staying so adamantly anonymous. He should be proud.

"When they ask, I'll just say, 'Do you really think I could do something like that?' And that'll be the end of it. Look how surprised you were."

He was probably right. Dammit.

She rested her hips against the edge of the cupboard. "So this is what's been keeping you locked away the last two weeks?"

He finished another petal and grinned. "Miss me?"

"Hmph," she huffed, determined not to be charmed by his sideways grin. "No."

"Not even just a little bit?"

"Not even."

"Come on, Jess. You know you love irritating me and pointing out my faults."

Her cheeks flamed, because she knew that's exactly what she'd done. "If I was . . . am . . . hard on you, it's because . . ."

He put down the brush and faced her. "Because . . ."

She licked her lips, which suddenly seemed dry. "Never mind."

He peered at her closer. "No, I don't think so. Because why?"

She wanted to tell him, to make him understand that she wasn't deliberately trying to find fault. "Look, you know that I dated Mike Greer for a while, right? It's just . . . that he . . ." Oh, for God's sake. Years of therapy and she couldn't even say it? She lifted her chin. "That he abused me."

"Abused you," Rick parroted, his gaze locked on her face. "Verbally?"

She nodded, just a little.

His voice took on a dangerous edge. "Physically?"

She swallowed. Nodded again.

"The bastard," Rick said calmly. Too calmly. "The goddamn bastard."

The fact that Rick was showing such control gave her the strength to tell him the truth. "There's more, you see? Mike is an alcoholic. Whether or not he ever admitted it, I don't know. But he had this way of looking absolutely charming to the world and then he'd start drinking and before I knew it he'd fly into a rage. Over nothing. A single glass in the sink and I was a terrible housekeeper. A thank-you to the guy behind the counter at the deli and I was a whore flirting with other men. He got very good at hitting me where it wouldn't show and I got good at applying makeup and wearing turtlenecks and long sleeves."

Rick's mouth had gone tight, but Jess felt the floodgates open up. It was such a relief to tell someone after all this time—someone who wasn't Josh. A friend.

"So you see, Rick, watching you go off the rails, watching you drink yourself stupid, and knowing that deep down you have so much rage at the world? That pretty much scares me to death."

He didn't come closer, but it felt like he had as he frowned. "So when you judge me, it's because you're afraid of me?"

"Afraid for you," she corrected, reaching out and putting her hand on his arm. "I don't want you to end up like that, okay? It's not who you really are. You're not Mike, but seeing your anger and your drinking, it brings back terrible memories for me."

"Jesus, Jess . . ."

"Are you an alcoholic, Rick?"

He stood there, dumb, and she felt horrible for asking so bluntly but relieved, too, that it was all out in the open. "I am not trying to be cruel," she said softly. "I saw you that day you came to work. You left the party after the wedding. I'm asking honestly. Because if you need help I want you to get it."

She could see the struggle happening inside him. It was in the dark confusion in his eyes, the way he held himself stiffly beneath her touch. "I don't know," he whispered hoarsely. "I know I was drinking too much, but it had become my anaesthetic. I promised my mom, though. I promised her I would stop and I have. That morning I showed up at your place? I couldn't sleep the night before. I wanted a drink so badly I would have done just about anything to get one. Instead I came down here and painted. I worked most of the night until the worst had passed. I didn't get much sleep at all. I wasn't hungover, Jess. I swear to you."

His brutal honesty touched her, and without thinking she took one more step and put her arms around him, pulling him into a hug. She believed him. She really did.

His arms came around her and he lowered his chin to her hair, the stubble on his face tugging slightly on her curls. He was warm and solid and he'd just allowed himself to be the most vulnerable she'd ever seen him. His right hand cupped her head and stroked down her hair, just once, but it was enough to change the hug into something different. An awareness flowed between them. She noticed that his shirt was old and the fabric soft, that he was only a few inches taller than she was, which made their bodies mesh together quite conveniently. He smelled like that unique scent of clean laundry and men's aftershave that women found impossible to resist, with the added afterthought of paint and solvent. Jess knew she should pull away, but she couldn't. Not yet.

It felt too good. When had she last been touched like this? It was only an innocent hug but it was pure, devoid of agenda or anger.

"Jess," he murmured in her ear, a warning.

She briefly recalled their dance at the wedding and how good it had been to be in his arms, even though he'd kept a respectable distance. Her head was telling her to run and not look back. But her heart wasn't. Was she being an utter fool?

She pulled back enough that she could see his face. She had to tell him this was a mistake, that she'd been rash. Instead her gaze caught his and she couldn't speak, couldn't look away. His left arm held her close and his right hand cupped her head and then slowly, ever so gently, he ran the side of his thumb down her cheek, dropping his gaze to her lips.

His thumb rested on the side of her chin and she was mesmerized by the depths of his eyes, the slow fire burning there as he moved closer, closer . . .

Was she drifting in to meet him? Impossible. And yet her eyelids started to flutter closed and her stomach got that swirly, weightless feeling that a girl gets when a boy is about to kiss her.

The first touch of his mouth on hers was feather-light, testing. Jess held herself perfectly still. But Rick had to know she'd take some thawing, because he rubbed his lips persuasively over hers, taking little tastes that melted her resolve and dulled the voice in her head as her senses took over.

"Jess," he said again, and the way he said it was with such wonderment that Jess's heart took flight. She opened her lips, just a little, but it was all the encouragement he needed. He nudged and coaxed until she relaxed against him and met his tongue with her own.

And oh, mercy, it was amazing. She stopped thinking altogether and let herself feel, just this once. He tasted like sweet coffee and cinnamon and his hand slid into her hair. She ran her fingers over his shoulder blades, holding him close, until he pushed his weight forward just enough to make her take a step backward. Then another until they met with the storage cupboard and she could rest her weight against it.

And still they kissed, drinking their fill of each other and listening to the sound of their labored breathing in the narrow space.

Finally they either had to stop or take things a step further. Jess felt so alive, so feminine and womanly, something she hadn't felt in a long time and it was tempting to see where things might lead. But she hadn't totally shut off her brain and she knew better than to let things get out of hand. Rick either felt the same or sensed her hesitation, because the kiss gentled, tapering off into a light grazing of lips again before the contact broke.

She felt sorry the moment there was space between them.

But Rick kept his arms looped around her hips, and in a surprisingly tender move, touched his forehead to hers. Confused, she lifted her gaze just a bit and saw his eyes were closed, his thick lashes touching his cheeks. A wave of tenderness swept over her. Their one and only kiss before this moment paled in comparison to this one. It had been innocent and carefree, but this . . . this was more. This had a decade of pain and wisdom behind it, making it all the more amazing.

Jess reached up and smoothed a rebellious curl away from his temple, feeling more affected than she was comfortable with. This wasn't supposed to happen. She wasn't supposed to get sucked into caring for a man clearly so damaged. In her deepest dreams, Jess envisioned herself meeting a man like her brother-in-law, Mark, or one of her cousins, someone who didn't have his own demons to fight, someone who wasn't one drink away from being an alcoholic. In other words, the opposite of Rick Sullivan.

Which was easy to say—when she was alone in her loft thinking about hypotheticals—and way harder when she was standing in the circle of Rick Sullivan's arms in the late afternoon.

"Wow," he finally said, the word barely more than a breath.

"Um, yeah," she replied, trying to put things back on a more normal footing. She leaned back a little so his hands slid from the hollow of her back to her hips. "Wow is right. That was even better than the last time."

"You were keeping score?" he asked, his eyes widening while his lips took on that cocky edge that she loved.

"Don't let it go to your head," she admonished. "We were young."

"A lot has happened since then," he admitted. "For both of us."

"We can't do this, Rick. I can't." She stepped away and out of his loose embrace. She didn't quite know what she regretted more—actually kissing him or putting a stop to the possibility of ever kissing him again.

He smiled a rogue's smile and she felt herself melting. "We just did," he pointed out.

Yes, they had. And it had been amazing, she admitted to herself. "I mean, we can't do this again."

The smile slid from his face. "You don't trust me."

It sounded so terrible, and yet it was true. "It's not

all you. I don't trust myself, or my judgment." Her judgment had left a lot to be desired in the past. What if she made the wrong decisions again?

His dark eyes held hers. "Yet you trusted me with the truth about Mike."

She blinked. "That's different," she said quietly. "I shared that with a friend. It's a lot different when there are hearts at stake."

He scoffed and looked away. "As if I could ever break your heart."

"Don't sell yourself short."

Silence filled the room as Rick looked back at her, his lips dropped open in surprise. Jess wanted to disappear but at the same time she'd made a promise to herself not to avoid honest and important conversations.

"Jess, I . . ."

"I care about you, Rick," she said softly. "We've known each other for years. And I've always had a bit of a crush on you. Even as a kid." Jess paused, smiling softly. "Remember when you worked for that landscape company? You used to wear ratty jeans and work boots and had a huge farmer tan."

"No matter how hot it got, we always had to wear our work T-shirts and no shorts," he replied with a note of nostalgia.

"I don't think there was a girl in Jewell Cove who didn't have a crush on you at least a little bit."

He shook his head and laughed a little. "Now I know you're kidding."

"I'm not," she insisted, her voice firmer.

"That was ten years ago. Look at me, Jess. I'm not the same man I was when I left. We both know it."

"Yes," she agreed. "We do. And I'm smart enough now to know it has very little to do with your injury and a lot more to do with what's happening inside."

His cheeks colored a little. So she was right. There was more going on with Rick than adjusting to life as an amputee.

"There are things I want, Rick. I'd like to get married and have kids someday. I'd like to be in a relationship where I'm not always waiting for the other shoe to drop. And right now I seriously doubt you're the guy to give me that kind of stability. You don't know what you want."

Rick nodded, but he didn't look happy about it. "I hate that he did that to you, you know," he said, steel lining his voice. "If I'd been here . . ."

"You can't play that game," she said. "You just can't. You'll drive yourself crazy. Believe me, I've done it a thousand times. There are things I would change, too."

She looked up at him. In so many ways he was the same Rick she'd always known, and in others he was different. He smiled less, frowned more. Kept to himself rather than be the life of the party. Was alone with his demons rather than being out with his friends.

"So what do you say we forget about what just happened and I'll tell you the real reason why I came over?"

"You mean it wasn't to annoy me and probe into my psyche?"

He caught on quickly. Jess smiled and shook her head. "No. I want your help with something and in exchange I promise to keep your identity a secret."

"Sounds intriguing." He didn't sound convinced.

She went to the box she'd brought in and took out

the package of glass ornaments. "Christmas ornaments. The church women are having their annual bazaar in a few weeks, just before Thanksgiving. We're always in need of donations for the craft sale."

"You want me to paint Christmas decorations."

She beamed. "I do. Your work is gorgeous. I know you'll do a fantastic job."

He sighed. "Anything else?"

"I'm glad you asked." She reached into the box again and withdrew a glass candle holder. "I usually do these up with some ribbon, or maybe hot glue and little stones and gems. But you could do some really neat things here. Mistletoe and holly and poinsettias, that sort of thing. What do you say?"

"Jess, really? For the church sale?"

"It's a good cause, Rick. The money goes back into the group coffers. Last year we bought a new dishwasher for the kitchen and donated a bunch to a mission in South America."

"I'm not sure I have time . . ."

She put the glass holder back in the box. "You said yourself that the demand for your work isn't as high right now, not like in summer. Besides, you've finished putting in my shelves. I'm busy, but I still take time to put together several items *and* I volunteer on the day."

"It's a bunch of old ladies making doilies."

"Are you calling me an old lady, Richard Sullivan?" She put her hands on her hips.

That finally cracked a smile. "You are anything but old, Jess."

Rick went to the box and withdrew a glass orb, turn-

ing it in his fingers. "You're trying very hard to insinu-
ate me back into this town," he said, not looking at her.

"Because it's your home. Because people will be here
for you if you let them."

"Are you so sure of that?" He put the ball back in the
package. "Not everything is easily forgiven."

"You have sins you're hiding?"

His gaze was inscrutable. "There are things I don't
talk about, Jess. Things I don't ever want to talk about.
You start letting people get close, and secrets have a
way of getting out. The town can get pretty small."

Didn't she know it. Rick's comment about Saint Jess
all those weeks ago had touched a nerve. She filled her
days with projects because it was better than being
alone. But she never aspired to be perfect or be held up
on some sort of pedestal. Still, small towns like Jewell
Cove were also supportive in times of need. They stood
by their own. "It might be small, but you're one of us.
You'll see. If you let me put your name on it, they'd sell
like hotcakes. Guaranteed."

He sighed. "Okay, you win. I'll do it."

"You will?"

"After I finish the door for Tom and Abby. And without my name attached to them. Got it? This is a onetime
thing for the church."

She smiled suddenly. "That's great! All you have to
do is let me know when they're done, and I'll come and
pick them up."

"You don't have to look so pleased with yourself."

"Oh, but I am." She looked around his studio. "One
day you won't feel like you have to hide all of this.

What's the old saying about putting your light under a bushel?"

Rick treated her to a sarcastic smile. "If you break out into a chorus of 'Let It Shine,' this conversation is over."

Jess realized that they were standing there grinning at each other, and she was tempted, so tempted, to rewind about ten minutes and start over with the kissing bit again.

"Well . . . I guess I should go." Funny how she didn't sound as much in a hurry as usual.

"I'm sure we both have work to do," he replied.

She glanced over at the door, his latest project that was both stunning and generous. "Think about telling Abby and Tom it's your work. They won't judge. I promise."

"Good-bye, Jess."

She met his gaze one last time.

"Bye, Rick."

He didn't follow her to the door, or watch out the window as she drove away, but she couldn't escape the feeling he was watching her just the same.

It bothered her to realize how much she didn't really mind.

CHAPTER 11

Jess locked up Treasures and made her way down the hill to the waterfront. She had a date tonight with Sarah, Abby, and Mary for pasta and tiramisu at Gino's. She'd been hiding away too much lately, giving her classes, manning the store, working on making Christmas stock. She'd stitched so many tartan stockings in the last two days she could practically see plaid behind her eyelids. They were beautiful, but the wool was not her favorite material to work with and just before leaving she'd let her attention slip and she'd stabbed the pad of her index finger with a kilt pin.

Jess let out a breath. The days seemed so short now and the streetlamps were already glowing, guiding her down the hill. Her breath formed clouds in the air and she pulled her scarf closer to her chin, warding off the November wind that blew off the water.

She was close enough to Gino's that the scent of tomato and garlic hung in the air, urging her to walk faster. Jess was nearly to the little ramp leading to the doors when they swung open and a woman came out, a takeout bag in her arms.

For a moment Jess didn't recognize her. She wore a funky peaked cap and a dark red leather jacket, along with slim jeans and knee-high boots, giving Jess a fleeting jolt of fashion envy. Then her gaze settled on the woman's features and it felt as though all the blood drained out of her face.

Of all the people to run into tonight, it had to be Mike Greer's sister.

Pamela's gaze burned down on Jess. "I should have known I'd run into you."

Jess bristled at the resigned tone. She felt like saying, *Then why didn't you stay where you were?* but she already knew the answer. Pam had come home because her mom was dying. That was reason enough for Jess to curb her tongue.

Very calmly, Jess took a step back and straightened her spine. "I'm very sorry about your mother," Jess offered quietly. No matter what Mike had done, she'd never held a grudge against the rest of the family. She'd never said a word against Mike, either—even though Pam had made it clear at the time that she considered the breakup Jess's fault.

Pamela nodded. "Thanks," she said as an awkward silence descended on the pair. They'd never been close. Pam had to be a good six, seven years older than her brother, always several years ahead of Jess in school. She'd gone off to university in New York before Jess and Mike had even started dating. Jess didn't figure he'd been singing her praises to his sister in the years since.

The door to the restaurant opened, expelling more rich scents and the sound of relaxing music. Sarah came out. "Oh good, Jess, you're here! We were wondering what happened to you. You didn't pick up your phone." Sarah finally seemed to pick up on the tension and her smile faded. "Everything okay?"

"Fine." Jess smiled, while her lips felt stretched holding the artificial expression. "I'll be there in just a second."

Sarah went back inside and shut the door after one last worried glance. Without so much as a good-bye, Pam stalked off, leaving Jess standing in the circle of light by the entrance.

Everyone was inside waiting. Jess wished she could take a few minutes to pull herself together but taking any more time was going to cause even more questions. She took a deep breath, adjusted her handbag on her shoulder, and pulled open the door.

It was warm and welcoming inside and she saw the girls sitting at a table in a corner. The place was quiet—starting in mid-October, cribbage and dart tournaments were held on Tuesdays at The Rusty Fern. She pasted on a smile as she made her way to the table. The worried looks on the girls' faces made her nervous, but she'd push through. She always did.

"Hey, sorry I held you up. I was talking to someone outside."

Sarah snorted. "Yeah, Pam Greer. And it didn't look like a pleasant conversation. Are you okay?"

Jess hung her coat on the back of the chair. "Of course I am. What's the special tonight?"

Abby reached over and touched her arm. "Sarah filled us in on who she is. Sister of your ex, right?"

"Yeah." Ex was such a mild word for Mike but it was the best one.

Mary used her straw to poke at the slice of lemon floating in her water. "Sarah said he left town when you broke up and hasn't been back. Did you break his heart?"

This was what she'd tried to avoid. After the first month or so, the speculation had stopped. For a long time now it was almost as though people had forgotten about Mike.

But all it took was one awkward conversation outside a restaurant and she was forced to fabricate answers. She hated lying to her friends. Especially to Sarah. They shared a lot as sisters, but they hadn't shared this. The sunshiny Sarah was just finally starting to come around again. Too much time had passed to open that whole can of worms.

"It was just weird, that's all. And I think it's worse because it's the first time she's been home in a long time and she's sad and scared about her mom. I'm not going to worry about it."

"You sure?"

"I'm sure. Now let me look at this menu so I can decide what to eat. I'm starving."

She opened the menu and began scanning the items, even though she knew it by heart after all these years. If Pam was home, it was only a matter of time before Mike returned.

The idea of running into him on the street like she'd just run into Pam made her stomach turn sickeningly.

Once they'd placed their orders, Abby brought up her new door. "Hey guys, guess what? Rick Sullivan refinished our sun porch door and you should see it! He didn't just refinish the wood, but the glass is all painted with blackberry bushes and blossoms. It's gorgeous, especially when the sun hits it."

"Wow!" Mary snagged a breadstick from the basket on the table. "Who did that for him?"

"That's the funny thing. He did it himself. Turns out Rick's been doing some painting in secret for a while now."

A warm glow centered in Jess's chest. Oh, good for him! He'd told them the truth, and she was absurdly proud of him.

"Painting? Rick Sullivan?" Sarah gaped. "You're kidding. I can't picture that guy with a paintbrush!"

"I know. Turns out he started doodling a bit when he was hospitalized, and then tried painting some stuff on glass. Don't say anything, though, okay? I mean, we're all family here, but I got the feeling he's pretty shy about it."

Mary laughed. "Rick? Shy? Right."

"Art's a pretty personal thing, when all's said and done," Jess said mildly, unfolding her napkin.

Abby peered closer at her. "You're not surprised, are you?"

Jess picked up her water glass and took a drink.

Sarah's eyes widened. "You knew?" She leaned forward in her chair. "When did you find out? You and Rick barely speak to each other!"

"They didn't seem to mind dancing together at the wedding," Abby pointed out.

"Though Rick did leave before Jess," Mary said.

"I knew. But he swore me to secrecy. The door *is* beautiful, Abby. I saw it when he was working on it. He does really great work." She smiled at everyone. They did not need to know about the kiss. No one needed to know. Not ever.

"You're blushing."

"I am not," she insisted. "It's warm in here."

Sarah raised a skeptical eyebrow.

Jess grabbed a breadstick from the basket and tore off a piece. "Look," she said, lowering her voice. "I've known Rick for a lot of years. But I dated someone with a drinking problem and I'm not about to jump into that again. Besides, Rick and I have always just been friends. More like a brother, really." She dunked the bread into olive oil and balsamic vinegar and popped it in her mouth.

Sarah chuckled. "Right. That man's never looked at you like a sister. Especially graduation night."

Breadcrumbs caught in Jess's throat and she started coughing. Her eyes watered and she reached for her glass, desperately hoping to wash the crumbs away. Oh my God. She'd never realized that Sarah had known about her crush, or that Rick had kissed her all those years ago.

Mary and Abby were positively transfixed at this little tidbit.

"You saw?" was all she managed to say, covering her face with her hands.

"Yeah, I saw you kissing behind the sand dune. I

didn't say anything to Josh though. He would have had a fit. But it wasn't as private as you thought."

She shook her head, utterly mortified. "It's not like we . . . you know. It was just one kiss." One kiss and Rick had walked away.

Sarah reached over and squeezed Jess's hand. "I'm just giving you a hard time, sis. I mean, I'd just started dating Mark. Besides, if you and Rick had been together maybe you wouldn't have gone out with that asshat Mike."

Like she needed reminding.

"I think you broke his heart, Jess. Though I always felt it was good riddance to bad rubbish. There was something about him that just wasn't right for you."

"Can we talk about something other than Mike or Rick?" She changed the subject. "Mary, how're you feeling?"

"Good." She smiled and patted her rounded belly. "Out of the feeling disgusting stage and not yet into the beached whale stage."

Abby laughed.

Mary looked up at Sarah. "Maybe this isn't the best topic of conversation, either," she said hesitantly.

"It's fine," Sarah said, waving her hand. The waitress came with their meals and for a minute they halted their conversation as the bowls of pasta were put before them and fresh Parmesan sprinkled on top.

Jess relaxed and speared a tender crescent of tortellini. She was ravenous and the first bite exploded on her tongue, pasta and tangy tomato and cheese.

The topic changed and the rest of the meal passed with tales of Abby's honeymoon in Paris and Mary's dilemma about whether or not to find out the sex of the baby. Tiramisu and coffee were served and Jess's belly was as full as her heart. She had good friends. A wonderful family.

The old strategy of protecting herself was wearing thin and all it took was one look around the table to know why. There was Abby, still in the honeymoon stage, her eyes sparkling all the time. Mary and her perma-glow from carrying a child inside her, and even Sarah's wistful smile as she talked about her kids and the possibility of trying to get pregnant again.

Jess had thought she'd done all the hard work. She'd faced her fears and was just waiting for the right guy to come along. And still she felt she was somehow missing out on it all.

Maybe there was no such thing as the right man at the right time—at least not for her.

CHAPTER 12

It wasn't unusual for Rick to drop by the house on Blackberry Hill to visit Abby and Tom. He'd done so several times before the wedding and a few times since. But today he was exceptionally nervous. Abby had invited him up to look at a window she was considering having him paint in the library, and with Rick's low bank balance, he couldn't afford to say no. After assessing the window and pointing out two other spots where he could install custom-made pieces, Abby tried to convince him to stay for coffee. Despite how much he liked Abby, sitting around drinking coffee from fine china in the Foster House was the last thing he wanted to do this afternoon. He was feeling jittery and closed in. God, he wished he could go out on the ocean.

"I should get going. I'm working on a project for Jess and I'd like to finish before she comes around nagging at me."

"Jess, huh?"

He scowled. "She twisted my arm to get me to do some holiday stuff for the women's bazaar coming up. Promised to keep it all quiet and stuff. You didn't tell anyone, did you?"

Abby's face took on an overly innocent expression and Rick frowned. "Abby?"

"Well, I had dinner with Jess and Mary and Sarah. But they're family and Jess already knew. They promised not to say anything. I was just so excited about my new door." She smiled hopefully.

He sighed. It was probably going to get out sooner or later. He liked painting for a hobby, but taking on jobs was more like work and he was afraid he'd lose the fun of it if it became a job. There were lots of times that escaping into a project was all that kept him sane. Especially nights when he couldn't sleep, when the memories crowded his brain a little too closely.

"Listen, about Jess," Abby said, and her face turned serious again. "She had a run-in with Pam Greer outside Gino's. She said it was fine but she was really upset, I could tell. I think she's really dreading seeing Mike when he comes home. Just keep an eye out for her, okay?"

His insides seized. How much did Abby know? Jess was so quiet about her past but Rick knew it had been bad. That she had a reason to be afraid of her ex. Keep an eye out? Damn straight.

"Don't worry about Jess. This town loves her. Everyone will have her back."

"I hope so." Abby cupped her mug and worked it in slow circles on the tabletop.

"Something on your mind, Abby?"

She met his gaze. "Promise you won't think I'm crazy?"

His stomach clenched. "Are you sure you want to ask *me* that? I've gone off the rails and it wouldn't take much to send me there again."

"There's something about Jess. I can feel things about people, Rick. I never really realized it until I came here, and it's a long story . . . but there's a sadness that surrounds her. I don't know what it is."

"She didn't used to be that way." The Jess he'd known had been bubbly, carefree. "She lost her dad at a pretty sensitive age."

"It could be that, I suppose," Abby replied. Her eyes were soft with concern. "But I think it's more than that." She stopped spinning the cup. "Just keep your eyes open, okay? She's a strong woman but everyone needs a guardian angel now and again."

He chuckled a little, a good show considering the bitterness inside him. Kyle could have used a guardian angel watching over him in Afghanistan. Maybe then he'd still be alive. Maybe then Rick would still have his hand. "Do you have a guardian angel, Abby?"

"Of course I do," she answered, a glow lighting her cheeks. "I have Tom. He pulled me out of that barn, remember?"

Right. How could he have forgotten that the Prescott barn had fallen in a lightning strike? Abby had been inside. She was lucky she got out with just cuts and bruises.

"I'm not sure I'm a good choice for a guardian angel," he contradicted.

"I think you're the perfect choice."

Her easy confidence touched something inside him—a feeling of warmth knowing she believed in him and then something that was like guilt from knowing how badly he'd failed in the past.

"Well, I'd better go. Thanks for the coffee and the info."

He stood up and so did she. "It was no trouble. You'll let me know about the projects we discussed?"

"As soon as I work up some drawings."

She walked him to the door and waited while he slipped on his shoes and grabbed his jacket. "Don't worry about Jess," he said. "I'll look out for her."

Abby closed the door behind him. "Oh, Rick." She sighed to the empty foyer. "I think you need her as much as she needs you," she said softly.

A raw wind brought with it small, hard drops of rain. Of all the months of the year, Rick hated November the most. The days were short and the trees were bare, their gray, gnarled branches like bony fingers against a bleak sky. Even on the rare sunny day, the vibrant colors of earlier months were gone and not yet replaced by a pristine blanket of snow.

Rick got out of his truck and zipped his jacket to the neck before reaching across the seat for a cardboard box, the flaps folded over to protect against the damp.

The street in front of Treasures was empty, except for Jess's car, which was parked in the narrow drive to the side of the building. Not much wonder. Today was the sort of day to stay inside where it was warm and dry. Even the normally colorful buildings looked drab against the steely waves of the harbor.

Shoulders huddled against the cold, he made his way up the steps and along the back boardwalk to the entrance of Treasures.

The bell above the door gave a cheery ring as he stepped inside. Jess was sitting behind the cash register and she looked up when he walked in, her face lighting up.

Whooomp, went his heart against the wall of his chest.

Whoa.

"Hey," he said, his voice sounding unusually loud in the quiet.

"Hey yourself." She stood up, putting aside a huge mound of knitting. "What brings you by? Are those the ornaments?"

"They are." He shouldn't be so pleased by the way her eyes sparkled at him. "I thought I'd deliver them myself, since you have to work around shop hours and I'm more flexible."

"That was nice of you." She stood up, pulling the hem of her sweater down over her jeans. She held out her hands. "Gimme," she said, waggling her fingers. "I want to see."

"You have someplace with more room?" he asked, looking at her crowded countertop that held the cash register, a rack of magnets, hand-crafted bookmarks, and a jar of saltwater taffy—not to mention the huge bundle of yellow knitting she was working on. "What are you knitting?"

"Oh, that?" She lifted a shoulder and touched the pale yarn. "It's a blanket. I started it when we found out Sarah was pregnant. I couldn't bear to take it all out, so I'm finishing it. I'll find a use for it somewhere."

"Is there anything you can't do, Saint Jess?"

The nickname came out before he could stop it, but to his surprise she didn't get her back up about it. She just laughed a little as she looked up at him.

"I can't paint on glass. So let's go back into the workroom where there's lots more space and you can show me what you've done."

Jess tried to calm the rapid beat of her heart. She'd been sitting at the counter, knitting away—the weather was so atrocious chances were she'd go without a customer all afternoon. She usually enjoyed looking out the wide windows, even in bad weather—the changing moods of the sea were so wild and unpredictable. But not today. Today she'd been restless and without the focus needed to do anything that required too much attention. So she'd pulled out the blanket, made a pot of tea, and settled in, letting the rhythm of the pattern lull her to a more comfortable mind-set.

And then the door had opened and Rick had come through it in a bluster of wind and rain. And what was boring and ordinary was suddenly brought to life. That was not good news.

Neither was it good that when she looked into his eyes she felt the jolt right down to the soles of her feet.

But when Rick lifted the flaps of the cardboard box,

she forgot about everything else and just stared in amazement.

"The ornaments first." He reached in and took out the first box—and then took out two more boxes. Forty-two glass balls in total, each one individual and stunning.

"You bought more."

"I was having fun. And I had more ideas than ornaments, so I made a trip to the department store."

She lifted the lid and gently examined the first ornaments. This box held the clear glass ones painted all in red and green designs. The globe in her hand had delicate trails of holly and berries. Another was painted with cascades of poinsettias and green-and-gold ribbon. There were several Santas—near chimneys, holding presents, stuffing stockings. Then he'd taken iridescent shredded paper and stuffed the clear balls full and painted adorable snowmen and penguin scenes. The next boxes were even better—they were painted on colored balls and looked amazing. The red ornaments were lavishly decorated with pyramids of Christmas trees, presents, Bethlehem stars, and cedar boughs with gold ribbon. The frosted white ones made a perfect background for snow scenes, and Rick had used blue tones to paint a night sky, a church scene, more snowmen, and tiny skaters spinning around a pond.

Jess put a hand to her mouth, swamped with emotion. It defied logic. Rick had been the outdoorsy, smart-ass jock growing up. He'd been a tough Marine. But this—this was more than cute holiday scenes. She could see his heart in his work. In the simplicity, in the comfort of the traditions, in the beauty. There was a gentleness to them—to him—that she'd never seen before. Her eyes began to sting and she blinked quickly to rid them of the tears that welled up.

"Jess? What's wrong? Don't you like them?"

She carefully put the ornament in her hand back in the box and told herself to get a grip. Nothing had changed. He still could have the power to break her heart. She couldn't let herself fall under his spell.

But then she met his eyes and she saw the vulnerability there as he waited for her verdict. She reached out and grabbed his right hand.

"Don't like them? They're gorgeous. They're perfect. I don't know how you . . . it's just that . . ."

"You? At a loss for words?"

She gave a little laugh. "I know. You've rendered me speechless."

"And you haven't even seen the candles yet."

He let go of her hand and reached into the bottom of the box.

They were better than the ornaments. One tall pillar holder was painted with a scrolled Santa's list. There were wreaths and holly boughs and flowers and one Mason jar that was simply stunning coated in a fall of delicate snowflakes. Then he'd taken some of her taper candles and painted them in candy-cane stripes. A thick creamy pillar candle that had been sitting on a special plate was now wreathed with tiny holly leaves and berries and the plate had been painted a solid, sparkly gold.

"You painted the candles."

"I told you I had ideas."

"This is incredible. Rick, there's more than enough here for the bazaar. Will you let me carry your work?

Even if it's not your bigger designs, I'd love to stock this stuff for the holidays. Do you think you could do a few more?"

She looked up at him hopefully.

He tilted his head, looked at the mess on the table, and back to her face again. "You really like them that much? I thought they might be a little . . . I don't know, juvenile."

"Are you kidding? They're more than stunning. And they're all one of a kind. At least let me try it. Let me keep one box of assorted ornaments and half a dozen candles in the store. If they sell—and they will, mark my words—then you'll consider doing a few more."

"I don't know, Jess . . ."

"The Evergreen Festival is the second weekend of December. If I sell out by Thanksgiving, will you do more for festival weekend? The store will be crazy busy."

He dithered for a moment but she put on her most hopeful look. "All right," he relented. "But only if you sell out by the end of Thanksgiving weekend."

Jess was confident the deal was solid. "Perfect." She put everything back in the box. "I'll price these, start a page for you in the consignment book, and get them on the shelf right away. Is a seventy-five percent consignment rate okay for you?"

"Is that what you usually charge?"

It wasn't. She normally took thirty-five percent of the proceeds, but she knew Rick would insist on the same rate and she wanted to help him a little. He was out of work, after all.

"Yup," she lied.

"Then you have a deal." He checked his watch. "I suppose I should get going. You'll want to close up soon."

It was after four and she normally closed at five during the week in the off-season. Not only that, but she was glad for the company. Ever since the run-in with Pamela, she'd been oddly restless.

"Closing up's no problem. All I have to do is lock the door and turn over the sign."

"Oh."

There were no classes tonight either. The hours stretched out in front of her, long and lonely. "Do you have plans for dinner?" The question popped out of her mouth before she even really thought about it.

"Dinner?"

Heat crept up her cheeks. "I mean . . . I was going to make some pasta or something. You're welcome to stay. Unless you have other plans."

He raised an eyebrow. "Let me check my social calendar," he joked. His eyes narrowed a little. "Are you sure this is a good idea, Jess?"

"Why not? We're friends, aren't we?"

Right. Just friends. So why didn't it feel that way?

"Friends," he said, and shrugged. "I guess I could. You're probably a better cook than I am."

She grinned. "Let me close up, then. I'll be right back."

It only took a moment to lock the door and turn over the sign. Jess hit the switches and the store went dark, lit only by the shadowy light from the windows. This was dinner with a friend. It was not a date. So why did it feel like one?

Because of that stupid kiss. Because while neither of them wanted to admit it, there was something simmering between them. She'd backed off so many times where Rick was concerned. She'd been downright rude to hide how she really felt. So how far was she willing to let things go?

It was just pasta. It would be fine.

Rick was puzzling over a box of items when she went back to the workroom. "This looks interesting," he commented, sorting through the supplies. "Wood circles, cloth, ribbon, clothespins. What are you making with this?"

Jess smiled, happy to be diverted from her train of thought. "On the Saturday of the festival, I'm holding a kid's craft class in the afternoon." She opened the drawer underneath the box and took out a completed item. "It's a wish list ribbon. You decorate the disk, then glue the ribbon to the back and put on a magnet. Each child will get six clothespins to decorate. Then they cut out a picture of what they want for Christmas, or write it down, and clip it on the ribbon. Cute, right?"

"Definitely cute."

"I'll run the class while Tessa and my mom man the store. It'll be a bananas day, but worth it." She held out a hand. "You want to come through? If you don't mind waiting for me to cook, that is."

"I get to see the inner sanctum?"

His words made her even more nervous. It had been a long time since she'd brought a date through to her apartment. The past few years she'd gone out with a few nice men, but things had only progressed so far when she'd broken it off. It hadn't been right . . .

As much as she told herself this wasn't a date, it kind of was. They weren't family. They'd kissed, for God's sake. They were both single. And dammit all, they were both aware of something buzzing between them. She was sure of it.

"It's just a loft. Not much to it."

But she found herself wondering what he thought as he stepped inside her private quarters of the enormous house. It looked far cheerier in the sunlight, but today the gray weather had followed them inside, making it dull and dreary. She turned on a lamp, chasing out the dimness with a soft, inviting glow. For autumn she'd tucked away a lot of the aqua and apricot accents and replaced them with warmer tones of dark red and gold, like the soft throw draped over the back of the sofa, assorted candles, and a few throw pillows.

"Nice place," he said, directly behind her. Close enough that she jumped a little at his nearness and goose bumps popped out over her skin—the good kind, too. She had to stop being quite so aware.

"Thanks."

"It's very you, Jess. Comfortable and classy. A bit of peace in a wild sea." He walked to the windows and looked out. "God, what a view. It's like having the ocean at your fingertips. She's a mean mistress today, isn't she?"

The dingy waves were tipped with whitecaps. It would be wild outside the shelter of the cove. "My father used to say that," Jess answered softly.

He turned around. "You still miss him, don't you?"

She nodded. "Of course I do. Not like I did. It's more fond memories now. It'll be that way for you, too. It takes a while."

"The house is so quiet without my mom. I keep expecting her to walk in the door and read me the riot act for leaving my clothes on the floor. How ridiculous is that? I haven't lived at home since I was twenty."

"When it's final, there's no turning back," she replied. "No do-overs or fixes. It can be tough to accept."

"Did you have regrets?" Rick held her gaze and she was caught staring into the depths, wondering how they managed to get from sniping at each other to sharing intimate details in only a matter of weeks. The truth was, she'd never hated him. Been scared for him, yes. Disapproved of how he handled things? Definitely. But never hated. They went too far back for that. And she was starting to realize that she'd been so very angry because she cared about him more than she should.

"I made lots of mistakes," she admitted. "Josh was oldest and the only son. Sarah was the baby of the family. It seemed everyone worried about them a lot. I just kind of held back at first, happy to be off everyone's radar. But then I missed my dad and I'd held my grief in for so long I didn't know how to talk about it. So I looked for attention. Not all of it was good attention, either."

Indeed not. Her marks had started slipping. She'd changed how she dressed and hung out with different people. Her father's death had taken what would have been normal teenage angst and amped it up a notch . . . or three.

The room suddenly seemed smaller, the air thinner. Where were they going with this?

"And then what happened?"

They both knew what happened.

"Mike," he said darkly.

The wind was picking up and the rain spattered against the wide windows, sounding like little grains of sand hitting the glass.

And still Rick's dark eyes held hers, tethering them together even though he was in front of the window and she was beside the sofa. She was tempted. So tempted.

Instead she forced herself to turn away. "It's cold in here. I'm going to build a fire."

She grabbed some kindling from beside the fireplace and in seconds it caught, the flames snapping and leaping behind the screen. Her heart felt like it was going to hammer its way out of her chest. *Dinner my ass,* she thought. She'd invited him up here but the last thing on her mind right now was dinner. Time with him was what she wanted. What she'd been wanting for weeks now. Time to explore what might be happening between them, away from the eyes of any of their friends or family. It scared her to death but it was exciting, too. He'd changed so much this fall, pulled himself together, and she'd waited a long, long time to have this feeling again.

He appeared beside her, took a log from the stack, and put it on top of the kindling. Then another. The licking flames caught the wood, curling the bark of the birch log with a snap.

His hand—his prosthetic—cupped her elbow and urged her to her feet, and when she stood up he turned her to face him.

"If you don't want this, tell me now."

Her tongue was tied in too many knots to reply.

His right hand slid to the base of her neck, beneath

her hair. The move was slightly dominant but in a totally sexy way. Rick was a man who would take charge but never be about control.

As Jess's breath caught in her throat, he pulled her closer, against his hard body, and stole all her thoughts as he kissed her.

CHAPTER 13

This wasn't a gentle kiss like before. There was no hesitancy, no caution, no testing the waters. It was full-on, lips and tongue, bodies pressed together and acknowledging a mutual need.

"Jess," he murmured, sliding his lips down her jaw. "What are we doing, Jess?"

Neither of them really expected her to answer. Instead she just gloried in the liberating feeling of kissing him. Of being in his arms.

And the awesome realization that Rick—equally damaged and complicated Rick—was the one person who could finally make her feel this way. Charged. Excited. Yearning.

His left hand was against her lower back, holding her firmly against him while his right slid down over her ribs and over, just a little, so that his thumb caressed her nipple through her sweater. "Did you really ask me up here for dinner?" he whispered in her ear, making her shiver deliciously.

"Are you questioning my motives?" She might have sounded serious except the last word came out on a breathy sigh as his thumb flicked again.

"I'm absolutely questioning them," he answered. "You say stop, I'll stop. But Jess . . . God, I don't want to."

Brown eyes met blue. This was the moment, then. They could stop it right now and that would be the end of it. He was leaving it in her hands. She could walk away and not risk embarrassment or getting hurt or the million other things she was sure could go wrong. That was exactly what they'd agreed, wasn't it?

Or she could put herself in the hands of the only person she'd come close to trusting. From the way his heart was beating against her palm and his zipper was pressed against her hip, she knew exactly where this was heading.

"I'm nervous," she confessed. "There's something different about what we have, you and me. I don't want to mess that up . . ."

He lifted his left hand. "I don't even know if I can brace myself up on this thing or not." His lips thinned and he shook his head. "I'm nervous, too, you know."

"You haven't since . . . ?"

"No," he confirmed, "I haven't."

She let that thought settle. Dangerous, wild-card Rick Sullivan had been celibate for months. But he wanted to make love with her. To her. And she'd always wondered what it might have been like if they'd gone all the way on the beach that night. Now was her opportunity to find out. She meant it when she said the "what if" game was pointless. But how often did you get a second chance? What if she never got a third?

Jess slid her hand down the center of his chest, stood on her tiptoes just a little, and kissed him, a sweet, slow kiss that she hoped left him in no doubt of her answer. Then she took him by the hand and led him through to her bedroom, closing them in a cocoon of privacy where they could shut out the world.

Rick grabbed the hem of her sweater and pulled it over her head, leaving her standing in the semidarkness wearing nothing but her lace bra. More kisses followed after that; hot ones that he trailed over her cheeks, down her neck, along the tender skin of her collarbone, his tongue dipping to trace the line of lace as her breath accelerated.

"Tell me if it's too fast," he said, his voice a husky rasp as he reached for the button of her jeans. "God, you are so beautiful, Jess. So beautiful."

That he thought so sent a wave of pleasure over her. He pushed her jeans over her hips and she stepped out of them, stunningly aware that she was in front of Rick in her underwear. Maybe it was because she'd known him for years. Maybe it was the gentle heart she saw in his art that he kept hidden behind his tough-guy façade. Either way, Jess was beyond ready. It was time.

His fingers touched the scar on her belly and he pulled away, surprised.

"It's a long story," she whispered, chagrined that she'd forgotten about it. "Just ignore it, okay?" She reached out for the buttons on his shirt and undid them, one by one, hoping it was sufficient distraction.

"Jess," he said quietly, putting his hand on her wrist before she could push the fabric off his shoulders. "There are scars."

She kissed the side of his mouth. "We all have scars."

But she wasn't prepared for what she saw when she spread his shirt wide and slid it over his shoulders. It was far worse than the four-inch pink line on her abdomen. At least half a dozen jagged scars marked his torso from navel to shoulder, healed but uneven and seemingly random.

Her throat swelled. "What happened?"

"Shrapnel," he answered briefly.

He'd told her once that he'd been in the hospital for more than his hand. Dear God, how much had he suffered?

She traced each mark with her finger, then leaned forward and kissed one gently. When she looked back up at him, his jaw was tense and his eyes were closed.

"You okay?"

His lashes fluttered. "I'm okay. Your fingers feel good."

So she ran her fingertips over the skin of his chest, his shoulders, his strong back. It was so warm, so firm and their bodies brushed together, making all her nerve endings come alive. His lips grazed the curve of her neck and she gasped. She wasn't just ready emotionally to take this step. Her body was speaking loud and clear.

She unbuttoned his jeans and within seconds they were both standing beside her bed dressed in nothing more than their underwear, breathing hard.

Jess reached behind her back and undid the clasp of her bra, letting it slip down her arms and to the floor.

Rick's eyes darkened to almost black, and she held his gaze, the connection between them so strong it seemed as though they must already be touching.

"I don't have protection," he said hoarsely.

She hesitated for a minute and counted days in her head. "It's the wrong time in my cycle," she said, her voice shaking. "We'll be okay."

"You're sure?"

"I'm sure. I don't want to wait." She reached for his hand and placed it on her breast. "Don't make me wait."

He didn't. They slid onto the bed and Rick wasted no time slipping her panties over her hips. The duvet was soft beneath her and she closed her eyes, luxuriating in the feel of his lips on her skin, touching her in sensitive spots until she thought she could barely stand it. She was on fire by the time he slipped off his underwear and settled himself above her.

"Open your eyes," he commanded, and she did, to find his face close to hers. A shadow of stubble roughened his jaw and she thrilled all over again to see how his pupils widened as she gave her hips an experimental grind against him. He braced himself on his right hand and left elbow, and she reached down between them and guided him home.

"Mmmmm," she hummed. Rick began moving slowly inside her before he groaned quietly into her neck, his control snapping as he began to push harder, faster. Oh God, she'd missed this. Missed the rush, missed the intimacy, missed the connection with another human being. This was better than she ever remembered—pure, uncomplicated. She closed her eyes and let herself feel, get swept away by the sensations washing over her.

The feel of his body against hers, the sound of his breathing, the taste of salt on her tongue when she kissed his shoulder.

"Jess," he murmured. "We need to reverse positions."

Rick's arm came around her and he rolled them over until she was sitting astride him, feeling rather exposed and slightly self-conscious about having to take the lead. But he put his hands on her hips and urged her just a little, and that was all the prompting she needed. Rocking against him felt so good that she quickly forgot any inhibitions and let her body take over until she was trembling all over.

When the orgasm hit she was unprepared for the force of it and she cried out, collapsing against his chest while her hips thrust against his, taking him over the edge with her until his head was thrown back against the pillows and he found the same fulfillment.

Their breathing slowed. The sweat began to dry, leaving Jess chilled. Reluctantly she slid off his body and disappeared to the bathroom.

She saw herself in the mirror and wide eyes stared back. Her skin was flushed and her hair a tangle of curls, tiny damp ones spiraling from her temples. Her lips were slightly swollen and she was naked as the day she was born. She'd been well and truly loved. So much so that she felt like crying, but she wouldn't, not in front of Rick. He'd think she was upset when she wasn't—she was simply overwhelmed with emotion.

It had been utterly fantastic. Freeing and beautiful. More than she'd ever imagined.

She'd been staring long enough, so she went back to the bedroom.

He was still on the bed, also still naked, and she felt a blush crawl up her face.

He grinned, a hint of a dimple forming on his cheek. "Getting all modest on me now, Saint Jess?"

She smiled back, feeling ridiculously shy. "Considering we're both naked, I don't think the saint thing applies," she answered. She nudged back the covers, crawled underneath, and rested on her elbow. "I'm a bit cold."

He got beneath the blankets with her. "Doesn't feel that way to me," he said, putting his hands behind his head and looking particularly satisfied. He gave her a sideways glance. "You look good naked, Saint Jess. Better than I thought you would, and that was a pretty damn good fantasy."

Her lips dropped open. "You thought about that?"

"Of course I did."

They cuddled under the blankets for a few minutes, simply enjoying looking at each other, when Rick spoke again. "Next time I'll be prepared."

Her heart leapt. "You expect there'll be a next time?"

"I don't think we'll be able to avoid it. Once isn't going to be enough for me, Jess."

So what were they starting here? A relationship? She doubted that was what Rick wanted. Friends with benefits? She wasn't sure she was comfortable with that sort of arrangement either. And yet she wasn't in any hurry to get out of the bed and she was already thinking about when the next time might be.

"Me either," she said, her stomach fluttering nervously.

"There's one more thing you should know," he said,

holding her gaze. "We probably should have talked about it before. I haven't been with anyone since leaving the hospital, and nothing was flagged on my medical. I'm clean."

Oh God, he *was* honorable. And honest and tender . . .

"Mike was my last."

"Holy shit!" His eyes widened and his head lifted off his hand. "Really? But that was . . ."

"A very long time ago, yes."

"Big dry spell for you."

She nodded. It definitely had been. "I thought about it a couple of times, but it never got this far. Things always ended before we could get . . . intimate."

"Wow. I don't know what to say."

She waggled her eyebrows a little. "I might have been thinking about you a little bit, too."

He chuckled. "Well."

"Yes, well." She smiled softly.

They settled their heads on the pillows again. Rick's expression changed, his eyebrows pulling together a little. "Jess, do you think we could keep this between us for now? I'm not sure I'm ready for Josh to know I'm sleeping with his little sister."

Disappointment made her heart heavy. "You want this to be our little secret?" There was an edge to her voice. She wasn't quite angry, but wasn't exactly pleased either. "You ashamed of being seen with me?"

"No! Of course not." He looked shocked that she'd suggest such a thing. "I just . . . this is all new territory for me. And Jewell Cove is tiny. Whatever this is, or whatever it's not, we don't need an audience speculating about our every move."

She sat up, clutching the blanket to her chest. "So for now, you want us to sneak around."

"I want us to be private," he corrected. "That's why it's called a private life."

She'd been feeling so awesome, so amazing since being with him. Like she'd turned a corner. Hopeful. And now Rick was making her feel like they'd done something wrong. She looked away. Despite his problems, she wouldn't have hidden them away like a dirty secret. The fact that he wanted to stung.

"Hey," he said quietly, and spread out his arm. "Can't we just have a little time to figure out if there's an *us* before we spring it on the whole town?"

She slid down beside him, resting her head in the warm curve of his shoulder. "I guess," she murmured, and as the quiet moment drew out, her eyes grew heavy. The heady combo of sex and emotion was leaving her feeling quite drained and he was so cozy to curl up to. "You're probably right, you know. Everyone will have an opinion."

"Because they care about you."

"They care about you, too," she replied, stifling a yawn. She curved her arm around his ribs.

It felt very right, being held in his arms. She should get up, but if she got up this would be over. And she wasn't ready for that yet . . .

He tightened his embrace and kissed her hair, and she gave in to sleep.

Rick heard Jess's breathing level out as she drifted off to sleep in his arms. He was still trying to wrap his mind around what had happened this afternoon. Sure, they'd been doing this love/hate dance since early fall and lately it had been much more on the love side. And there'd been the kiss that had knocked him a bit sideways.

Yeah, he'd wanted to see her today. He'd wanted to see her face when she saw what he'd done with her ornaments but mostly he'd just wanted to see her.

But not in a million years had he thought they'd end up making love.

Jess was too guarded, too cautious.

And so was he. Right? Except maybe they weren't, because they'd actually done quite well as far as he was concerned. Jess was different and always had been. She wasn't the kind of woman a man could love and walk away from. Even if he knew he should. She deserved better and he knew it. Hell, the whole town and her family knew it, too. Which was exactly why he wanted to keep things on the down-low for now. The moment the world found out about them? Shit would hit the fan. Josh and Tom were his friends, but he knew they'd have plenty to say about it.

The gray afternoon shifted to evening dark and the streetlights on Lilac Lane came on, illuminating the tiny gap between the window blinds and the frame. He closed his eyes and took slow breaths, imprinting the memory of these moments on his brain. Her scent, like summer lilies; how warm and soft she was; her skin delicate and pale against the tumbling waterfall of her hair. She'd been so sweet—sweet and sexy and stunning. All that he could have asked for in a lover.

Jess was a giver. She could talk all she wanted about

Rick hiding his light under a bushel but she'd been doing the same thing. Not with her talents, but with her heart. She'd guarded it so carefully.

And the first time she opened up it was with him. He was honored and more than a bit humbled, but it was also scary as hell. It felt like she was asking more of him than he could give. He didn't want to disappoint her, and yet he suspected he probably would. Didn't he always?

Being with her was easy and frustrating and fun, and when they were together, he could relax and let the past go. Hopefully that was enough for now. "I won't let you down," he whispered quietly in the darkness. He would do the right thing. He'd make it work—if it killed him.

CHAPTER 14

"Jess."

She stirred, sliding further into the warmth surrounding her.

"Jess," came the voice again.

She opened one eye and realized she was cradled in Rick's arms.

"I fell asleep."

"You sure did." He smiled down at her. "Feel better?"

She stretched a little, pointing her toes toward the bottom of the bed. "I do."

"It's after six. I wasn't sure if you had a class tonight or not, so I thought I'd better wake you up just in case."

She chuckled. "That would be awkward."

"A bit."

"It's my night off."

"So you don't actually have to get out of bed."

The suggestion in his voice heated her all over. "Technically, no."

There was a growling sound from under the covers and they both started laughing.

"I think we might need to eat, though." She shoved her hair away from her face. "I did ask you to dinner."

"You've been a terrible host," he confirmed, reaching out and tucking a stray chunk of hair behind her ear. The touch was so affectionate she nearly swooned right then and there.

But they had to take things slowly, be sure this was what they both wanted, needed. There was a friendship at stake, so it would be better to feel their way through it and not rush.

Which was pretty funny considering they'd already skipped to the sleeping together part.

"As cozy as this is, I'm starving. How do you feel about pasta and chicken?"

"If I don't have to make it, it sounds great."

"Oh, you're helping. No slackers allowed here." She slid out from beneath the blanket and shivered. "I suppose our fire went out a long time ago."

"I'll build a new one." He got up and reached for his underwear and she was treated to a lovely view of his backside as he pulled them on. When he turned around she really got a good look at the scars on his chest and shoulders. He hadn't had an easy time.

Once she was back in her underwear, she went to her closet and chose comfy yoga pants and an oversized hoodie, her favorite relaxing wardrobe. She pulled her hair back and anchored it in a loose bun with an elastic. When she looked up, Rick was watching her with a smile on his face. "You look adorable."

"I look comfortable," she corrected. She hadn't felt

the need to dress up and impress him. They'd known each other too long. He'd seen her in far worse. With a start she realized that she could really be herself with Rick. How cool was that?

"Let's go. I'm starving."

Once Rick had a fire going, they worked side by side in the kitchen. Jess put water on for the pasta and then put Rick to work chopping vegetables while she stirred chicken in a skillet and built a simple sauce with cream, butter, and Parmesan. It seemed to take no time at all to finish creating the meal, and Rick set the table as she scooped up servings.

They chatted about nothing important as they ate, and when their bowls were empty Rick sat back and sighed. "Wow. That was good. Thanks, Jess."

"You're welcome. It was much nicer than cooking for myself." She smiled. "I didn't make dessert, though. I think I have some ice cream in the freezer."

"That'd be fine."

To her surprise he cleared the table while she got out the container of Rocky Road. They took their bowls to the sofa, and Rick patted the seat beside him. "Come here and snuggle up."

She curled up next to him, tucking her legs to the side as they took spoonfuls of the cold treat.

After a few minutes Rick spoke. "Can I ask you something, Jess?"

"Of course." His voice was low and serious and she bit down on her lip. This was all so new, so fragile. She didn't want to do or say anything to break the delicate balance they'd achieved today.

He knit his fingers together pensively. "I've been

doing some thinking about what you said about there not being a timeline for dealing with my mom's stuff."

She was a bit surprised by his choice of topic, but that quickly passed as a warmth spread over her. If she were honest with herself, she'd been a little afraid that sex between them would just be . . . well, sex. But Rick really did trust her. Of course he'd still be dealing with his grief and she was pleased he wanted to talk about it.

"It takes a while," she encouraged, giving him a squeeze. "It's not like making a list and checking things off. Sometimes you think you're doing great and then wham! A memory will hit you and take you back when you least expect it."

He nodded. "I know what you mean." His gaze looked far away for a few moments before dropping to meet hers. "I've been putting something off, but maybe it's time I took a step forward."

Intrigued, she sat up a little. "Oh?"

"Ian Martin handled Mom's estate. There was a safe deposit box key, but I haven't gone to the bank yet. It's the last thing I have to deal with, and . . ."

His voice trailed off and she thought she might understand what he was getting at. "And once you have, you're afraid you'll let go? And you don't want to do that yet. Because once you do, it's really final."

He nodded. "Yeah. I didn't know how to explain it, but that's it."

Her eyes misted over a bit, knowing he was hurting. "I think it's probably common. When my dad died, there were so many loose ends. And then one day I found my mom, sitting in the back garden, crying." She looked into Rick's solemn face. "When I asked her what was wrong, she said everything was settled, and it had finally hit her that he was really gone."

His arms tightened around her and they both held on, thinking their own thoughts for a few minutes.

"Do you know what's in the box?"

Another shake. "Not a clue. But all the legal documents were with the lawyer. I can't imagine what she'd want to put in a safety deposit box. It's not like we ever had money or anything expensive. It's a bit of a mystery, really."

He reached out and took her hand. "I should have a look inside. It's probably nothing important anyway. Knowing Mom, it'll probably be filled with my crayon drawings and baby teeth." He smiled fondly. "Maybe you could go with me?"

Jess leaned her head back against him shoulder, absently fiddling with his fingers, which were still twined together with hers. Being with Rick like this felt right, intimate. And while normally, she would shy away from using that word with someone so quickly, that ship had already sailed. If he didn't want to be alone when he opened the box, she'd be there with him.

"Of course I will. You make the appointment and I'll arrange to be there." He was trusting her enough to ask. And today she'd seen a less complicated Rick, and the changes in him urged her to trust him, too.

"We'll play it by ear," he said. "And now, I should get going. Wouldn't want to outstay my welcome."

Jess smiled and got up from the sofa, waited as he grabbed his coat and shoes and walked him to the back door of her workroom to say good-bye. They lingered there for a moment, both of them unsure about what to do next. Smile and wave? Kiss? What sort of kiss? Quick and casual, or long and lingering? Rick finally made a move, leaning in and kissing her, not too fast but not too long either, just a slow, complete kiss that left her weak in the knees.

She watched him go, a part of her thrilled and another part of her scared to death. With Rick it wasn't just physical. They'd known each other too long. Cared about each other too much for it not to have meaning. There was a gravity to being intimate with him that she wasn't sure she was ready for.

Scared to death didn't even begin to cover it. She was fully involved now, and she doubted he realized how much power she'd just placed in his hands.

He had the power to hurt her. She hadn't allowed that to happen since Mike . . . but the truth was, when it came to Rick, she hadn't had any other choice. When it came to Rick, her heart didn't listen to logic.

Rick didn't want to go home yet.

Being with Jess had been incredible. Better than he'd imagined. She'd been glorious.

He pulled his truck into The Rusty Fern. He was dying for a game of darts. He hadn't been inside for weeks now, and for good reason. He'd been avoiding the bottle and doing a good job of it. But he wasn't here for the liquor. He was here because he missed the guys, the social atmosphere. He could enjoy that, couldn't he? And forget the rest?

It was worth a try. He felt he was ready to pass this test.

Inside the bar it smelled of frying grease, grilling beef, and yeasty beer. Rick inhaled the familiar aroma and scanned the room. Bingo. Tom and Bryce were shooting darts, two pints of beer on a nearby table. Tom shot a triple twenty that caused Bryce to curse under his breath and take a sip from one of the glasses.

"Fellas," he greeted.

"Hey," Tom replied, his gaze wary. "What brings you by, bud?"

"The house gets a bit quiet. I was hoping for a game of darts and here you two are. Just waiting for an ass kicking."

Bryce chuckled dryly. "Bro, I'm already there."

"Hey, Rick." Tanya, one of the regular waitresses, came over with a tray of empties. "Can I get you something?"

He considered a single glass of beer. Perhaps one shot of rum—he could handle that, right? After all, it had been so long. Things were better now.

And then he thought of Jess, standing in the doorway to her place, looking soft and rumpled, and said, "Just a Coke, Tanya, thanks."

Neither Bryce nor Tom said a word but Rick thought he could see their shoulders relax a bit.

"Carry on," Rick suggested. "I'll play the loser. It's been a while, so it'll be good for your ego."

The game was over in minutes. Rick sipped at his soda and watched Tom aim a perfect last shot. "Looks like I'm playing the cop," he observed, a half grin playing on his lips. He nodded at Tom. "Clearly married life hasn't affected your dart game much. How was Paris?"

Good grief, was his friend *blushing*? "Paris was good, thanks."

Bryce chuckled. "Abby was telling Mary all about it. Apparently our boy here is very romantic."

"Shut up," Tom advised. "I'll go get the next round."

When he was gone Rick picked his darts and took a few warm-up throws. They started their game while Tom chatted at the bar. It'd be a while before they saw their round, but that was okay. Neither of them was empty.

"So what's new?" Rick asked, lining up for a shot. He let go and missed his target by a half inch.

"Not much. A few break and enters we've been looking into, but things have been pretty quiet. As they generally are when the tourist season winds down." Bryce smiled and took aim, his shot perfect. "The wild parties tend to slow down once school's back in and everyone's gone home."

"Mary's doing okay?"

Bryce grinned. "Better than okay. She's due December twenty-seventh, so give her another few weeks and she'll start complaining about being as big as a barn and not being able to see her feet."

Rick laughed. Bryce didn't sound as if he minded too much.

"She's driving me crazy about the baby's room, though. It's pink, the way it was for Alice, but we've moved Alice into a new room and she wants this one repainted. It's a boy this time," he said. "And she can't decide on a color. Says she wants a mural or some crazy thing.

Who in heck is going to paint a mural on our walls? Sure as hell isn't going to be me. Unless she wants stick people."

Another few shots and Rick conceded that he was indeed rusty. Bryce was wiping the floor with him.

Tom finally came back with their drinks. Rick could have used something stronger, but was thankful Tom had simply gotten him another Coke. As they paused to take a drink, Bryce put his hand on Rick's arm.

"You're not drinking," Bryce observed. "Is it wrong to say I'm proud of you?"

"Naw," Rick answered, taking another sip. "Bit awkward, but not wrong."

"You had a lot of shit to deal with," Bryce said, looking over at Tom. "I'm glad things seem to be coming around."

"Me, too," Tom added. "

Rick put down his drink, touched by his friends' loyalty more than he wanted to admit, yet feeling a strange pressure to live up to their expectations. "I'm fine. Let's just play some darts. I think I've spotted you a big enough lead."

They went on to play for another hour, laughing and joking. When Abby came in to get the guys, Rick offered to be the designated driver so they could hang out a little more.

He didn't want to go home. Didn't want to go there and face an empty house full of disappointments. But he was happy about one thing. He'd faced something that needed facing and he'd done it without alcohol. Another test passed. Hell, if he kept on this way he might actually get his life back.

* * *

Jess met him at the bank. He'd been sitting in the waiting area for a few minutes when she rushed in the door, her hair blowing around her head and a scarf twined around her neck. "Sorry I'm late," she panted, coming to a stop in front of him. "I got tied up with a customer."

He smiled. "It's okay. I haven't been here long. Thanks for coming."

She smiled reassuringly and he let out a breath. "Let's do this, then."

A cashier led them back to a private room, where the box was waiting. He produced his key while the cashier withdrew her guard key and the lid to the box opened.

The cashier left them alone, quietly shutting the door behind her.

"You ready to look inside?" Jess asked softly.

He wasn't sure. This felt so strange. He'd never felt like they had any secrets, he and his mom.

Jess put her hand over his. "There's no rush, you know. You can do this when you're ready."

There was no sense putting it off, he realized. It wouldn't change anything. He opened the lid on the box and looked inside. All that waited for him was a velvet bag. That was it.

He picked up the soft bag, held the heavy weight of it in his palm. He sat in the vinyl chair provided and eased open the drawstring, pouring the contents out into his hand. It was a necklace. A very old necklace with red stones, the dark metal of the settings marking it as antique and nothing new at all.

"What the hell?" He looked up at Jess. Her face held a mesmerized look, almost like she couldn't believe what he was holding. "What was my mom doing with something like this? It can't be real, can it?"

Jess swallowed. "It's beautiful. The color and the setting are a work of art." Her finger lifted and gently stroked the necklace in Rick's hand. "God, look at that. I think it is real, Rick. The collets and clasp are rose gold from the looks of it. I think it's real and very, very old."

"Real? But that's crazy. Why would my mom have something like this?"

"I have no idea. Maybe it's a family heirloom?"

Rick's frown deepened. "Jess, I don't come from the sort of family that has heirlooms."

She picked up the necklace, turned it over in her hand, and examined it.

"What is it?" he asked. "You've got this strange look on your face." He couldn't read her eyes right now and that troubled him.

"Would you like me to look into it for you?" she asked. "I can make some inquiries. Have it appraised, that sort of thing."

"Sure. You know more about this sort of thing than I do." He put the necklace back in the pouch and frowned before handing it over to her. "Are you going to be okay?" she asked again.

He shrugged. "I guess." He paused, swallowing hard, and looked down at the key in his hand—the key that had somehow felt like the last real connection to his mom—before turning back to Jess. "I think I was expecting more. Something more . . . meaningful and emotional. Only I don't know what. That probably doesn't make any sense."

She tucked the pouch into her handbag. "It doesn't have to make sense. You want to come over?" she asked. "We can grab some takeout and veg on the couch for a while."

"I'd like that."

They got up and left the box on the table, now empty. Jess took his hand as they went out into the main area of the bank, but he let go when he got to the desk again and spoke to the cashier.

He'd thought today would be about finally letting go of his mom, but instead he was left with more questions. Where did the necklace come from and what was its significance?

CHAPTER 15

Jess clutched the velvet bag in her hand as she knocked on Abby's front door the week before Thanksgiving. She tucked her chin into her scarf, protection from the cold, raw air that seeped into her bones, and shoved her gloved hands deep into her pockets.

She wasn't sure she was doing the right thing by coming here. The moment Rick had put the necklace in her hands, she knew she'd seen it before. It had been in the photo that Abby had brought by when she'd asked Jess to make her necklace for the wedding. That day she'd asked Rick if he wanted her to do some digging around, but she'd never told him her suspicions or that she was asking for Abby's help. There was no sense prompting questions if she'd gotten it all wrong, after all. The last thing she wanted to do was upset him.

Abby opened the door, a broad smile on her face. "Jess! Gosh, it's good to see you. Tom's working late and it's so quiet around here. Come on in."

Jess stepped inside the warm house and shrugged off her coat. Every time she visited she noticed something different about the mansion, some little detail that made it into the showpiece it was. As they walked down the hall, today's revelation was the porch door that Rick had painted. Even in the dim light, the colors were vibrant and rich.

He had so much talent.

"Come on in and I'll get us some cocoa or something." Abby led the way into the library that served a dual purpose as a den.

Jess stopped in the middle of the room. "No cocoa for me, thanks anyway," she said, a little nervous. "I actually came here for a reason. I have something to show you and I want to get your honest opinion, your first reaction to it."

"What is it?" Abby came forward, her happy face now wreathed in concern. "Are you okay, Jess?"

"I'm fine," she reassured her friend. "Come sit with me and I'll show you."

When they were seated side by side, Jess unfolded her hand and revealed the bag. She undid the string and slid the necklace out of the soft folds. The dancing light from the fireplace flickered over the heavy stones.

"Oh my gosh. That's stunning. Where on earth . . ." Abby's voice faded a little. "That looks like . . . but it can't be. I'd swear it's identical to . . ."

"I thought so, too," Jess said, and her stomach twisted, though she wasn't sure if it was excitement or disappointment. Why on earth would Roberta Sullivan have a Foster family heirloom? It made no sense. "Do you still have the picture of Edith and your grandmother?"

"Yes, yes, of course. I'll be right back."

Abby disappeared out the library door but returned in seconds, clutching a picture frame in her fingers. "This is it." She sat down again and held out the picture. Jess held the necklace so it formed a perfect oval. There was no question. If this wasn't the same necklace, it was a damned good imitation. The stones, the setting, everything . . .

"Where did you find this?" Abby asked.

"I'm telling you this in absolute confidence," she said quietly, the stones in her hand a warm reminder of the faith Rick had placed in her. "You can't say anything to anyone, okay?"

"Of course."

"It was in a safe deposit box that Roberta left Rick."

"What?" Abby's brow furrowed. "But why would Roberta have it? Was there any explanation?"

Jess swallowed thickly, knowing that her next words were going to betray Rick's trust, and yet she couldn't think of another way to explain the connection. "Maybe." She closed her hand around the necklace. "You promise you'll keep this to yourself?"

Abby's gaze locked with hers. "I promise, Jess. Good heavens, what could be so serious?"

Jess swallowed. If she wanted to help him, to help him get some closure, she needed answers. And this was Abby. Jess trusted her completely.

"Rick was adopted, Abby. Roberta and Graham Sullivan were your great-aunt Marian's last clients. That's really the only link I could come up with. The only connection Rick has to the Foster family was his adoption. And maybe it's something completely innocent. Maybe

Marian sold it to Roberta. Or maybe it was a gift, but . . ." Jess paused. "I don't know. I just have a feeling that the necklace is more important than that. Why else would Roberta have hidden it away for all these years?"

Jess would have sworn right then that Abby looked guilty of something. "What is it?"

Abby shook her head. "I don't know how to say this," she murmured. "Tom and I . . . we've known about Rick's adoption for a while. But we never said anything. We didn't know if Rick knew, and we didn't know if we'd be violating a privacy law or something. We found out when Ian Martin brought by the last of Marian's things."

Jess shook her head. "Funny how Ian tends to be at the center of all this stuff. He had the safe deposit box key. Do you think there's a connection there, too?"

Abby sat back. "I couldn't tell you. But I can do some digging."

Jess thought for a minute. Technically she hadn't broken Rick's confidence because Abby had already known. But if she asked Abby to go ahead, it was a deliberate decision to meddle around in his past. What if they discovered something they didn't want to know?

Would it be better than not knowing at all? And maybe it wasn't a bad thing, in which case Rick deserved some happy news, didn't he?

"I think he needs to know in order to really move on," she finally responded. "The whole reason he went to the bank was to get it over with. Now he's left with more questions, you know?"

Abby laughed. "You have no idea. I went through a lot of questions when I arrived in Jewell Cove, and it took me a while to sort through the answers. And there are still things that are a mystery to me, and I know I'll probably never know the entire truth. But I know enough."

"It's probably better not to mention this to Rick until we know more," she suggested. "He's had a real rough go, dealing with Roberta being gone and adjusting to his injury. No sense stirring something up if it comes to nothing."

Once more Abby's frown deepened. "Are you sure? He might not like us nosing around."

The dark, guilty feeling slipped through Jess again, but she shook it off. "He said it was okay if I looked into the necklace. And besides, he's been doing so much better lately. The last thing I want to do is cause him to have a setback, you know?"

Abby nodded. "I get that." She leaned a little closer to Jess. "You and Rick, are you . . . ?" She didn't say the words but Jess knew what she was asking. Just as she heard Rick's voice in her head, asking her to keep things quiet for now. Discreet. She'd already said enough today without adding to it.

"I'm just helping out a friend, Abs."

"May I have a closer look at it?"

Abby held out her hand and Jess placed the necklace in Abby's palm.

Abby examined the stones. "It's real, I'm sure of it. And old. And it does look the same . . . though to be fair, who's to say that the one Edith had was the only one?"

They looked at each other. Both knew that the chances of there being identical antique ruby necklaces in the same small town were slim at best.

Abby straightened her spine and handed the necklace back to Jess. "I'll do some investigating, see what I can find out."

"Thanks, Abby. I appreciate it."

"No worries." She smiled. "I've enjoyed looking more into family history. I'll call you if and when I find out anything."

"And you'll keep it private? Rick hasn't told anyone that he's adopted."

"Except you."

Yes, except her. It was another indication of how close they'd become over the last several weeks. They were really starting to trust each other, and it was a feeling that took some getting used to. But it was a good feeling, too. Jess was starting to think that the reason her past attempts at romance had failed was because she hadn't trusted anyone enough to let them see the real her.

"I know you said you two weren't, *you know*," Abby said significantly. "But you're falling for him, aren't you?"

Jess let caution be her guide. "You're just caught up in newlywed glow," she accused with a laugh. "And think that everyone should be as much in love as you are."

Abby raised an eyebrow. "Funny. Rick said the same thing the day of the wedding. I think you both doth protest too much."

Jess laughed. "On that note—I'd better get back. Thanks, Abby. And remember, secret."

They walked to the front door and Jess got her coat, shrugging it on and buttoning it to the top. Abby took the scarf and looped it around Jess's neck. "I'm pretty good at keeping secrets," she said, and all levity was gone from her face. "Don't worry."

Rick's truck was parked in Jess's driveway when she arrived home. Her heart gave a leap at seeing him again, standing by her back door, and the searing kiss he treated her to made her knees go weak. She considered telling him about the afternoon's developments, but he pulled her into his arms and the conversation with Abby was swept out of her head.

Dawn on Thanksgiving morning was a non-event, thanks to a heavy fog rolling into the harbor. Jess got up, took a hot shower, and then started on her contribution to the family dinner: Grandma Collins's corn casserole and cranberry sauce.

By the time she'd put the berries on to boil and the casserole in the oven, a weak autumn sun was trying to burn away the fog. Rays filtered through the wispy clouds, and the air was so still that the boats that were docked at the wharf were perfectly reflected on the water.

This was one of the reasons she loved Jewell Cove. No matter what time of year, it was still the most beautiful place she'd ever known.

Thanksgiving was a big deal, and this year everyone was going to Sarah's for dinner. Treasures was closed for the day, and tomorrow Jess would be run off her feet during the annual Black Friday sale. Granted, the shops in Jewell Cove had nothing on the bigger cities with their chain stores, but they all held holiday sales just the same.

She was pulling on her favorite cashmere sweater when a thought hit her. What was Rick doing for Thanksgiving? He had no family left in Jewell Cove. They'd been spending more and more time together, but Jess hadn't brought up the holiday, not wanting to upset the happy balance they'd found. They had fun together and tended to steer away from topics that would bring them down.

Except she really should have made sure he had plans before now.

She picked up her cell, found his number, and hit the call button.

He answered on the second ring.

"Hey," she said softly. "What are you up to?"

She heard a bit of a clatter in the background before he answered. "Just working on something. You?"

"I was wondering if you had any plans for today."

"I'm just working," he answered.

"No dinner plans?"

"Well," he said, "I have a frozen turkey dinner in the freezer. I figured I'd pop that in later."

"That's disgusting," Jess replied. "It's Thanksgiving. You need a real dinner. With mashed potatoes and gravy and my mother's stuffing."

"Breezes is open. I'm sure Gus has turkey and the fixings planned."

Stubborn man. They were technically seeing each other but he was so determined to keep their relationship private that he refused to even acknowledge the hint.

"We're all going to Sarah and Mark's this year. Why don't you come?"

There was a pause on the other end. "With your family?" he finally asked.

"Why not?" she asked cheerfully. "Good heavens, you're practically family anyway. And there'll be a mountain of food. After you have a dozen, one more person at the table is nothing." They'd kept their relationship discreet, as per his wishes. She knew what she was asking. If they went together, questions would be asked. Assumptions made. Would that really be so bad?

"What I mean is . . ." His voice lowered a little. "Are you asking me to go with you, Jess?"

She cradled the phone close to her ear. "I suppose I am," she replied. This was a new step. Asking him to a family holiday was pretty much her way of saying they were a couple.

"You're going to tell your family we're a *thing*?"

Jess frowned. She was perfectly fine with showing up together, and she was actually okay with the idea that they were a couple. But Rick's resistance spoke loud and clear that he wasn't ready yet. A little voice inside her said he might never be, but she ignored it. "Why do we have to define what we are?"

"Because you know someone's going to ask."

She sat down on the sofa and leaned back. "I don't think they will. It's just dinner. You're included in a lot of family events. The invitation just came from me this time. And I can say that I knew you didn't have plans and invited you to come along."

"Which is strictly true."

"Right." She let out a breath in relief.

"Except . . ."

Her breath halted.

"Except what?"

"Except that I can't stop thinking about you, Jess. And there's a chance your family is going to see right through me."

Her heart did a happy flip. Maybe he was just private when it came to his personal life, because he made little statements like that and she lit up like crazy. "There'll be too much commotion." She hoped. Their feelings were too new and confusing to try to explain. Still, she wanted him to go. The thought of him sitting home alone on Thanksgiving, only a few months after losing his mother was just wrong. "Come on, Rick. The boys will be there. You know you'll hang out with them anyway. You can watch football and eat pie until you burst."

There was a sigh on his end. "What time?"

"We're supposed to be there at one thirty, dinner at two."

"I guess I could go."

"I'm driving since I have food. I'll swing by and pick you up."

"I can always walk. It's only a few blocks."

"Hey. I could use a spare pair of hands." She no longer considered his prosthetic even a disability. It was just part of who he was.

They would walk in together. People could make of that what they would. This way she had someone to help with her dishes.

"Okay then. I'd better finish up here and have a shower."

The simple mention of him having a shower brought an image flying back into her brain and her sweater suddenly seemed a bit warm and cloying. "Right." Her voice sounded slightly strangled. She was on the brink of offering to come over and help scrub his back when his voice sounded in her ear again.

"Jess? Thanks. I mean, this will beat feeling sorry for myself at home, you know?"

"You're welcome. And don't be late."

She hung up the phone, unable to stop a smile from spreading across her lips. Then she dialed one more number. She'd give Sarah the heads-up that there'd be one more for dinner.

Jess carried the casserole while Rick took the Tupperware holding the cranberry sauce. Several cars were already in the yard: Abby and Tom's, Bryce and Mary's, and their parents, Barb and Pete Arseneault's. Jess knew Josh and Meggie would have walked over to Sarah's. With Mark and the two kids, they were up to a dozen before Jess and Rick.

She rang the bell but then reached out and opened the door without waiting. "Hello, we're here," she called out over the racket already taking place.

Rick came in behind her and shut the door with his hip. "Holy cow," he said behind her. "I forgot what a madhouse a Collins event can be."

There was an ear-piercing scream followed by giggles. Jess grinned and looked over her shoulder. "Matt and Susan are playing with Alice. My guess is toddler hide-and-seek." Sure enough, Suzie came dashing by on her way to the laundry room to hide while Matt's voice counted, slowly, followed by incoherent calls by Alice, who was walking but not yet talking.

"Come on, let's put this stuff in the kitchen," she said.

They walked through and found Meggie, Sarah, Barb, and Mary working—one at the stove, one at the sink, and two standing at the butcher block. "Jess!" Meggie saw them first and put down her spoon. "And Rick, so glad you could join us. Let me take that for you. The boys are all in the den."

"Thanks, Mrs. C," he answered, handing over the dish. "Sure smells good in here."

"That's my turkey," Sarah answered. "I brined it and it's going to be delicious." Her tone dared him to say otherwise, and Jess saw him smile.

He was startlingly handsome when he smiled like that; the rest of his face relaxed and his eyes were warm like melted chocolate. His gaze shifted to her, almost to ask if it was okay to go find the guys and that weightless feeling fluttered around again. "We'll call you when dinner's ready." She nodded. "Thanks for carrying my stuff."

He followed the noise of the television, and Jess took a quick moment to admire the rear view as he walked away.

"Je-esss," said Sarah, reaching for the casserole holder and plunking it down on the butcher block.

"What?" she asked innocently. Maybe a little too innocently, because Sarah's gaze turned razor-sharp.

"You said you asked Rick because you didn't want him to be alone on the holiday."

"That's right. He just lost his mom, and he doesn't have any other family." She snagged another glass bowl and used a spoon to help transfer the ruby-red cranberry sauce into Sarah's decorative china.

"Right."

Jess remained nonchalant. "Rick's been a part of our family events for a long time anyway. Heck, he was Tom's best man and you invited him here for Josh's homecoming."

"Yes, I did. But I'm not single, am I? And you most definitely are. And so is he. I saw the way you were looking at each other just now. What's going on?"

Her sister was like a dog with a bone. But Jess had expected this. Sarah had been married for a long time. She tended to play both mother and matchmaker whenever possible. Jess didn't usually mind because she knew it always came from a good place.

"We're close, that's all. We've been talking more because he's been doing a little work for me. You don't need to read more into it than there is, sis."

"Friends, huh?" Sarah put her hands on her hips. "Might I remind you that at Josh's party, you were pretty upset I'd invited him as he was a 'bad influence.'"

Darn it.

Mary stepped in to Jess's aid. "Bryce says Rick's cleaned up his act a lot. He hasn't had a problem with Rick since before his mother died. I'm glad you invited him, Jess. No one should be alone on Thanksgiving."

Jess snapped the lid back on the container of sauce. "I agree. Now, what can I do to help?"

Sarah was taking the stuffing out of the bird and Mary was finishing setting out plates and cutlery while Jess went to work mashing potatoes. Her mother sliced

fresh buns and put them in a wicker basket while Aunt
Barb spooned pickles into tiny dishes. "Jess," Meggie
said quietly, low enough that Jess was sure it was so no
one else could hear. "Are you sure about Rick?"

"What do you mean?"

Meggie put down the knife and put her hand on Jess's
wrist. Jess looked up into blue eyes that were very much
like her own. Though Meggie's hair was graying, the
resemblance was striking. Jess had always been rather
pleased that she got her mother's looks. She'd wished
she had more of her mom's strength, though. She'd become a single mom of teenagers and dealt with the grief
of losing her husband and done it all with grace and
patience.

"I saw how Rick looked at you. And how you looked
at him. There's something happening between you. I
just want you to be sure, okay? I love Rick, but he's
been struggling. And I've waited a very long time for
you to take this step. I don't want to see you get hurt
again."

Jess blinked several times as emotion welled up
inside her. She met her mother's gaze and gave her a
watery smile. "I love you, Mom. And I promise it's
okay. I'm being careful. Not rushing into anything and
keeping my eyes wide open."

"I know you are. I just want you to be happy."

"I'm working on it." She gave the potatoes one final
mash. "What do you think, okay?"

"Perfect," Meggie answered. "Why don't you call the
boys and round up the kids? We'll get everything on the
table."

Jess stuck her head into the den and took a second to

imprint the scene on her heart. Her favorite men in the world were gathered in this room—doctor, teacher, cop, soldier. All of them friends, brothers, and protectors of those they loved—whichever was needed at the time. And one was something more. Lover. Rick was sitting next to Mark drinking soda from a can and scowling at the television, grumbling about a bad call. Being with him changed everything.

She just wasn't sure what she wanted to do about it.

Rick half-turned to put his empty on an end table and saw her standing there. For a few moments their gazes caught and clung, the connection between them as strong as ever. He was out of his ratty T-shirt today and instead wore jeans and a button-down shirt in soft blue. She hadn't noticed earlier but he'd had his hair cut, too. It was neater along the sides and back, but she could still see the hint of curl there.

And the moment drew out . . .

Josh shouted at the television and Jess blinked. "Um, we're ready to eat, guys. Hope you're hungry."

"About time," Bryce said. "I'm starving."

Jess reluctantly dragged her gaze away from Rick and went to find the kids. By the time she had them with their hands washed and heading to the kitchen, Sarah was shooing everyone to the table while she put a huge pitcher of water in the center. Jess had Alice on her hip, and she inhaled the scent of baby lotion, made stronger by the exertion of the baby's games with her cousins.

"Let's get you in your high chair, hmm?" she asked, giving Alice a kiss on the cheek. Mary was seated next to the chair, ready with a bowl of mashed potatoes, carrots, and sweet potatoes. It only took a moment for Alice to start banging her hands on the plastic tray, clearly excited about what was about to come her way.

Mark, as head of the hosting family, said a brief blessing and then they all dug in.

Bowls were passed and glasses filled until everyone had a bit of everything. Jess marveled that Josh and Tom managed to keep all their food on their plates without the use of sideboards to keep the gravy from dripping off. Beside her, Rick was loaded up with vegetables and turkey and one of Meggie's fresh buns. "You're going to have to roll me home after this," he said, picking up his fork. "I haven't eaten like this since . . ."

He hesitated, and Jess's heart went out to him. "Since Roberta cooked for you?"

He nodded. Put the fork in his mouth and chewed but Jess knew his mood had taken a hit.

"You still have family. You have people who care about you."

"And yet you were the only one who thought to invite me today."

"Well, I care about you." She kept her voice low and stared down at her plate, making a show of spearing a few golden circles of carrot.

And then she reached over, not caring that it was his prosthetic that she was touching, and squeezed his hand.

Two tables had been set up—one being the dining table with all its leaves inserted, which sat eight comfortably and right now held a crowded eleven. Another card table had been set up nearby, where Mark and Sarah ate with their kids. The noise from separate con-

versations kept the volume at a steady hum and Jess
watched out of the corner of her eye as Rick managed to
cut his turkey, somewhat awkwardly but successfully.
Pete regaled the group with a tale of his latest fishing
trip and Bryce had his own stories to share about life as
the police chief. Someone asked about the sale the next
day at Treasures; Meggie assured Jess she was coming
over to help out but only for a few hours because she
wanted to take advantage of the markdowns around
town as she was hoping to get some holiday shopping
done.

Jess looked around her and felt so very blessed. No
matter her troubles, no matter her mistakes, she had a
wonderful family. She looked up and met Josh's gaze
and he smiled at her, looked at Rick, looked back at her,
and winked.

She winked back.

CHAPTER 16

When the main course was over, it was time for pie. The kids went to work clearing the table and loading the dishwasher while pumpkin and pecan pies were taken from the cool back porch and a golden apple pie was taken out of the oven where it had been warming. They were all lined up on the butcher block for cutting when Sarah let out an "Oh, no!"

Everyone looked up.

"I forgot ice cream."

Jess couldn't have cared less if she had it or not but the chorus of dismay from the rest of the family was downright ugly. "You can't have warm apple pie without ice cream," Josh said with a frown. "It's just not Thanksgiving!"

"Really, Josh? What are you, four?" Jess raised her eyebrows and teased. "It'll be fine."

"I can't believe I forgot it. And the market's closed." Sarah looked truly distressed. Jess sighed. Only Sarah would consider the lack of ice cream a national emergency. She did have a tendency to be a bit of a perfectionist, especially when it came to hosting anything.

Rick interrupted. "I bet the G and S is still open. It doesn't generally close on holidays. I can go get some, if you want."

"Really?" Sarah's face lit up. "We can let dinner settle for a few minutes, can't we, guys?" She looked down at baby Alice, her cheeks smudged with sweet potato and peas. "I mean, poor Alice might like dessert, too."

Jess snorted. A tub of yogurt would have done Alice just fine but when Sarah got something into her head . . .

"We'll go, won't we, Rick? It won't take long. I could stand to walk off some of that stuffing anyway."

"Back in a flash," he agreed.

They put on jackets and shoes and headed out the door, making their way to a side street where the G & S Convenience was open pretty much every day of the year. The afternoon had warmed up a bit and neither Jess nor Rick seemed too concerned with hurrying back. Jess in particular was happy to be out of the commotion for a few minutes alone with Rick—even if it was simply walking to the store.

"So, did you get the third degree?" Rick asked, ambling along with his hands in his pockets.

"A little," Jess answered. "Sarah mostly. She's nosy. And my mom was a little concerned. Aunt Barb didn't say much."

"Concerned how?"

Jess shrugged. "Just doesn't want me to rush into anything. Not when . . . well, we both know it's no secret

I had quite a dry spell." She looked sideways at him and sent him a crooked smile. "You?"

"A bit. Mark and Pete didn't say much, and Tom and Bryce gave me some shit, but Josh was a bit more, stern, maybe, than I expected. He's pretty protective of you."

"Josh was there that night," she reminded him. "And he's my big brother, not my cousin."

Rick took his hand out of his pocket and reached down, lacing his fingers with hers. "He asked me if we were a *thing*. I said define *thing*." He chuckled. "Poor guy couldn't do it. Couldn't come right out and ask if I was sleeping with his sister, so he said if I hurt you he was going to mess me up bad."

"And you said?" She kept her hand in his. It felt good.

"I said fair enough." He squeezed her fingers. "Except I'm not quite sure what we are either."

"We'll figure it out on our own time," she said, but he stopped in the middle of the sidewalk.

"That's what I figure, too. I mean, there's no rush, is there?"

They were face-to-face now and she looked up at him. "No rush at all," she answered, but couldn't help but be a bit disappointed. It had taken her a while to be ready to be in a relationship again. It wasn't much fun feeling like she was dragging him along with her, perhaps a little reluctantly. What was he so afraid of?

She stood on tiptoe and, regardless of any potential audience, gave him a kiss. She twined her arms around his neck as her body pressed against his, and his hand rested on the curve of her back, pulling her close.

"Jess," he said, his chest rising and falling faster than before. "We're in the middle of the street."

"You really don't want people to know we're seeing each other?" she asked, frowning a little.

He stepped back just a little, but enough that she felt the cool November air surround her once more. "I think you've forgotten how gossipy this town can be." His dark gaze met hers. "It was only a few months ago that you were pointing out what everyone thought about me, Jess. Do you really think that's changed? That the people of Jewell Cove suddenly think I should be polishing my halo?"

She hadn't really thought of it that way, but he was right. He'd made some mistakes, and quite visibly. As a result he'd faced a fair bit of censure. She really couldn't blame him for not wanting his every move scrutinized and judged.

Jess reached up and touched his face with her hand. "I understand," she said softly. "I just want you to know, Rick, that I'm sorry for how hard I was on you, and that I'm not afraid of people knowing we're together. Whenever you're ready for that."

"Thank you," he said. "For being patient with me."

She laughed and lowered her heels, tugging on his hand. "Don't get used to it," she joked. "My patience has a sell-by date."

"Mine, too," he replied, giving her a jostle with his elbow and making her laugh. "So let's get this ice cream. The sooner dessert's over, the sooner we get to go home." He waggled his eyebrows suggestively.

Up ahead the convenience store was deserted in the late afternoon. Jess took in the empty street and parking lot, before nudging Rick. "Looks like everyone else in Jewell Cove is still sleeping off their food comas."

Rick smiled and, in a heart-fluttering move, brought her hand up to his mouth for a quick kiss. "Good for us. I like being alone with you."

Jess didn't say anything as they closed the distance between them and the parking lot, but she couldn't remember a Thanksgiving afternoon she'd enjoyed as much as this rambling walk with Rick.

A car pulling into the station broke the comfortable silence, stirring up a cloud of dust from the gravel. She gave a little cough, but her breath froze in her lungs as the car door opened and a man got out, slamming the door behind him.

She'd forgotten. Somehow it had slipped from her mind that this was Thanksgiving weekend, the perfect time for Mike to come home from *wherever* to see his family. Even in a community as small as Jewell Cove, Jess could go days without seeing acquaintances. What were the chances of running into each other at exactly this moment? Damn Sarah and her stupid ice cream.

She halted, catching Rick up short and pulling him back. She could tell the moment he noticed Mike because his hand tightened on hers reassuringly.

Maybe Mike would go into the store without seeing her and it would be fine.

Her heart beat wildly. She told herself that she had no reason to be afraid right now but her adrenaline had already kicked in, igniting her fight-or-flight response. "We can go," she whispered to Rick. "Sarah can go without her ice cream."

Mike was walking across the parking lot with long

strides, and she was nearly in the clear when he put his hand on the door, pulled it open, and looked over his shoulder at the same time. When he saw her the curl of panic tightened in her stomach. It felt like it was centered directly behind her scar, the spot where he'd cut her all those years ago.

He let go of the door.

"Don't run," Rick said quietly. "I'm here. You've got nothing to worry about."

She watched Mike start toward her and fought the urge to cower. She hadn't seen him since that night. Since Josh had threatened him, stitched up her wound, and driven her to the shelter. Perhaps she should have faced him before now, because the sight of his face did frighten her. Her body was tensed, ready to flee. It was only Rick's hand clutching hers that kept her rooted to the spot.

Mike's face was impassive, unreadable, and he stopped a few feet away, his gaze locked on hers. In that moment, looking into the face that had haunted her for years, Jess realized she was done cowering. She'd had years of healing, friends, and laughter, and she wasn't going to let him take anything away from her ever again. At that realization, something eased inside of her, and she took a breath and straightened her spine, her eyes holding his. She was determined to do this with her chin up.

"Jess," he greeted, his voice as smooth and charming as ever. He smiled, his teeth perfectly white. *Come into my parlor, said the spider to the fly . . .*

"Michael," she answered coolly.

"You must be surprised to see me," he continued.

She knew exactly what he was saying. He'd broken

his promise to Josh to never return to Jewell Cove. With his mocking smile, he was telling her he knew and didn't care.

"Not really. I know your parents wanted you and Pam around for the holiday. I'm really sorry about your mom."

Something flickered in his eyes at the mention of his mother, but he cleared it away quickly. "Yes, well, I really should have come to see her sooner. No real reason for me to stay away, is there?"

Jess wanted to shudder at the thought of him moving back to Jewell Cove. She'd come a long way but having him live in the same small community would be torture.

"Except a promise you made," Rick pointed out, his voice hard. "It's extenuating circumstances right now."

Mike's gaze flickered to Rick. "Jesus, Rick Sullivan. I didn't even notice you there."

Pompous ass, Jess thought, keeping her hand firmly in Rick's.

"You always did have tunnel vision," Rick replied calmly. "Now why don't you get what you came for and go back home? I'm sure your family is waiting."

Mike's eyes hardened. "Oh, Jess and I have some catching up to do."

"Not in this lifetime," Jess answered. "Stay away from me, Mike."

He turned his smile on her again. "Now, Jess, is that any way to treat an old friend?"

"You are not an old friend," she said, her voice barely above a whisper.

His expression turned sharp. "That's a bit harsh considering all we shared." He reached out to touch her hand, but Rick pivoted a little and stopped Mike's hand with his own.

Mike looked down at Rick's prosthetic on his forearm and chuckled. "Really, Rick?"

"Let's just go," Jess whispered furiously. "Please, Rick."

To her relief Rick let go of Mike's arm, though he shifted a little so that his body shielded her from any contact with Mike. "What do you want?" Rick asked, looking Mike in the eye. "Are you trying to intimidate her? Scare her? What is it? Because she's not alone this time, Mike. You think Josh messed you up? That's a shadow compared to what I'll do if you so much as touch her."

"Christ, Rick. Don't get yourself worked up. I was just saying hello."

"No, you weren't. You were playing games. And it stops right here."

Mike, to Jess's relief, backed up a step. But he wasn't done. He addressed Jess once more. "You know, my staying away was based on you keeping your mouth shut and not spreading damned lies about me. Who've you been talking to, Jessy? All of Jewell Cove or just lover boy Rick?"

"Back off, Mike." Jess lifted her chin and issued the order with more force than she'd realized she possessed.

Rick let go of her hand and she instantly missed the security of his touch. He took one small step closer to Mike. He didn't threaten, but then he didn't have to. His body language said it all.

Mike put his hands up, palms out in a supplicating gesture. "Jeez, easy there, tiger. You're awfully protective."

"Damn straight."

A quick glance around told Jess that their little conversation in the parking lot hadn't gone unnoticed. The day clerk was watching them intently from his window. The poor guy was probably scared they'd start a brawl in the parking lot on his watch and on Thanksgiving no less.

"Go home, Mike." Jess's voice came out stronger than she expected.

Mike raised an eyebrow. "Really, Jess? You and this gimp? You can't be serious." He started laughing.

Jess couldn't quite believe how well Rick was holding his temper. He'd always been a bit of a hothead. And he had a tendency to act first and repent later. But right now, despite the tension she knew he was feeling, he was solid as a stone, putting himself between her and Mike and refusing to rise to the bait. Even when he was called a gimp to his face.

"He's more of a man than you'll ever be. I know you're in town to see your mother and that's fine, but leave me the hell alone."

"It's a free country. You never know where I'll show up."

Those words marked Rick's tolerance point. He reached past the zipper of Mike's jacket to the shirt underneath and gripped it in his hand, twisting so that Mike's chin went up, stretching him so it looked like he had a chicken neck.

"You. Will. Not. Touch. Her. You will not show up at her place. If you see her in town, you'll cross to the other side of the street, do you hear me? And if you so much as look at her or utter one word it won't be just me you have to deal with. It'll be Josh, and Tom, and Bryce."

All the charm and confidence fled from Mike's face as it reddened with anger. "Don't dictate to me, little man. All it'll take is one phone call to the police and I'll have you up for uttering threats."

Rick gave the collar a shake. "It's not a threat, it's a promise. And go ahead. Call the police. Bryce is the chief now. Let's see how he reacts when he finds out you smacked his cousin around, huh?"

He let go of Mike's collar and took a step back, still half-blocking Jess's body with his own.

Mike shook his shoulders in an attempt to undo the twisting that Rick had exerted on his clothing. He looked over Rick's shoulder, staring at Jess.

"Get gone," Rick suggested. "While you still can."

A cruel smile crept up Mike's face. "Don't worry," he said, backing up. "She's all yours. You can have the bitch. She was never much good in bed anyway, so you'll be a perfect match, Gimpy."

Jess was sure that all the blood drained out of her head. She saw gray dots behind her eyes for a few seconds and felt herself weave from light-headedness. But it only lasted a moment because the next thing she knew Rick had pulled back his right arm and let it go again, his fist connecting with Mike's nose.

Blood spurted as Mike doubled over, one hand resting on his knee while the other cradled his wounded face.

Rick turned around briefly and Jess saw barely suppressed rage on his face. "Go inside and get the ice cream," he ordered.

Her feet wouldn't move. She was frightened *and* intimidated, but most of all she didn't want this to escalate into something bigger. Rick was a big man and Mike—well, she knew firsthand that Mike could throw a wicked punch. The last thing on her mind was her sister's dessert. She was way more concerned about a fistfight in the middle of the G & S parking lot.

"Jess. Now. Go inside." His voice was hard and commanding. "Mike and I have a few things to get straight."

She met his gaze and for once she didn't argue with him. She hurried into the store, grabbed the first carton of vanilla ice cream she saw, and paid for it without ever looking at the cashier.

"Are you all right?" a soft teenage voice asked her from behind the counter. "Do I need to call someone for you?"

She shook her head wildly. "No, it's fine, really." She peered through the door and saw Mike stalking off to his car again and her body relaxed a fraction. "It's all good now. Sorry for the disturbance."

"Receipt in the bag okay?"

It was such a mundane, ordinary question that Jess barely registered it. "Oh, yes, fine," she stammered, distracted, then grabbed the bag and went back outside.

Rick was waiting for her. "Let's go," he said shortly, and stalked off toward the sidewalk.

"Wait up!" She hurried after him, totally freaked out about what had just happened. In her mind she'd wondered what it would be like to see Mike. If he'd changed, if she'd be afraid, what he'd say. If he'd ignore their past or if he'd be hostile and aggressive.

Now her body trembled wondering how it would

have gone down if she'd walked to the store by herself. It was back to this now. Being afraid to be alone. And boy, did that piss her off.

"Rick, wait!"

He hesitated, long enough for her to catch up with him again. "Sorry," he said, his voice tight. "I'm a little keyed up. I didn't realize how fast I was going."

She reached for his hand and then drew hers back as she felt wetness on her fingertips. The punch to Mike's face had ripped his knuckles, making them bleed. "Stop," she pleaded. "Let me look at your hand. Rick . . ."

"You can look at it once we're at Sarah's. The ice cream is melting." He started walking again, not much slower than before.

It was a cool November day and it was a ten-minute walk at best. The ice cream would be fine. But Jess could tell that Rick wasn't. He was agitated, full of adrenaline. Not much wonder. He'd held his cool remarkably well at first. And even when he'd stepped in, he hadn't lost it the way Josh had that first night.

She couldn't escape the look of Mike's mocking face as he'd said, "You never know where I'll show up." He was a master of intimidation. If he wanted Jess to be looking over her shoulder, this was the perfect way. The rest of the words she didn't care about. The insults didn't matter. But the fear . . . that was his objective. And until she stopped being afraid, he would always win.

"Wait. Rick, goddammit. Wait just a minute, okay?"

She stopped, put her hands on her knees, and felt the shakes start, the aftermath of the adrenaline rush. Her breath came in short gasps and she dropped the grocery bag on the ground. It was over and she was fine.

She knew that. She just needed a minute for her body to get the memo and steady out.

She heard Rick swear and then his arm came around her. "I'm sorry, Jess. I'm so wound up I don't know what to do with myself. Take deep breaths. Maybe we both need a few minutes to get ourselves together, huh?"

She focused on breathing and let him pull her into his embrace, working on slowing her heart rate. "You gonna be all right?" he asked roughly.

Jess nodded against his shoulder. "Yeah. Delayed reaction I guess. What you did back there . . ."

"I'm sorry. I didn't want to . . . I mean, I know you've got to be sensitive to violence, but I swear he knew how to push my buttons and . . ." He cursed again, and she smiled.

"It's okay. I could see how hard you were trying."

Rick pulled back a little and looked down into her eyes. There'd been so many emotions today but right now she looked into Rick Sullivan's face and felt as safe and loved as she'd ever been. He pushed a bit of hair back from her face with his hurt hand. "What makes people like that, do you think?" he asked. "The Greers are normal people. I can't imagine Mike learned that at home."

Jess shrugged. His hand felt so good along the side of her face and she reached up and covered it with her own. "I don't know. I wondered if he had changed, you know? Sometimes I wondered if some things had really happened or if I imagined it. But it did and he hasn't changed and . . ." She shivered all over, then took a deep breath and pushed out of his arms a little, determined to be stronger. To not give Mike one more ounce of power over her.

She met Rick's gaze. "What did you say to him? When I went inside?"

His thumb touched the corner of her mouth and he kissed her, a soft, brief kiss that was tender and healing.

"I told him that I'd already seen hell, and I'd go back there in a heartbeat if it meant protecting you from the likes of him."

Sarah was on them the moment they went back inside the house. "What in the world took you so long? We've been waiting for ages!"

Jess's temper flared. "Give it a rest, will you?" She barely had the door shut and someone was in her face. The afternoon had been stressful enough without family getting on her back about something as trivial as dessert. "Here, take your ice cream."

Sarah's face registered hurt and Jess felt sorry and yet there were so many emotions swirling around inside her that she wasn't quite capable of dealing with Sarah's feelings, too. She closed her eyes and took a deep breath as Sarah did an about-face and went to the kitchen before Jess could apologize.

"Are you going to be okay?" Rick's voice was low and concerned. "Do you want to go?"

"I just need a minute. I forgot how chaotic it is when the whole family is together."

"They care about you."

She opened her eyes. "I know they do. I'm sorry."

"Don't apologize to me." He smiled down at her. "I get it, more than you can imagine."

Jess looked up at him and felt so thankful for him.

Rick never pushed. He just accepted and supported. How could that be when he had his own issues? Issues he didn't talk about, she realized. He knew more of her secrets than she knew of his. Perhaps that was why he was so accepting of her refusal to spill her guts.

Right now she was just grateful he was with her. She walked into his embrace, wrapping her arms around him and snuggling close for a few seconds. "Thanks," she said, pulling back. "I just needed that for a few moments."

"Anytime." He moved his hand off her ribs and winced.

"Damn!" Jess grabbed his hand and examined his knuckles. "I forgot about your hand. Let's get it cleaned up and get some ice."

Rick didn't protest; there was blood drying on his knuckles and the joints were slightly swollen. Jess led him into the kitchen, while the curious eyes of Sarah, Meggie, and Barb followed them. From the shouting coming from the den, Jess figured there'd just been a touchdown. Wordlessly she turned on the cold water and stuck Rick's hand underneath the spray, washing off the blood.

"What happened?" Meggie was the first to break the silence and come over while the other two women stopped slicing the pie and watched. "Rick, what did you do to yourself?"

"Could you get a bag of ice, please, Mom?" Jess looked up at her mother calmly. Even though she didn't want to tell the truth, she was starting to realize there might not be a way around it. Just not right this minute, though. She blinked away a few tears as she gently brushed Rick's knuckles. This was his painting hand, she realized. She looked up at him. "Do you think anything's broken?"

He shook his head. "Just bruised, I think." He flexed his fingers a few times. "It all works. Just hurts like the devil."

Sarah stepped forward. "There's an ice pack in the freezer. That works better than a bag." She opened the freezer drawer and took out a blue pouch. "This'll wrap right around it." She frowned. "I'll get Josh. He should have a look at it, make sure you didn't break anything."

"Thanks," Jess said, much calmer now. She took the ice pack, grabbed a dish towel, and wrapped the whole thing around Rick's hand. "How does that feel?" she asked him.

"Better," he said.

"Hey, didn't someone say we were finally having pie? What's the holdup?" Josh came out of the den before Sarah had a chance to fetch him, grumbling the whole way until he saw Rick standing with his hand wrapped up. "What'd you do to your hand?"

"It's nothing, just a few split knuckles."

Josh gaped. "You managed to get in a fistfight going to the store for ice cream? Who the heck with?"

Rick met Jess's gaze. How could they not answer questions? And yet answering them meant giving explanations. Was she ready for that?

Rick nodded a little, urging her on. "I think you need to tell them. They need to know what's happening, and why."

And all Jess wanted to do was pretend it *wasn't* happening. But she knew he was probably right. It wasn't like they were going to get out of the afternoon without some sort of explanation.

"There's something I need to tell you all," she said, feeling a little sick to her stomach from simple nerves. "Maybe Matt and Suzie can look after Alice for a bit?"

Meggie looked alarmed, and so did Aunt Barb. "Josh, why don't you get the guys," Rick suggested. "Sarah, why don't we dish out the pie and sit down?"

Jess was grateful to Rick for taking charge. Barb went to get Mary and Jess heard her offer the kids a few dollars apiece for looking after the baby for a while. Before long everyone had pie and they were sitting around the table. But no one was eating. Jess sat at the head, and without saying a word Rick pulled up a chair and sat beside her in a unified show of support.

A long silence filled the room as Jess struggled to find the right words to say. Rick jumped in, leading off the discussion. "I busted up my hand today when I punched Mike Greer."

Jaws dropped all around the table.

Rick looked directly at Bryce. "If he comes to you asking for an assault charge, it's okay. But I don't think he will. He was pretty threatening and I'm sure he'd like to keep things under the radar. Just giving you the heads-up."

"Holy crap," Tom said, frowning. "I never took you for the jealous type, man. I mean, Jess and Mike were over a long time ago."

Jess's fingers twisted beneath the table. Clearly everyone did think that she and Rick were a couple. She'd address that later. One revelation at a time.

"It wasn't jealousy," Jess said, her voice catching

and she cleared her throat. "Mike got in my face. He tried to intimidate me."

"But you've been broken up for years," Meggie insisted. "Surely he's over that by now."

Jess looked over at Josh, whose eyes were soft with understanding.

Rick's hand slipped over to her thigh and squeezed reassuringly.

She lifted her chin, determined not to look down this time. "When Mike and I were dating . . . when we moved into the cottage . . ." Big inhale, long exhale. She could do this. "He was abusive. I didn't want to face it. I got used to making excuses for him. And he could be so charming. I actually started to believe things were my fault. But then there came a point where I knew I couldn't stand it anymore. Problem was, I didn't quite know how to get out of the situation. He was everywhere. My whole family is here. To escape him I would have had to leave Jewell Cove, and yet staying in the same town with him was unthinkable. We got in a fight one night and he . . ."

She broke off. Fought for air. There wasn't a sound from the group around the table. They all seemed stunned into silence. Rick's hand was still on her thigh, though, and when she looked at her brother he gave a small encouraging nod.

"He came at me with a knife."

Those words unleashed a flurry of responses, both of dismay and anger from her family. She looked over at Rick. He looked down at her tummy and then back up into her face, questioning. He remembered, then. Remembered asking her about the scar the first night they'd made love. This was the part he hadn't known. She gave a nearly imperceptible nod, and his gaze swiveled to Josh. Jess watched as the two men communicated silently. It wasn't hard to figure out what was being said.

"Okay, okay," she said, raising her hands. "Look, I'm fine now. That was the night Mike left town. Mom, remember how I called and said we'd broken up and I was with friends for a few days?"

Meggie nodded, her fingers over her lips. "You sounded so strange. I was relieved the relationship was over, you know. There was always something about Mike that didn't sit quite right, but I couldn't put my finger on it. Oh, honey. I wish I'd known. I could have helped you . . ."

"Josh helped me. He interrupted us that night and took care of Mike. Josh is the reason Mike left town. Then Josh stitched me up and drove me to a shelter until I was ready to come home again."

Rick didn't know all of this either. She felt his gaze on her face as he asked, "The shelter . . . that's the real reason you know the director there, right?"

She nodded. "That's right. Catherine looked after me and got me the help I needed."

Josh leaned forward and interrupted the group. "Getting back to Rick. I'm assuming you ran into Mike today?"

Jess nodded. "We all know how sick his mother is and that they moved her back here for her last days. Mike and Pam are both home for the holiday. I was hoping to avoid seeing him at all, but no such luck."

"He was a total asshole," Rick put in. "All charm

and smiles and veiled threats. When it was clear he was trying to intimidate Jess, I stepped in." He lifted his hand. "It was worth it. He needs to know she's not alone this time. This is why you all need to know what happened: Maybe he was just blowing off steam. But I think it would be good if Jess's family had her back."

There were murmurs of approval around the table. "Of course we will," Abby said staunchly. "Whatever you need, Jess, you let us know."

"Thanks, everyone," Jess answered, overwhelmed by the love and support around the table. "I'll be fine, though. No need to fuss over me."

"There's every need," Mark replied, and everyone around the table nodded. "Don't minimize it, Jess."

Aunt Barb nodded. "You don't have to be strong all the time, you know."

Jess's lip wobbled a bit. Why had she waited so long? She should have had faith in her family. Should have trusted them to stand beside her.

Should have been less ashamed.

"Thank you," she whispered. "I love you guys."

A few throats were cleared discreetly, and then Bryce folded his hands on top of the table in front of him. "Do you want a restraining order?"

"That's not a bad idea." Rick nodded in agreement.

Jess shifted in her chair and folded her arms. There was support and then there was taking over and that was exactly what she didn't want. "Look, we all know how effective restraining orders are. It's just a piece of paper."

"But if there's a restraining order, he'll get busted if he comes around you and I doubt he wants to get arrested. Imagine how his mother would feel knowing her boy was in lockup for that?"

Jess waffled a bit. "That's true, and I'm not saying I'm not open to the idea." Indeed, the idea of taking proactive steps was bolstering. It felt better to be in control of a situation. But there were other things to consider. "I wouldn't want to do that to Karen. She's got enough on her plate with her illness, and this is about Mike, not her. Besides, I don't feel like shouting my history around town like a town crier, you know? I'm sure Rick's reminder was enough to make him back off. Let's face it, it's been years since we were together. He's not really interested in me . . ."

"You think this is about interest?" Bryce interjected, his brows a hard line. "It's not and you know it. It's about control. He lost that control once. He could be really pissed about that."

If Bryce was trying to scare her, it was working, no matter what she said out loud. Maybe it wasn't such a bad idea . . .

"I'll think about it," she repeated. "Besides, I don't think he's home for long. There's probably not much point." At least that's what she would continue to tell herself. She wouldn't let him get to her again.

As she looked around the table, she saw ten members of her family with set expressions of resolve. Suddenly she didn't feel so alone. Support was close by if she needed it. All those years ago she hadn't wanted to worry anyone. Besides, her silence was part of the bargain for Mike leaving. It had been worth it.

That agreement no longer held up. Even if she understood the reason, he had come back to town and keeping quiet was no longer a requirement.

"Let's just eat some pie, okay?" She forced a smile and picked up her fork, though eating was the last thing she wanted to do. "It's Thanksgiving. We're all healthy, we're all together for the first time in ages, and it's going to be fine." She scooped up a bit of pecan pie and popped it in her mouth with far more enthusiasm than she felt.

For some reason she felt like she needed to make this okay for her family. That she had to show them that she was all right and could handle it.

The conversation was far more hushed, but they followed her lead. In the midst of the noise Rick leaned over and whispered in her ear. "Good job," he said.

"Thanks." Oddly enough, she did feel better. Maybe the old saying was right. Maybe confession was good for the soul.

CHAPTER 17

It was six o'clock and dark by the time they finally left Sarah's house. Rick's hand was throbbing now; the ice pack long gone and the swelling in his knuckles back with a vengeance. Hitting someone in the face with bare knuckles was a lot different than in the movies. Jess pulled into his yard and put the car in park. "Sorry about this afternoon," she said quietly.

He looked over at her. She was bundled into her fall coat with a soft scarf looped around her neck and matching gloves on her hands. When she'd invited him to dinner he'd had no idea that there'd be so much excitement.

"Don't apologize. I'm glad I was there."

"I'm glad you were, too." She hesitated and then met his gaze. "Rick, I'm really sorry about how I acted last spring and stuff."

He shook his head, pleased with the apology even

though it wasn't necessary. "I deserved it. I was a mess. Some days I still am."

"But you're handling it better."

"Yeah, I am. I deserved the things you said, Jess. You were right. I think I just had to work through it."

"I should have helped rather than criticize."

He smiled then. Did she know how amazing she was? "And you think I would have taken help? I thought you knew me better than that."

It got a smile out of her anyway. She laughed a little and agreed. "You're right. Anyway, thank you. For standing up for me. For being beside me when I told everyone. Your support meant a lot."

He ignored the pain in his hand and reached out, touching the side of her face. "I'll always be there when you need me," he replied.

"Rick, I . . ."

"Do you want to come in, Jess?"

Their gazes clung for a long moment. The heat in her gaze told him she understood what he was asking. What it meant. Something had changed between them today. Sex was one thing. Opening up to someone, having a relationship . . . that was something else entirely. But this was Jess. She already knew most of his secrets. And she was still sitting here. With him. What surprised him most was that he felt ready to take this next step.

"I think I'd like to come in. I think I'd like that very much."

"Even after today? Even after seeing Mike? It had to bring back memories." He understood that better than she might think. He had plenty of moments where the past snuck in and knocked him flat. Dreams about Kyle and the night he'd been beaten so badly. Dreams about the day of the firefight, right up to the moment when the grenade exploded and everything went dark. He knew it was all in the past, but it didn't stop the reactions. They called it PTSD. He knew it wasn't limited to soldiers.

Jess lifted her hand, too, and placed it on his face, mirroring his touch. "It did, yes, but you're not him. I know that." She paused. "You know, I didn't want to tell the family. I guess I thought I deserved to deal with it on my own, kind of a punishment for being so stupid . . . so weak. By the time I understood it wasn't my fault, I didn't see any need to worry them. But you knew I needed to and you were right." Jess leaned over the console and kissed him. "Thank you," she murmured against his lips. "I feel so much better now."

"Your family is pretty great."

She smiled. "Yes, they are. And they care for you a lot."

It was all the urging he needed. He got out of the car and went around to open her door. She left her empty and washed dishes in the back and only grabbed her purse, then took his hand as they walked to the house.

He let go of her hand long enough to get the keys from his pocket, and unlocked the door. Stepping into the kitchen, he flicked a switch, letting light into the darkened room.

It was barely seven o'clock. They hadn't eaten dessert until four, after a huge meal midafternoon. He could suggest turning on the television, he supposed. Offer her something to drink. Tea. She liked tea, he remembered. Maybe he imagined sweeping her off her feet and carrying her to his bedroom, but the last thing he wanted was for her to think that was the only reason he'd asked her in.

"I can put on some tea if you like."

She put down her purse and smiled softly at him. "Tea? Is that why you asked me in?"

His cheeks felt hot. What the hell? He was nervous and she looked as cool as a cucumber, smiling at him that way. He had no answer for her. Nothing that he could think of that didn't sound utterly stupid or inappropriate.

She stepped up to him so they were face-to-face. "Are you nervous, Rick?"

"I shouldn't be."

"I'm glad you are." She leaned forward and kissed him again, a feather-light touch of lips that stole his breath. "I'm glad you don't take anything for granted."

He closed his eyes for a moment, willing himself to take it slow and not rush anything. "Nothing should ever be taken for granted. It can disappear in the blink of an eye."

"I know," she murmured, her fingers teasing the hair at his temples. "But we're here now."

He swallowed. "I guess I wanted you to know that for me, it's more than just sex. I just want to be with you, Jess. In whatever way you need."

"I need to feel alive, Rick. I need to feel alive and strong and secure. I was hoping you could help me with that."

He ignored the pain in his hand and curled it around her neck, pulling her closer so he could kiss her properly.

Her body melted against him and she made a soft sound in her throat. Damn, she was sweet. Sweet and sultry, innocent and earthy all at once. Jess Collins was a whole lot of woman and at this moment, with her in his arms, he felt a protective possessiveness he'd never felt before.

Somehow they made it to the stairs with their lips still joined. Rick swept her into his arms and she leaned against his chest. Slowly they made their way up the stairs, Rick constantly aware of the side of her breast pressed against him and the way her lips nuzzled at his neck. Good God, she was going to be the end of him if she wasn't careful.

He hadn't redecorated his room, and for a moment he realized that it wasn't exactly romantic with the boyish spread and posters still tacked on the wall. Jess didn't seem to mind, though, as he put her down carefully on top of the covers.

Before things went further, he opened the drawer of his nightstand and took out a condom, putting the foil packet on the top of the stand. He wanted her to know. Know that he was prepared. Know that he would take care of her . . .

And he did. Twice, before sleep finally overtook them as they curled together under the bedding.

Jess rolled over, her eyes slowly opening as she came awake. The bed was empty beside her, and a quick glance at the alarm clock next to the bed told her it was eleven fifteen.

She was naked under the blankets and she stretched

luxuriously, feeling the soft cotton against her skin. It was such a revelation to have a physical relationship based on mutual pleasure. On giving and receiving.

A sliver of light was visible at the bottom of the bedroom door. Rick was up. Maybe it had simply been too early for him to go to sleep. Or maybe he'd needed some space. Things had been pretty intense there for a while. Intense and awesome.

There was a T-shirt on a nearby chair, so Jess rolled out of bed and pulled it on. She was tall enough that the shirt barely covered her bottom, but she didn't care. On quiet feet she padded to the door and gently opened it. The light was coming from the bathroom across the hall. The door was open and she could see Rick standing at the sink.

"Couldn't sleep?" she asked.

He spun around, startled by her voice and the smile slid from her face.

She'd never thought. Never considered or expected. He'd removed his prosthesis, and the stump of his arm was visible.

"God, I'm sorry. I didn't mean to interrupt you . . ."

His face went blank, devoid of any emotion. "I thought you were asleep. I take it off at night. The batteries need to charge and I have to look after my skin."

"I didn't mean to intrude . . ." Lord, she felt like such an idiot. She didn't know where to look. She was curious about his arm but didn't want to stare; she was acutely embarrassed and couldn't meet his eyes.

"It's okay if you freak out a little. You weren't expecting to see me without the arm."

He looked so tough, so wounded as he stood in front

of her dressed in nothing more than a pair of boxers. The scars on his chest still looked angry, even after all this time, and it was impossible to ignore the missing limb. He'd been through so much.

"I'll be done soon."

She stepped closer. "What do you have to do?"

His jaw tightened. "I have to clean the socket, charge it up, wash my arm, and moisturize it."

"Can I help?"

There. At her offer, there was a flicker of emotion. He wasn't as immune as he was pretending to be. But he'd accepted her. If she was going to be with him he deserved no less from her.

"Jess . . ."

She entered the room and saw soapy water in the sink. She grabbed the washcloth, wrung it out, and with her heart in her throat, reached for his arm, lifting his elbow so that his handless forearm was extended her way, over the basin of the sink. Gently she applied the cloth, wiping along his arm, slowly soaping the skin and rinsing away the suds. The air in the room grew heavy, weighted with emotions and unanswered questions. Jess put the cloth back in the water and reached for a towel, patting the skin dry.

Then, without saying a word, she reached for the lotion on the counter and squirted a healthy amount into her palm. Slowly she worked the lotion into the skin.

The muscle and bone were firm beneath her fingers and she massaged the lotion into his warm skin. Rick's eyes were closed, his breath slow and steady. She hoped that what she was doing felt good. That it helped relax the muscles in his arm. She kneaded with her fingers, starting above his elbow and working her way down.

"Do you ever get phantom pain?" she asked softly, still kneading.

"Sometimes. Not as often as I used to." His voice was gritty. "That feels good, Jess. Real good."

"I'm glad." She got more lotion and started over. "It hurts me to think of this happening to you. It must have been so hard."

He shook his head. He turned a bit, resting his hips against the vanity, allowing her better access to his arm and relaxing his shoulders. "The physical stuff wasn't as bad as the other," he replied. "That's what most people don't get. Yeah, adjusting to an artificial limb's a challenge. It's not what keeps me up at night, though."

Her heart gave an odd little thump. "What does keep you up at night?"

His eyes opened. "People."

Keep your fingers moving, she reminded herself, wanting to keep him talking. She sensed they were on the verge of something important. "Anyone in particular?

"Does there need to be?"

There was an edge to his voice that reached out to her. "I think so, yes," she answered, her fingertips stroking the soft skin now. "I think that something happened that keeps you up at night. Something that you try to escape, or at least cancel out, first with your drinking and now with your painting." She stopped rubbing and looked up into his face. "Am I right?"

"You trying to psychoanalyze me, Saint Jess?"

The nickname told her she was on the right track. "Maybe I get it, Rick. I started doing all these crafts and projects to keep my mind and hands busy after I left Mike. It was important that I was able to make something, to build something that was maybe not necessary but added a bit of beauty to a world that could be pretty damned ugly. I made it my livelihood, but I think it's pretty cool that I was able to take something that started out as a kind of self-therapy and now make my living at it, you know?"

She put her hands around his forearms, linking the two of them together. "I know your painting is your therapy. I wish you'd talk to me, though. Tell me what happened."

He pulled his arms away. "I'm doing better. I'm not sure bringing it all up again is such a good idea."

Rick put the lotion back in its spot and tidied the supplies on the vanity. Jess's heart ached for him. He was so defensive she knew whatever he was keeping inside was still eating him up. "Rick, you helped me, more than you know. Won't you let me return the favor?"

He put the cap on the rubbing alcohol and then turned back to face her. "You don't want to know, Jess. It's not pretty."

"Of course it's not. If it were pretty, it wouldn't be hurting you so much. What really happened when you were wounded? Why is it so hard to forget? If it's not the injury, what? Did you lose someone important?"

"Dammit, Jess!" His patience at an end, Rick snapped out the words and pushed his way past her to the door. She sighed as his feet hit the stairs heavily, taking him to the lower level of the house.

With soft steps she followed him in the dark, down the stairs and past the porch door to the living room beyond. She found him sitting on the sofa, his elbows on his knees. She couldn't help but notice his arm, an obvious physical reminder of so much else going on underneath the surface.

"Rick," she said quietly, going to him and sitting beside him on the sofa. The only light in the room came from whatever filtered through the windows from the streetlamp two houses away. "You don't have to do this alone."

"You wouldn't understand."

She snorted then. "Oh come on. You think just because I didn't go through exactly what you did that I can't understand? That I don't know what it's like to lose someone I care about? That I don't have guilt, or regrets, or understand emotional trauma? Do you really think that?"

"Jess, I . . ."

But she kept going. "I lost my father. He was the one man I counted on for everything. He was the rudder of our family and suddenly he was gone and no one knew how to function without him. The last thing I wanted was to make things worse, add grief to a bad situation, so I kept my mouth shut and tried to make things better behind the scenes. But I needed love, too, you know? By the time I graduated, I had such a low sense of self-worth that I was ripe for the picking for someone like Mike Greer."

She took a breath, met his black gaze in the semidarkness, and pressed on. "I wish I'd been better at dealing with my feelings. I wish I'd had better self-esteem. I wish

I'd realized that I was capable of more. You want regrets? I've got them by the bucket load. Mike took more from me than any man ever should. You think this scar on my belly is bad? It's nothing compared to the scar in here"—she pressed her hand to her chest—"and the guilt I carry around every damn day."

"Jess," he said again, softer this time. "I don't know how to do this."

"None of us does," she replied, her throat raw. "You just do it."

Quiet descended over the room until Jess heard Rick sigh deeply. "His name was Kyle."

He'd started, and now she had to tread carefully to make sure he kept going. "Kyle?" she urged.

He nodded. "He was a good kid. A good soldier and a good friend. A brother."

Rick stopped for a minute, but Jess simply waited for him to continue.

"We became buddies. He was young and fresh-faced, from a farm in Kansas and had a wicked sense of humor. Nothing seemed to get him down, you know? And that was saying something considering where we were. And sing; man, could that kid sing. Just when you thought you couldn't stand another minute, he'd break out into some stupid song. Usually Weird Al, so we'd get laughing. And in the absence of that, he'd make up his own words."

"He sounds great," she murmured, wondering if he realized how his voice had warmed talking about his friend.

"We were nearly done with our tour when someone found out he had a partner at home."

By the way Rick said *partner*, Jess immediately got what he was saying. "Kyle was gay."

"Yeah."

The warmth was gone from his voice now, replaced by a hard edge. "I didn't give a shit. It wasn't like he was running around the camp hitting on us, you know? He was like a little brother. The guy was in a relationship. But there were a few in our unit who didn't feel the same way."

"There was trouble?"

"He got the shit beat out of him."

The room fell utterly silent.

Finally Rick spoke again. "The next day, we were out on a patrol when we were ambushed. Kyle should never even have been along, but he was so determined they wouldn't get the best of him, you know? He refused to say a word about who attacked him, covered up his injuries. He just took it on the chin and kept going. But it slowed him down and he got hit. I was running out to get him when an RPG hit the vehicle he'd been using for cover."

Jess couldn't imagine the horror of such a thing, or what it must be like to be in that kind of extreme situation. "What happened to him?" she asked gently.

"He died," Rick answered, his voice flat, devoid of any emotion. Jess now understood that the detached tone meant he was protecting himself from feeling too much. "When I woke up I was in a hospital, full of holes, and minus one hand just above the wrist."

So he'd seen his friend die, and then he'd been wounded himself so that he was powerless. "I'm so sorry," she whispered, putting her hand on his knee and squeezing reassuringly. "But it wasn't your fault. You know that. You were trying to save him."

Rick's haunted eyes searched hers. "But I didn't. I should have reported what I knew to our CO. I should have tried to protect him. He never should have been with us that day, only I kept my mouth shut."

And she could tell that no amount of talking or urging on her part was going to change his mind. He blamed himself, and that was that.

"Whatever happened to the guys who assaulted him?" she asked gently.

Rick's face twisted with distaste. "Nothing, as far as I know. I never went back. And I never said anything, either. I thought it was better to let it go and not kick the hornet's nest, you know? Stuff like that has serious ramifications. And since Kyle hadn't meant for people to find out, I told myself that he wouldn't want his name dragged through an investigation. Nothing would bring him back . . ."

Jess cuddled closer, leaned her head on his shoulder. "It makes sense," she answered.

"Maybe it does, but talking about regrets . . . I can't help thinking that I should have gotten him some kind of justice. Or I should have looked out for him so he wasn't hurt at all, and would have been at the top of his game. I failed him all the way around, Jess, and I can't stop thinking about it."

She wrapped her arms around his middle. "You can't do that to yourself, Rick. I'm sure he would understand . . ."

But he pushed her away. "*I* don't understand. And

the hand thing? Yeah, it's a pain in the ass, but the drinking? I see his face at night, Jess. When I'm sleeping. When I was drinking, I'd go to sleep and not see anything. Of course the hangover was a bitch, but I could forget for just a little while."

"But you stopped." She smiled encouragingly.

"Because my mom made me promise. It's pretty hard to deny your dying mother anything. And I started painting more instead. At night when I couldn't sleep. Anything to think about something other than his face. Jesus, he was just a boy."

He'd lost so much. It wasn't much wonder he'd been an emotional wreck. Jess's heart went out to him, sitting with his elbows on his knees in the darkness. He'd come a long way, too. He'd found a job, looked after his mom, stayed off the bottle, and he'd become someone Jess could rely on. All the while being all alone, with no support system to speak of beyond Tom and Josh. Rick was so much stronger than she had given him credit for.

They sat together for a long while, letting the night settle around them. The heating was turned down for night and the temperature outside began to dip, and Jess gave a little shudder as she started to chill.

"Come upstairs," Rick suggested. "We'll crawl under the covers and stay warm. It's silly to stay down here."

"Maybe I should go. My big sale starts tomorrow and I need to be in the shop early . . ."

"I'll set the alarm and get you there in lots of time. Promise."

The idea of being wrapped in Rick's arms all night

was alluring. Things were moving forward in a big way. It did seem like they were heading into relationship territory.

"Jess?"

She put her hand in his. "Okay. But you have to set your alarm for early. I mean it. Like six o'clock."

He chuckled. "I'm usually up by then anyway. Old habits."

They got up and she followed him to the stairs. Before long they were under the quilts, snuggled in against the cold. It felt so surreal, being here, being in his room, in his arms. Like she belonged.

That was perhaps the scariest thing of all, and at the same time the most exciting.

Rick stared at the dark ceiling for a long time after Jess's breathing evened out. God, what a day. When he'd agreed to go to Sarah's for dinner he'd pictured food and football. Instead he'd been put through the wringer.

Mike didn't scare him, but he sure as hell scared Jess and that made Rick see red. It had taken all his self-control to not beat the man to a pulp, but he'd held back knowing how much it would distress Jess. All except that one punch. It had been smart, sending Jess inside for a few minutes. Because Rick had taken that time to make it very clear what would happen if Mike came within a hundred yards of Jess.

Not that Mike would listen. He was too full of himself for that. Too used to getting his way and using intimidation to ensure it. Of course, he didn't think Rick would follow through. And that was Mike's biggest mistake.

Rick would protect Jess no matter what. Tomorrow Josh, Tom, and Bryce would be getting phone calls. As long as Mike was in town, he didn't want Jess alone.

Which was why he'd asked her in tonight. He just hadn't expected it to end in a baring of souls. Part of him felt better, finally talking about Kyle.

But other parts of him were scared shitless. It wasn't just sex with Jess. It was more. It always would have been. But damn, she had a way of getting too close. In the past he would have backed away and let her go home. But not tonight. Not after everything that had happened today, so he'd brought her back upstairs and held her close and wondered how the hell he'd managed to get caught up in this mess.

CHAPTER 18

By eleven o'clock, Jess's store was packed.

Whoever said Black Friday sales were limited to department stores and online giants had never been on Jewell Cove's Main Street the day after Thanksgiving. Sure, some ventured into the bigger shopping areas and outlet stores for major deals, but one thing was for certain: the residents of the cove turned out to support their local businesses.

Jess was run off her feet already, and she took a moment to gather her hair up in a loose topknot just to keep the warm weight of it off the back of her neck. Her Christmas stock was going fast, but so was her supply of jewelry, candles, and yarn. If customers weren't decorating for Christmas, they were buying presents or planning knit and crochet projects. Best of all, Rick's items were flying off the shelves.

"Jess, have you got any more of those peppermint-scented pillar candles?" Georgia McKinnon, the new fourth-grade teacher, looked up hopefully. "I love those candles."

Jess did a quick check and discovered the spot on the shelf was empty. "You hold on a minute, and I'll check the back," Jess assured her. She glanced at her mother, who was tidying the yarn shelf for the third time that morning. "Mom, will you watch the register?"

Meggie gave her the thumbs-up and Jess disappeared into the back—only to come face-to-face with Rick.

She pressed her hand to her heart. "Oh my goodness, you scared me! What are you doing back here?"

"I came in a while ago, but you were stocking your soaps and didn't see me."

She flushed a bit. Rick had dropped her off shortly after six and had come in with her, indulging in some very long and distracting kisses before announcing he had some errands to run. She'd tried to hide her disappointment . . . it had been amazing, waking up with him next to her. Seeing his lashes on his cheeks as he slept, feeling his body curl around hers in the moments before he woke . . . that was special.

The truth was, she suspected she was falling in love with Rick. Not that she was in any particular hurry to say anything about it. It was so new, far too early to start dissecting feelings when their relationship still felt tenuous.

Still, looking up at him as he stood in her workroom, she felt a familiar glow that seemed to happen whenever he was around.

"It's crazy in here today. I'm going to have to see if Tessa can work an extra few days just so I can replenish some of my stock. And here I thought I was finished sewing those blasted tartan stockings." She grinned.

"I thought you could use some help today, but if I'm in the way just let me know. I can take a hint."

She shook her head. "Not in the way at all. I can use the help. Just let me check on an item here and I'll be right back."

She grabbed a half-dozen candles to restock the shelf, pleased at both the offer and his presence. Within moments she'd sold two peppermint candles to Georgia and was back in the storeroom again.

"Let me give you the nickel tour," she suggested, meeting his gaze. She couldn't get distracted; there was too much to do. Maybe she'd cook for him later to show her appreciation . . .

Jess opened the door to the stock cupboard. "In here you'll find tissue for wrapping delicate items and shopping bags, which we keep under the counter at the front. This," she pointed to a small cardboard box, "is cash register tape in case it runs out. If you can check to make sure we have lots of everything under the counter, that'd be great."

"Yes, boss," he intoned seriously, a little smile twitching at the corner of his mouth.

She smiled back and led him to a storage room where she kept her stock. She flipped on a light and led him into the narrow space between several rows of shelving.

"This is my stock. Everything is tagged, so it just needs to go on the shelf. This section is jewelry, and it's organized very specifically so that nothing gets mixed up or knotted." She gestured further. "Along here are my soaps, each container marked with the scent, and the same with the candles. Scent, then size. Yarn is here, and this whole shelf is quilting fabric. Along here we have sewing and knitting supplies. Then the consignment items . . ." She hesitated, looking over her shoulder at him to make sure he was still following along. "Each one is marked by name, not item. And finally, we have the fun section. Kids' stuff for the kid corner. Puzzles, toys, that sort of thing. I've got a sale on puppets and brain twisters today, so those might disappear faster than usual."

"How on earth do you keep track of all of this?"

Jess laughed. "My favorite thing. Paperwork. Add in accounting and staying in the good graces of the IRS, and there's more of it than I'd like."

"Have you thought about hiring an accountant?"

"Maybe, when the shop is doing a little bit better. I try to do as much as I can on my own to reduce my overhead."

"Like living here?"

"Beats having rent on two places."

"Right."

They backed out of the closet. Jess was a little disappointed he hadn't tried to sneak another kiss along the way, but on the other hand she really should get back to the front of the store.

"So, are you up to it?"

"I think I can handle it. I'll check the bags and tissue first, how about that?"

On impulse, Jess went up on tiptoe and kissed his

cheek. "That sounds great. Don't forget to pimp your ornaments either, Rick. They're almost gone and I want a new supply for the Evergreen Festival."

With a wink she disappeared back into the store.

The business was brisk but Jess was always aware of Rick nearby, talking to the customers, straightening shelves, opening the door for them, or helping Meggie— who was significantly shorter than Jess or Rick—reach items on some of the upper shelves. Once, when Jess was at the cash register ringing in a particularly large order, Rick stepped up and wrapped each fragile item in tissue and bagged it. She could smell his body wash or whatever he was wearing, the scent becoming familiar now the more time they spent together. During a lull, he grabbed a broom and swept the floor, and at one o'clock they realized no one had had lunch and he zipped off to the café to pick up sandwiches and coffee for everyone. When he got back, Jess let Meggie and Tessa eat first, and when they were done she and Rick went to the back room to eat together.

"Is it always this crazy?" he asked, opening his carton and picking up half of his turkey salad sandwich.

"Not at all. Well, sometimes in the summer it gets crazy, when the tourists are here and the weather's good. It's been particularly busy today, which is very good for my bottom line."

"I'm really impressed, Jess. I'm starting to see how much work goes into this place and how you handle it with, well, 'ease' is probably the best word. You must really love it."

She beamed at him. "I do. It's not perfect, and it can

be a bit of a challenge owning your own business, you know? But I can't imagine doing anything else."

Opening her own carton, she grabbed her sandwich and took a bite of fresh bread, still slightly warm. Wiping her mouth on a napkin, she laughed. "I should have known turkey would be on special the day after Thanksgiving," she said. "No one makes turkey salad like Gus."

"I bet there's a secret ingredient."

"Probably."

"If there is, he'll take it to his grave." Rick finished his first half in record time. "If Gus ever leaves, I don't know what they'll do."

For a few more minutes they ate, comfortable with the silence between them. When the last crumb was consumed, Rick sat back and rubbed his belly. "That hit the spot."

Jess nodded. "It did, but I should get back. Both Mom and Tessa are leaving at three. I need to take advantage of their help while I've got it."

"I'll stay until closing. So you don't have to be here alone," he added.

There was something in the way he said it that twigged with Jess. What was his underlying reason? To help? Or to make sure she wasn't alone? This couldn't be about Mike, could it?

She dismissed the thought and wondered if she might be just a little bit paranoid. They'd made their point to Mike yesterday and up until now he'd kept his promise to Josh. Meeting had been unpleasant and damned uncomfortable, but a day later she was able to see things more clearly. Rick was just here to help. Maybe he wanted to spend more time with her after last night. The thought sent a warmth rushing through her and she smiled a little to herself. Besides, an extra set of hands for the remainder of the afternoon would be very welcome.

"Since I haven't paid you for today, how about you stay for dinner? I can promise there won't be turkey on the menu."

Rick closed up his container and brushed his hands together. "How can I refuse an offer like that?" he asked, getting up and pressing a kiss to her forehead.

"Besides," he murmured, his lips close to her skin, "it gives me more time with you."

The warm feeling remained throughout the afternoon as Rick stayed and they closed up the store together. She'd been right after all. He simply wanted more time with her, and nothing could have pleased her more.

After the holiday craziness, the next days settled down a bit and Rick worked on a few of his made-to-order projects. Right now he was replacing the last hinge on the front of the grandfather clock in Abby and Tom's hall.

The workmanship was solid, but the age of the piece dictated he be incredibly careful. He'd even questioned Tom's judgment in tinkering with it at all, voicing the opinion that altering the glass on the door would affect its worth. But Tom had argued that he and Abby weren't worried about that, and so he'd removed the door, taken it to his studio, and painted a simple design of an apple blossom branch holding a pair of fat chickadees.

Tom stood behind him, watching the progress. "Dude, you continually surprise me," he said.

"I get that a lot." Finished, Rick looked over his shoulder and grinned. "Hope your wife likes it."

"She will. Listen, are you busy tonight?"

He thought about the boxes of ornaments he had ready to go to Jess's. "I can make time. I've got to drop a few things off at Jess's . . ."

"A few things, huh? How are things with you two?"

Rick chuckled. "Things are none of your damned business, bro."

A full-throated laugh echoed through the hall. "Right. Well, good for you guys. It's about time. For both of you."

As much as Rick was enjoying being with Jess, he wasn't sure he was ready for everyone to pair them off as a big thing. "I'm just looking out for her, that's all," he insisted. He stood up and brushed his hands on his jeans, wondering if he was as transparent as he felt.

"I hope not, Rick. She deserves more than someone keeping an eye out, you know? And if you're playing around with her . . ."

"Relax," he said quietly. "A guy can do both, you know. But you didn't hear that from me."

Tom relaxed, but only slightly. "Anything happening with the asshole?"

"Not that I can tell."

"Hopefully Mike will be out of town soon and she won't have to worry about it."

"Amen to that," Rick agreed. "So, what's up with tonight?"

"I was thinking it'd be nice for you and Jess to come to dinner. We haven't really had anyone over since the wedding, and now that you and Jess aren't sniping at each other all the time . . ."

Rick laughed. "Yeah, yeah. I get it."

"So what do you think?"

"I'll have to check with her. She'll have to close up first."

"Just give Abby a call when you know for sure. Hopefully I'll see you later. I'd better get down to the job site before my foreman fires me." He grinned and clapped Rick on the shoulder.

When Rick stopped at Treasures to deliver his ornaments, Jess was alone, knitting on the yellow blanket again.

"Wow, it's almost done," he noticed, looking at the long waterfall of lacy yellow yarn.

"Getting there. Snatching time to work on it is tricky. At this rate I won't finish it until Christmas."

He lifted the box. "Brought you some stuff as promised. Since you just happened to sell out last weekend."

"Oh, great! I'll take anything you can spare." She moved to put down her knitting but Rick shook his head.

"Don't get up. I'll put this in the back."

He put the box on the back worktable and then came back out front. "Listen, Tom and Abby have asked us over for dinner tonight. You up for it?"

She looked up. "I guess so. What's the occasion?"

"According to Tom, there isn't any. Just hanging out."

If she was with him he didn't have to worry about Mike . . . who was still in town even though Thanksgiving was well over. The only thing that kept the "boys" from pressing him to go was the knowledge that Karen had taken a turn for the worse and it would probably soon be over.

"I'll call Tom and let him know," Rick said, leaning over the counter and giving her forehead a quick kiss.

"That's okay. I'll call Abby. I should ask if she wants me to bring anything anyway. Pick me up at six?"

"Perfect." It would give him time to go home and get cleaned up properly.

At six on the dot he was at her back door and she was ready. They drove out to Blackberry Hill while small flakes of snow fluttered in the air. The wind blew from the north and Rick looked over at Jess, bundled up in her wool coat and pretty scarf and felt his heart constrict. God, she was so beautiful. Too beautiful for him. He couldn't help feeling that something this good wasn't going to last.

The house on Blackberry Hill was stunning. For the first time in several years, it was decorated for the holidays. Now that Thanksgiving had passed, Abby had gone all-out with the decorations. Evergreen boughs with wide red bows festooned the railings between the stately pillars and again on the faux widow's walk. A gigantic wreath hung on the door. The house looked different in the evening, when everything was lit up by a fairyland of tiny white lights, and a floodlight highlighting the front columns. It was good to see it brought to life again.

Rick parked and went around to open Jess's door. "Thanks," she said, and he noticed a little flush to her cheeks.

"What, you don't think I have manners?" he teased.

"Oh, I know you have manners. It's not that. It feels a little weird. Us," she clarified.

"Weird good or weird bad?" He looked over at her as they walked toward the house.

"Weird good. Weird different." She shrugged. "A few months ago I never would have thought we'd be on friendly terms, let alone . . ."

"Sleeping together?" he finished for her.

Her blush deepened. He liked it.

"Yeah, that," she replied.

He put out his hand and stopped her from climbing the steps. "You," he said quietly, "are incredible. I hope you know that."

"Rick," she said, and his heart constricted at the wistful tone of her voice. For the first time they were going somewhere as a couple. Thanksgiving had been different. It had been less of a statement. More of a test run.

Tonight was one couple having dinner with another couple. It was another first for them. "I'm not in any rush. We take things one day at a time, right? Just like we always have. I just wanted to say it. You're a special woman, Jess. Don't ever let anyone take that away from you."

He squeezed her arm and they climbed the steps to the landing. He thought about his words, knowing he'd unconsciously added "even me" to the end of that last sentence. Jess was wonderful, and he'd started to understand that he trusted her but he still didn't quite trust himself. He'd made progress, he knew that. But the rough times weren't necessarily over and not everything was coming up daisies.

They knocked, using the big brass door knocker and stood back. Jess smiled over at him. "Do you know the first time I was inside this house after Tom renovated it, I was here for a sleepover?"

He grinned. "Really? At your age?"

"It was after the picnic at Sarah's. We brought out pizza and wine and ended up crashing here. I walked through the halls gawking at everything."

The door opened and Abby stood there, smiling at them. "Hello you two! Gosh, it's good to see you. Come on in."

She led them through to the parlor, a pretty room done in warm yellow with antique furniture and draperies the color of rich merlot. A fire burned cheerily in the fireplace. Unlike the modern additions to the library, this room was like stepping back in time.

"Do you ever feel like you're living in a time warp?" Jess asked, perching on the edge of a silk settee.

Abby laughed. "Yes. I don't know what's going to happen when Tom and I have kids. The rug in here is original. Can you imagine spilling grape juice on it?"

Rick looked at the light in her eyes and knew the idea didn't really faze her a bit. "You're not . . . already, are you?"

Her eyes twinkled at them. "Not yet. Not that we know of," she amended.

His buddy Tom a dad? The image seemed to fit for some reason. Tom was ready, Rick realized, but he wasn't sure if he'd ever be ready for kids.

The front door slammed and Tom's voice rang out. "Hello! Anyone home?"

Rick watched as Abby's whole face lit up at the

sound of her husband's voice. The two of them were so in love it was sickening.

Tom stuck his head inside the room. "Hey, sweetheart." His first smile was for his wife. Then he looked at Rick and Jess, sitting side by side on the settee. "And hey to you, too," he added, shrugging out of his heavy jacket. "Glad you could make it."

"Now that we're all here, Jess, why don't you give me a hand in the kitchen and Tom can show off his new shop to Rick."

The women disappeared in a flurry of conversation and Rick found himself out in the old carriage building, admiring Tom's woodworking shop, while Jess and Abby talked about God knows what. Their first dinner date as a real couple. The idea should have scared him more than it did.

He was falling in love with Jess Collins and had no idea what to do about it or where to go from here. All he knew was that he didn't want it to end. Problem was, he was very aware that good things never lasted forever. Especially for him.

CHAPTER 19

Jess paused at the door, wondering if she should ask Rick in. She wanted to. The evening had been wonderful, the two of them visiting with Abby and Tom, and she couldn't remember when she'd laughed so much. It had felt like a normal relationship. At least, it had once she'd had a moment to speak to Abby. There was no news on the necklace yet, so she'd relaxed and let herself enjoy the visit.

And now Rick had walked her to the door. Her stomach flipped from nerves, but the good kind. They were embarking on something here, something important. And both of them were so afraid to talk about it and jinx anything.

She turned and found him standing remarkably close to her, close enough she had to tilt her chin up to look into his dark eyes. "Are you coming in, Rick?"

She heard the breathless tone of her voice and her

nerves jacked up another level. "Yeah, I'd like to come in," he answered, voice low and husky.

The back door opened into the workroom, and Jess left the lights off while Rick locked the door behind him. In the inky darkness Jess took his hand and led him to the loft steps leading to her living space. Once inside, she reached for the lamp but he stopped her with three little words that made her heart thump with anticipation.

"Leave it off."

She dropped her purse and turned around to face him. It only took a step for him to be inches away. Jess half expected him to gather her up in his arms and whisk her away with a steamy kiss, but instead he lifted his hand and framed her cheek with a tenderness that stole her breath.

She leaned in to the cup of his hand, her eyes sliding closed. She had never imagined he could be so tender. It was a revelation that made him doubly dangerous and drew her in like a moth to a flame.

Only then did he kiss her, taking her lips with an assurance that set her pulse skipping. He took his time, letting the kiss draw out until she felt herself melting against him, her arms sliding up over his shoulders as their bodies pressed together.

She reached for the buttons of his shirt, undoing them one by one and sliding her hands over the warm expanse of his chest before pushing the cotton over his shoulders. All she wanted right now was to feel the heat of his skin against hers. But when she gripped the hem of her sweater, Rick stepped back. "Wait," he said, his voice husky in the darkness.

He went to the window and she realized with a little embarrassment that the blinds were open and the wide windows facing the street would reveal them to anyone who bothered to look up. Rick tensed, staring outside for a few moments before gripping the cord on the roman blinds and releasing the folds, enclosing them in privacy.

"Are you all right?" His jaw was set at a hard, tense angle and his eyes seemed extra intense in the shadowy light.

He didn't answer, but came straight to her, pulled her body flush against his, and kissed her with an intensity that was at once frightening and thrilling. She let out a little squeak as he swept her up into his arms and carried her to her bedroom.

Tonight would be all-out, no-holds-barred, baring-of-souls lovemaking. Jess trembled, standing on the precipice of taking this gigantic leap. It wasn't about being *the first time since Mike* or *a new step* . . . She touched Rick's face, met his gaze, and knew, deep down, that she'd tumbled down the slippery slope of falling in love with him.

She loved Rick Sullivan. She probably always had.

They left the lights off but the glow of the streetlamps cast enough shadows that Jess was able to see all of Rick's features as they undressed in the dark. The glow in his eyes, the outline of his lips, the hard line of his jaw, the broad dips and curls of his shoulders and arms. The moment he slid inside her she cried out. Nothing she'd ever experienced had ever felt as right as this moment, and they held there, letting the impact settle over them.

Each movement, each pulse and beat was a tattoo on her heart. When things got too intense they slowed it down, determined to make it last as long as they could stand it. Sweat slicked their skin and Jess straddled his hips, her hair cascading down her back as she rocked against him and his hands gripped the flesh just below her waist. It wasn't until he reached down to the spot where they were joined that she lost control, trembling and shuddering around him, calling out his name in the darkness.

The tremors were subsiding only a little when he swore, his fingers digging into her hips as he thrust upward, her still-sensitive skin throbbing as he reached his own orgasm.

Then there was only the sound of harsh breathing in her bedroom as they recovered.

Something had changed tonight. Something important and big and amazing. Rather than ruin the moment by speaking, Jess curled up against his side, still naked, and rested her head on his chest.

I love you, she thought to herself, wondering if it was too soon to say the words. But they had already been spoken in her heart. If Rick wasn't there yet it was okay. The way they'd come together tonight had not been one-sided. Rick would say the words when he was ready. The lack of them didn't take anything away from the connection they shared. It went deeper than anything she'd ever experienced.

I love you, she thought again, as her eyes drifted closed.

* * *

Rick made sure she was completely asleep before sliding out from beneath her embrace and reaching for his jeans.

He left his shirt off and walked quietly out to the living room, lifting the blind and staring out into the darkness.

The car was gone. The face was gone. But Rick knew. When they'd first returned, when Rick had moved to shut the blinds, Mike had been standing across the street looking in.

Rick took his cell from his pocket and dialed Josh.

"It's after midnight. What do you want?"

"Hello to you, too," Rick said quietly.

"If this is a call to come pick you up somewhere . . ." Josh sounded supremely irritated. "I have early appointments tomorrow."

"Shut up for a minute and listen."

"I can't hear you very well. Speak up, will ya?"

Rick pressed two fingers to the bridge of his nose, deliberating. "I can't. Jess is asleep."

Silence hummed along the line, but Rick heard the quiet condemnation anyway. So much for discreet. Every time he turned around, his relationship with Jess was a little bit more public.

"I'm at her place," Rick finally said. "And when we got home, Mike was waiting across the street. I wanted you to know."

"Shit." Josh left off the *you're sleeping with my sister* attitude momentarily and let out a big breath. "You're sure?"

"I'm sure. I don't like her left alone. I'll be hanging around a lot. I don't trust that guy as far as I can throw him."

"Me neither."

There was a long silence. "You tell Bryce yet?" Josh asked.

"Not yet. You dealt with Mike before, and you're her brother."

"And you're sleeping with her."

Rick swallowed. He'd known this would eventually come up. "I think I love her, Josh. I think I have for a long time. I just don't want to rush things and screw it up."

"And having sex isn't rushing?"

He glanced toward the bedroom—no sign of movement yet. "Give me a break here. We're figuring things out. We've both got bigger issues than sex to get over."

"She's my sister," Josh said hoarsely, as if that said it all. Because it did.

"And I'd die before I let Mike Greer lay a finger on her again. You can trust me on that."

"I believe you. I might not be entirely happy about how things are, but I believe you."

"And you'll talk to Bryce and Tom?"

"You can count on it." There was a pause. "Look after her, Rick. She's had enough to contend with. Don't you hurt her, too."

With his past history, Rick knew he shouldn't be offended, but he was just the same. He forced back the defensive words that sprang to his brain and said instead, "Don't worry. I won't."

Another beat of silence and Josh asked quietly, "So you love her, huh?"

Rick swallowed thickly. "Yeah."

"Well, goddamn." There was a low chuckle. "Keep me posted, okay?"

"Will do."

Rick clicked off the phone and moved to the window, staring out at the inky shape of the cove and the docks jutting into the water of the harbor. There was something else he had to do, too. He'd been putting it off long enough.

But not tonight. Not now. He'd pick a better time. Right now he just wanted to crawl back into bed with Jess and pull her warmth against him.

When he did that, he felt like everything would be okay.

Rick made a habit of staying as close to Jess as possible during the days that followed, insisting that she needn't look for extra help when he could lend a hand. He spent most of his nights there, holding her close in his arms, and when he ran out of reasons to see her during the day, he brought his paints over and worked on some candle and ornament projects—she was selling out of them at a surprising rate and the holiday festival was fast approaching. The light in her living quarters was great, and Jess set up an area for him with a worktable and stool. Quite often he'd go out and pick up lunch for the two of them and bring it back, and on the nights she taught her classes he cooked something simple and had it ready for when she was done.

It was all very domestic and homey and Rick knew he should be running in the other direction as fast as his feet would carry him. And yet he didn't, because being with Jess felt disturbingly right.

But Mike was still out there, and until that whole problem was resolved, Rick would keep his real feelings to himself. They had time. Besides, he told himself, it wasn't like Jess was in an all-fired rush to make any huge declarations either.

One night after they'd made love, Rick traced his finger over the line of Jess's scar, running diagonally across her stomach. "You ever going to tell me the story behind this?" he asked. He leaned over and kissed the pink, slightly puckered skin. "And not the edited version you gave your folks?"

Jess put her hand on his hair and sighed. "The night I left Mike . . . he cut me. Not badly, and Josh stitched me up. But it was scary. I knew then that I could never be tied to Mike in any way ever again."

"Jess," he whispered, awed.

"Don't look at me like that. I was so blind. So foolish and . . . God, I made so many mistakes."

He studied her face, seeing the hesitation there and something more. Fear? "It can't be that bad, Saint Jess." He tried an encouraging smile.

"That name." She frowned. "I'm so far from being a saint, it isn't funny. I've done things . . ."

He waited. Let her explain on her own terms and in her own time. She'd done the same for him and he owed her the same courtesy.

All he did was reach out and take her hand again, feeling the smaller palm against his own. The last few weeks he'd almost completely forgotten about his own disability. Life had felt . . . normal. He had Jess to thank for that. Whatever she was about to confess wouldn't change that one iota.

Her voice was small as she began. "You never think it'll happen to you. You say you would never stand for that kind of treatment and you'd get out if you found yourself in that situation . . ." She looked down. "I wasn't strong enough. I wish I'd done so many things differently. And I know I can't go back and change things and I know it wasn't my fault. Still. I should have been smarter. Stronger."

Rick had been staring at their joined hands but at those words his gaze snapped to hers. Her blue eyes were shimmering with tears. God, she was hurting so much. If he hadn't hated Mike Greer before, he definitely did now.

"Oh, Jess," he said softly, and scooted up the mattress so he was beside her. He opened his arm and she snuggled into him. He couldn't offer her much. He didn't have a lot of money, he was as damaged as she was, and his employment prospects were limited. But he could offer her comfort.

"Are you disappointed in me?"

What a question. "No, of course not! You could never disappoint me."

She lifted her chin so she could look up at him. "Are you sure? Because I disappointed myself. I just didn't know what else to do."

"But look at you now," he insisted. "You overcame it. You went back to school and built this great business for yourself. You did beat him, Jess." He put his finger under her chin and lifted until she met his gaze. "Take it from me. Sometimes you can't do it by yourself. I thank God that Josh was there that night. And I'm so proud of the woman you've become."

She was crying now, broken sobs against his shoulder as he held her close and felt his eyes sting in response to her pain. He let her go on, knowing she needed this the same way he'd needed to talk about Kyle. "Shh," he soothed, rubbing her arm and kissing her hair. "It's okay to let it out."

After a few minutes her crying lessened and she pushed away, turning her tearstained face his way. "I go for ages where it doesn't bother me, but lately . . . I think being with you, and then seeing him . . . it brought back a lot of stuff I haven't had to think about in a while." She gave a self-deprecating smile. "All the time and therapy in the world doesn't erase the fact that people, if they knew, would ask how I could be so stupid."

He gave a short laugh. "I hope you don't include me in that group. I'm the last person who should ever pass judgment on anyone. Ever."

He got up and slid beneath the covers with her, cradling her close.

Her shoulders relaxed and she turned into his arms once more. They lay that way for a long time, just holding onto each other. They talked a while longer in the dark, and then got up to actually get ready for bed. Jess brushed her teeth while Rick recharged his battery for his arm. It was nothing for her to see him without it now. He had a toothbrush in her toothbrush holder on the sink. His shampoo was in her shower. His clothes were on her floor.

Hell, he'd practically moved in.

It should have bothered him more as they crawled into bed and pulled the covers up, cuddling together.

It should have. And it didn't. Because he trusted her. Because he loved her. And if things kept going the way they were . . .

He couldn't think that way. Not yet. One day at a time.

The hall in the basement of the church was teeming with people. It was Advent, and there were always more people who turned out this time of year for weekly services. Lighting the Advent candles was always a special event, followed by carols, and today the junior choir had sung a sweet rendition of "Away in a Manger." Jess had enjoyed it but missed seeing Rick at the service. He wasn't much of a churchgoer, so she'd given him some space and come to church alone.

Brian Greer sat at a table across the hall, with Pamela at his side. Jess breathed a sigh of relief. She knew Karen wasn't doing well at all, but Mike must have gone back to his life—wherever that was.

"Hey, sis!" Sarah came up to her and linked their elbows. "Matt and Susan want you to come sit with us. Suzie made the cinnamon cake and she saved you a piece to have with some coffee."

Coffee. Jess's nose twitched. Right now the thought of the dark brew made her stomach turn just a bit. "Maybe tea," she suggested, feeling odd. "I'm a bit tired, you know? Busy time of year."

"Have you been eating enough?" Sarah's brow furrowed as she led her along to their table. Sure enough, a plate with a piece of cake waited for her. Sarah was mothering, but Jess let her sister pull her along without much resistance. The last few emotional weeks had taken their toll . . . not to mention the lack of sleep now that Rick was at her place most nights since after Thanksgiving.

"Sure. It's just the holidays. Between the shop and the festival next week . . ."

"And Rick." Sarah grinned at her. "You two are really an item now, aren't you? I could tell when you brought him to Thanksgiving. Is it serious?"

Jess avoided answering by sitting down in the saved seat and smiling at her niece. "I hear you've been baking," she commented, picking up a fork. She tasted the cake and smiled. "Don't tell your mom, but I think it's better than hers."

Susan beamed. "Can I get you coffee, Aunt Jess?"

Again with the stomach flip. Jess smiled weakly. "How about a little tea instead, okay, sweetheart?"

"Coming right up." Susan popped away to grab a cup while Sarah stood chatting with Gloria Henderson.

The hall was decorated for Christmas, with lots of paper snowflakes dangling from the ceiling and a little Christmas tree propped on a table in the corner. Jess thought back to Tom and Abby's wedding in October and how so much had changed since then. Even though she'd been attracted to Rick before, if someone had told her they'd be practically living together six weeks later, she'd have laughed them out of town. With a slight shock, Jess realized that they'd first made love the day he'd brought over the ornaments, and that had been over three weeks ago. So much really had changed . . .

Over three weeks.

The cake in Jess's mouth turned to sawdust and she fought to keep chewing. Susan returned with hot tea and Jess sipped it quickly, trying to wash down the crumbs before she began to cough.

"You okay, Aunt Jess? You don't look so good. Is it the cake?"

Jess was getting rather good at pasting on fake smiles, and she treated her niece to one. "Of course I'm all right, honey. The cake is great. I just got a crumb down the wrong hole is all."

"I hate when that happens." Suzie's ponytail bobbed. "I'll get you some water."

She darted off again and Jess took a few moments to count days. She distinctly remembered telling Rick not to worry about condoms their first night together. That the time of the month was wrong . . .

Except accidents happened.

She didn't need to freak out. It'd been a stressful past few weeks, and she and Rick had been careful since then. But then there was the smell of the coffee, the way she'd been so tired lately, nearly falling asleep mid-afternoon during the most inane tasks. And her breasts were tender.

Then again, that could all be PMS, too. No need to go into an all-out panic.

Either way, the last place in the world she wanted to be was here.

She got up and touched Sarah's arm. "Hey. I think

I'm going to blast off. I need an afternoon of quiet before the week starts again."

"You're not coming to Uncle Pete and Aunt Barb's for dinner? Everyone's been invited."

"I'll call her. I'm just really tired, you know? With the festival next week, I need to finish up a few things."

"You can't take a few hours for family?"

Sarah wouldn't give up. It was straining Jess's patience. "Look," she replied in an undertone. "I have the shop to worry about, and the workshop for the kids, as well as my food donations for the hall lunch. Cut me some slack, okay?"

Sarah had the grace to look guilty, which in turn made Jess feel guilty. "Okay, okay. Relax. You want me to save you some cheesecake?"

Jess wanted to scream that no, she didn't want any damn cheesecake, but instead, she just shook her head.

"I'm good," she answered. "I promise I'll call and give my apologies. See you later, okay?"

She scooted out before Susan even made it back with her water.

The air was a Decemberish, raw cold that seeped into her bones, blowing in off the water with a relentlessness that made her ache. It took no time at all to drive to Josh's. By the time she made it to his door it was open and he was standing in the breach. She must have looked terrible because his face was immediately drawn with concern.

"What's going on?" he asked quickly. "Is it Mike?"

She hadn't given Mike a single thought. "No, I haven't seen him. I have a favor to ask."

"Is it Rick? If he hurt you . . . I swear to God. I warned him about that."

She couldn't stop a small smile from tipping up her lips. "I love you, big brother, but it's not that either. Not really, anyway." She paused. "I need you to promise that no matter what, you don't say a word to a soul about why I'm here today."

"I swear. If you're in trouble I want to help." He stepped aside and let her inside the foyer.

A laugh bubbled out of her mouth as he shut the door behind her. Trouble was the clichéd word for it all right. "You have no idea." She sighed, met Josh's concerned eyes. "I came here because I need something . . . sensitive that I don't want to go to the town pharmacy for. You know how everyone gossips there, and there's no sense bugging Dr. Yang on a Sunday when you're sharing an office anyway." Jess paused, taking a deep breath. "Do you have pregnancy tests at your office?"

His eyes widened. "You think you're pregnant?"

Hearing the words scared her to death, especially since she didn't even know how Rick felt about her. She knew she loved him and thought he probably felt the same, but they hadn't made any promises or declarations. "I might be. I'm late. We've been careful, but the first time . . ."

He raised an eyebrow. "We maybe weren't as careful as we might have been," she admitted.

"Shit, Jess." Josh blew out a breath and sat down on a nearby bar stool.

"I know," she answered meaningfully.

"What are you going to do if you are?" he asked. "Does Rick know?"

"No, he doesn't know. I just realized I'm late and there's no sense saying anything until I know for sure. So are you going to help me or what? If I walk into the drugstore and buy a pregnancy test . . . well, nothing stays a secret for long in this town." That she'd managed to keep her share of secrets was tantamount to a miracle. She really didn't want to tempt fate.

She looked up at him hopefully.

Tenderness softened his features. "You know I will always help you. Always. Give me five minutes to run to the office."

"Thanks, Josh," she answered, thankful once again for her big brother.

"There's coffee on if you want some," he suggested, grabbing a jacket from a small closet.

"No, no coffee. Definitely no coffee."

His gaze settled on her once more, and it seemed like they both knew what the test was going to say. It was just a matter of physical proof.

Jess looked around Josh's place while he was gone. It was messy but not dirty, with clean dishes piled in a drying rack, a stack of laundered clothes sitting on a chair in the living room, a week's worth of mail strewn across the counter. There were no pictures of people— and particularly none of Josh with Erin. Either he was in the middle of one serious case of denial, or he really meant it when he said he was moving on.

He came back, handed over a small box, and pointed her to the bathroom. "The sooner you know, the better," he suggested. "Waiting sucks."

So on a bitter Sunday afternoon she found herself peeing on a stick in her brother's bathroom, waiting to see if the line turned to a plus or stayed a minus.

Rick might not be ready for fatherhood. They might not make it as a couple. But she knew, deep down, that he would love his child. It would be okay. It had to be.

She emerged from the bathroom holding the stick and met Josh's gaze. "Looks like you're going to be an uncle again," she said quietly.

CHAPTER 20

Jess paced the carpet in front of her sofa. She knew she should tell Rick right away. There had been enough secrets lately and he deserved to know. And yet she couldn't make herself drive over to his house and throw his world into more upheaval. Maybe it would be okay to keep the news to herself—well, between herself and Josh—for a little while. She could get used to the idea and then decide how to tell him.

She sank down on the cushions. Their relationship was so new. They had said repeatedly that they were going to take their time. Oh, what a mess.

She put her hand on her still-flat tummy, the warmth of her palm soaking through the skin. Still. She'd always wanted a family. While the idea of having a baby scared her to death, there was a little bit of her that was pleased . . . excited, even. A little life, growing inside of her. A miracle.

Her cell rang in the stillness and she jumped before

reaching for it and pressing the button to accept the call.

"Jess, it's Abby. Are you and Rick busy this afternoon?"

"I haven't seen him today. Why?"

"I have some news about the necklace. I was going to call Rick, but I thought that since you were the one who brought it to me . . ." There was a little hesitation in her voice. "Plus Rick could use some moral support."

"Oh, God. Is it bad?"

"I'd rather talk to you both in person. But no, not really bad. Just . . . surprising."

"I'll give him a call." Jess forgot all about her news momentarily. "Unless you hear otherwise, we'll be over this afternoon."

"Okay. Thanks, Jess."

Abby clicked off, and Jess sat a moment on the sofa. Not bad but interesting. She wondered what Abby had managed to dig up. But first she had to tell Rick what she'd done. And hope that he'd be happy about it.

She toyed with the phone but figured this was better done in person.

The air was cold, the bitter kind of wind that seemed to seep through any and all clothing right to a person's bones. Jess stood on Rick's front step, waiting for him to open the door. When he did her heart gave a mighty thump and the first thought in her head was, *I'm having your baby*. But she kept the words unspoken and smiled instead. "Can I come in? We need to talk."

His face took on a wary expression. "That doesn't sound good."

She went into the kitchen and instantly smelled something delicious. Her gaze was diverted to a metal pan of still-warm brownies on the stove top.

"You made brownies?"

"I got hungry and the bakery is closed on Sundays." He must have seen her ravenous look because he grinned and reached into the cupboard. "Would you like one?"

"Maybe a small one."

He started to cut and she went over and put her hand over his. "Not that small . . ." She shifted the knife over so the brownie was nearly twice as big as he'd been going to cut. Rick laughed, a deep rumble in his chest, and Jess felt the warm flush, knowing in that moment what it was like to be in love.

They sat at the kitchen table, and Jess took a few bites. As Rick poured her a glass of cold milk, she thought of how it was good for the baby and once more the words sat on her tongue. But first things first. Nervously, she put down her fork and reached for his hand.

"Rick, I need to tell you something."

"This sound serious."

"It might be. Remember the necklace you gave me?"

He nodded. "Right. You were going to see if you could find out anything about it."

"I thought I'd seen it before. And I was right. At least I'd seen one like it. So I did a little investigating."

"And what did you discover?" His gaze sharpened and he, too, put down his fork.

She swallowed. "I saw a similar necklace in a picture at the Foster House."

Rick's brow furrowed. "The Foster House? Then how did my mother get ahold of it?"

"That's what Abby and I both wondered. So I left it with her to do some digging around. I hope that's okay. I designed Abby's wedding necklace, remember? It was a replica of the one in her picture. That's why it seemed so familiar."

She paused, wondering how much to reveal. "Rick, I'm sorry. For getting someone else involved and not telling you what I'd done."

He let out a sigh. "It's okay. I mean . . . it's not like you shared it at one of your crafty meetings or whatever. It's just Abby. To be honest, I've been so busy the last few weeks I'd kind of forgotten about it."

She nodded, relieved. "Well, Abby called me a while ago. Said she has news about it. She thought we might like to go over there together."

"Sure, why not? It'd be nice to know where it came from." He smiled at her. "Letting go isn't as scary as it once was, Jess. I have you to thank for that."

Jess smiled at him and squeezed his fingers. She was relieved he wasn't mad at her for getting Abby involved, and doubly pleased that he wanted her by his side.

But she couldn't escape the feeling that he wouldn't be so content with it all if he knew she had told Abby his secret. Or if he knew she was hanging on to another surprise that was bigger still.

She was just waiting for the right time to tell him about the baby. That was all.

Once more Rick found himself in the foyer of Abby and Tom's house. He'd tried to resist tapping his fingers nervously on the steering wheel on the way over, but a few times he'd forgotten and he'd caught Jess looking at him strangely.

"I made coffee," Abby was saying, and she led the way down the hall to the kitchen. Jess took his hand and soon he found himself in the warmly lit kitchen, the rich scent of coffee and cookies in the air.

Tom was waiting, perched on a stool beside the butcher block. "Hey," he said, looking up. "I think winter's almost here by the feel of that north wind today. It could almost bring snow with it."

The weather? Rick supposed they needed to break the ice somehow. "It's bitter," he acknowledged, rubbing his hands together.

"Go ahead and fix your coffee the way you like," Abby instructed. She busied herself putting cookies on a plate and then put the plate in the middle of the butcher block. It seemed that counter space was going to be the center of operations, at least for now.

Rick sipped his coffee and munched on a shortbread cookie until he couldn't take the false joviality anymore. There was a thread of tension underlying everything and he needed to get things out in the open.

"So, Jess tells me you found something out about the necklace," he said, kicking off the conversation.

Abby nodded. "Yes, I did. Jess brought the necklace here, and we put it next to the picture of my great-grandmother. See for yourself."

She retrieved the photo from a nearby counter and placed it before him, spreading out the necklace beside it. There was no question—they looked the same. Jess peered around his shoulder at the rubies spread on the wood. "It really is an extraordinary piece," she murmured.

"Just because they look the same doesn't mean they are the same."

"Oh, I agree," Abby said. "So Tom and I took a drive into Portland and had someone qualified have a look at it. It's very old, Rick. And genuine. Dating takes it back over one hundred and fifty years."

Rick sat heavily on a nearby stool. "One hundred and fifty? I knew it was old, but not that old." He was staggered by the news. It made no sense that his mom would have something that old in her possession.

Abby met his gaze. "I know. I took along some of my own things I inherited with the house—notably an emerald choker and a diamond bracelet. Both were appraised and dated, and both are from around the same time period."

He frowned. "Are you saying they belonged to the same person?"

Tom shrugged. "We can't say that for sure. What we do know is that the dating puts all three pieces right around the time that George Foster settled here in Jewell Cove, along with my ancestor, Charles Arseneault, and Edward Jewell."

"There's more," Abby said quietly. This time she took out a yellow envelope and removed photocopies of pictures, laying them out precisely.

Rick didn't recognize any of the people beyond Edith Foster, but the woman in each picture was wearing the same necklace.

"Where did you get all of these?" He stared at the pages, some of the pictures very faded and a bit grainy.

"In the attic. I ran across some old albums when I first cleaned it out and I went looking a little closer." She pointed at the first picture. "This is Edith, of course. Then we have this one—Amelia Foster, Elijah's mother and wife to Robert. Then we have Martha, wife to Jed, who built this house. And finally, this one, dated 1864. George's wife, Elizabeth. Right at the end of the Civil War. And that's the last picture I have of the necklace. Not that we'd find pictures much earlier than that, anyway."

Rick's head was spinning.

"So how on earth did it happen to get into my mother's possession?"

He stared at Abby, who turned her attention to Tom and the two of them shared a significant look.

"This is where it gets a little bit complicated," Tom said quietly.

"What do you mean, complicated?" Rick asked, his voice low. He was dimly aware of Jess's hand resting reassuringly on his forearm. She'd been very quiet during the exchange and he turned to her now. "Are you believing all of this?"

He could see in her eyes that she did. "I don't think Tom and Abby would be telling you any of this if they weren't sure."

Which he knew. And which made his heart feel like it was sinking straight to his toes. Good God, had his mother *stolen* it? It seemed the only thing that made sense. But he couldn't believe that. She would never have done such a thing.

"I hired someone," Tom was saying. "To look into what might have happened."

"Hired someone," Rick found himself parroting. "Like a private investigator?"

Abby nodded. "Yes, a private investigator."

Everything inside Rick went cold.

Abby and Tom shared a meaningful look. Rick's temper bubbled. "Will you quit looking at each other that way? What aren't you telling me?"

Jess's voice interrupted. "Rick, calm down. I know it's a lot to process . . ."

"You don't know anything about me," he bit out. They'd hired an investigator? Like his mother had been some sort of criminal? Did they really think she was capable of stealing?

He ignored the hurt look on Abby's face. "Well?" he asked Tom.

Tom took out an oversized envelope. In it was a picture, and when Rick took it in his shaking fingers, his heart constricted.

It was the picture from the photo album. The one with Roberta and Graham and Rick and Marian behind them. But instead of reading "Meeting our son" on the back it read "The last clients of Foster House."

"We found that in a box of things Marian left to Abby," Tom said quietly. "Your birth date is June fourth, right?"

Rick's temper roared to life. "Wait a minute," he said, standing up. "You knew I was adopted?"

Even Jess looked surprised, but he wasn't sure why. He turned on her. "How much did you tell them, huh? I thought this was just about the necklace?"

His accusation hit her hard and she paled. "The adoption was the only thing I could think of that connected

Roberta and Marian." She stammered. "But they already knew anyway, because Marian left the picture."

He stared at her incredulously. "And you never thought to tell me any of this?"

"You said you didn't want to know about your birth family," she replied, but her voice shook.

"Oh, that's a convenient answer, and not worthy of you, Jess. How long have you been telling yourself that lie?" God, how it hurt. After all the secrets they'd shared, that she'd keep this from him.

He turned on Abby and Tom. "And you two. Yeah, I knew I was adopted. But guess what? I never hired an investigator. I never put my name on any damn list or tried to find anything out because Roberta Sullivan is my mother." He was starting to lose control and he gulped in a breath in a futile effort to calm down. "Jesus. It's bad enough that you knew and didn't say anything. But for you . . ." He looked at Jess. Her eyes were wide and her lips were trembling. Hurt mingled with the anger he was feeling at the moment. "For all of you to go behind my back? It wasn't your place. It wasn't your call."

He hated the helpless feeling rushing through him right now. Over the last several months, he'd screwed up a lot. He knew that. But he'd made his own decisions. He'd started to call the shots in his life after so many things had been taken out of his control. Kyle. Losing his hand. His mother. Only to have the people he counted on most strip that away from him again.

He'd honestly thought his world couldn't crumble any more when one final thought struck him right between the eyes.

"When did you get that envelope?"

Abby's gaze flickered away and Tom looked confused. "Excuse me?"

"When did you get it?" He'd raised his voice but seemed unable to lower it.

"In July," Abby whispered.

July.

"Rick . . ." Abby started to speak but Tom reached over and took her hand.

"We thought about talking to you about it, but then with Roberta being so sick, it didn't seem like the right time."

"The right time?" Rick exploded. "The right time for whom?"

"We wanted to protect you," Abby pleaded, her eyes reaching out to him. "You were struggling so much . . ."

He felt like his skin was shrinking and he might burst through it. "Oh, so you kept it from me for my own good? Poor unstable Rick. He can't handle the truth. Well, news flash, all of you. I knew the truth. And I didn't give a shit."

"Hang on," Tom said, standing up, his own anger flaring. "Last summer your mother was dying and you were getting arrested for public drunkenness every time you turned around. What kind of friend would have dropped that photo into the mix and left you to sort it out?"

"Right, because everyone else always knows what's best for me," he answered angrily. "I never thought you were the self-righteous type, Tom. Or you either, Abby."

Jess pulled on his arm and he turned to her. Her face was white and he felt a spear of guilt shoot through him and then got angry at that, too, because she made him feel weak. "And you. I tried to tell you last fall that I needed to do things on my own time. But oh no, Jess knows best, right?"

"Rick, that's unfair," Jess interjected. "You've been through so much. I didn't think it was right to ask you to handle anything more . . ."

Rick cut her off. He was so hurt, so angry, so confused, that he couldn't sort through any of his emotions. It was all too much. "I get it," he snapped. "Poor Rick is too broken, too fragile, to handle anything difficult. You want to know what's unfair? Try all of you trying to play God with my life like I'm nothing more than a puppet." He wrenched his arm away from Jess's hand. Everything in the kitchen held for a single, charged moment.

And then he knew he had to get out of there.

Rick grabbed his jacket from the coat tree on the way out the door. He was halfway to his destination before he realized he'd left Jess behind without a ride home.

CHAPTER 21

Jess waited until nine o'clock, but when she called again and Rick didn't answer, she frowned. He'd been so angry when he'd stormed out of Tom and Abby's. And she couldn't say she blamed him, but it didn't stop the fact that his words had hurt and she was worried about him.

He should have answered his cell or at least seen her calls. Which meant he was avoiding her. Avoiding everyone. It had been hours, and she was hoping he'd cooled off. Most of all she knew he shouldn't be alone right now. The last thing she wanted was for him to backslide into old habits.

She grabbed her bag and scooted out, jumping in her car. Another vehicle was parked down the street that she didn't recognize, and out of long habit she locked the door before even putting the key in the ignition. She wasn't paranoid. She was just cautious. Always.

The drive to Rick's place was short, and to her relief

his truck was in his yard. Over the past several weeks he'd been there for her in so many ways that now she wanted to return the favor. She knew he felt betrayed. Perhaps he was right. The people he cared for most had kept things from him and now he had to deal with them all at once. She didn't even blame him for leaving her out at Blackberry Hill, even though a very sober Abby had driven her back to town, completely apologetic for how things had turned out.

Jess took a fortifying breath as she went up the walk. Maybe he needed to talk, or maybe he just needed someone to sit with him while he sorted through his feelings.

The first knock at the door went unanswered, and she tried the knob, thinking maybe he really was in the porch painting. It was locked, so she knocked again, peeking in the window. After a few moments, Rick came into view and her stomach gave a slow, strange twist. A warning. She didn't have time to heed it before he opened the door, glaring at her.

"Um . . . I thought I should check in with you. See if you were okay. This afternoon was kind of intense."

"Jess." Rick sounded tired. "Not right now, okay? I can't sit through a pep talk about how everything will be fine. Because I keep thinking it will be fine, but then something else comes and knocks me on my ass. I made my peace with Roberta before she died, but you and Tom and Abby had to stir things up again. So for right now, just leave me alone."

A flash of anger rose to the surface and Jess looked back up again. "No. I won't leave you alone. I care about you, Rick. And I did what I thought I had to do. I won't let you push me away over this."

His face changed. The mask of hurt disappeared and was replaced by an arrogant, screw-you expression. "This isn't about *you,* Jess! This is about me and my life. This is about me dealing with *my* shit and wanting people to respect me enough to let me do that. I thought you were that kind of person, you know? But you're as bad as everyone else. You think you know best, but you don't. You still think I'm a wild card, don't you? What, did you come over here to make sure I haven't drowned myself in a bottle?" He shook his head with disgust.

His words hurt, deeply. She gasped in a breath but before she could say anything, he kept going. "Look, what we had was a sexual relationship, nothing more. I don't need your kind of help at the moment. In fact, I don't need your constant harping at all. Most of all, I'm not your little project to fix!"

"What we had?" Pain tore through her at the harsh words. Maybe she'd been wrong, but she'd been wrong for the right reasons! She was angry, too, and she lashed out in the only way she knew how. "Well, I guess if you don't broadcast a relationship no one's the wiser when it ends, huh? Smart strategy, Rick. Nice to see you planned ahead."

She turned to walk away. She couldn't do this, couldn't argue with him right now. She took the first step away from him, then another, trying to hold back hot tears.

She heard him let out a big breath. "Jess . . . I'm sorry. Shit. Don't go." His voice was instantly apologetic.

Her steps slowed and she closed her eyes, wanting to give him what he was asking so badly and knowing she couldn't. Her throat thick with emotion, she kept moving toward her car.

The car door appeared in front of her though Jess could barely see it through her tears. Fumbling with her keys she got the door open and slid in behind the wheel. At least she couldn't hear Rick anymore but he was still standing in the doorway.

She wouldn't back down. She'd be stronger this time. She'd be smarter. For herself and for her baby.

He was still standing there as she pulled away from the curb and headed not toward Lilac Lane but to Josh's house. She didn't want to be alone tonight, and Josh was the only one who knew. Who would understand.

And tomorrow she would start picking up the pieces. Again.

It was a Monday in December and Jess couldn't *not* open the store, so she left Josh's at seven thirty in the morning. They'd stayed up late talking, and she'd never been gladder to have her big brother. They'd talked about Rick, and Erin, and Mike, and Jess's pregnancy. When Josh asked about Rick, she'd simply said that it wasn't her place to tell, but he was justifiably upset. She left out the part where he'd referred to them in the past tense. That just hurt too much.

She was in a better state of mind when she headed home for a shower and clean clothes, though the hollow ache still persisted inside when she thought about how she and Rick had almost made it. Still, she'd be okay. She'd come through worse . . .

It wasn't until she was inside that she realized the

back door hadn't been locked. She was sure it had been when she left last night. Uneasy now, she crossed the workroom to the stairs to the loft and went up into her living space.

The door to the loft was ajar. She slowly pushed it open and then cried out at the state of the apartment.

Rick's paints and supplies, which had taken up residence in front of the wide windows overlooking the bay, were now smashed and scattered all over the floor. Her little tables with candles and other knickknacks were overturned, and her furniture was in utter ruin. Red and green paint had been smeared all over the white upholstery and dumped over the throw rug on the floor. She stepped farther in and covered her mouth with her hand. Her dishes, the ones that had belonged to her grandmother, were in shards on her kitchen floor. Books had been thrown out of her bookcase. All in all, her apartment was a disaster and Jess felt completely, horribly, violated.

But worst of all was the rough swipe of paint on her lovely white wall. *Whore,* it said, and she knew without a doubt that even if she'd agreed to the restraining order, it wouldn't have kept Mike away. He'd done this. He'd be the only one to call her such a repulsive name, to be this angry. He hadn't liked seeing her with Rick. And now he'd been where she lived, touching her things . . .

Anger such as she'd never experienced before burned through her body. Did he really think he could frighten and intimidate her this way?

Her hands trembled but her mind was resolute as she picked up the phone and called the police station. She reported the incident to the duty officer and then went to her workroom and paced until she heard the squad car pull up out front. He wouldn't win. Not this time.

She opened the door to Bryce and another officer who'd come to assist. She told them what she'd touched, and stepped out, not wanting to see the carnage any longer. Instead she made a sign and posted it on the front door stating the shop was closed for the morning. A quick check showed her that the office and shop hadn't been touched. It was only her living quarters. Whoever had done it—and she was sure it was Mike—had deliberately struck her where she lived.

Bryce had already come to the same conclusion. "You want me to look into Mike's whereabouts?" he asked quietly, pulling up a stool beside her in the workroom.

She nodded. "I should have listened to you at Thanksgiving. Should have realized how dangerous he was." Her insides were still quaking. She couldn't stop thinking about what might have happened if she'd been here alone.

"Where were you last night?" Bryce's cheeks colored a little as he asked, and hers did, too. He expected her to answer that she'd stayed at Rick's. It was written all over his face.

"I was at Josh's," she replied, trying to school her features. "I stopped by Rick's first."

"I see."

She doubted it.

"Did you call Rick this morning? I would have thought he'd have shown up by now, worried sick."

She looked away. "I just called you. That's it."

Bryce stayed silent, and she appreciated him not

throwing in his opinion. She was mixed up enough. And also feeling a little bit this morning like Rick was right. She hadn't trusted him. Neither had Abby or Tom. When the truth was that since Roberta's funeral he'd done absolutely nothing to show that he couldn't be trusted or responsible. He'd done everything right . . .

"He loves you, you know." Bryce finally spoke. "I don't know what's happened, but I know that for sure. You should call him. He'd want to be here for you."

"I doubt that." Not after yesterday.

But Bryce nodded his head. "I've seen Rick at his worst. I've seen him crying like a baby sitting on the docks, I've seen him be a loudmouth at the bar when they stop serving, I've seen him be a wicked asshole. But I've also seen him try hard to do the right thing. I've seen the way he looks at you. He loves you. Not a doubt in my mind."

The sound of boots pounding on the outside stairs made Jess look up. Rick stood in the back door, freshly showered though he hadn't bothered to shave. Droplets of water were still on his hair even though it was bitterly cold outside. It wasn't his appearance that hit her straight in the gut. It was the wild way he was looking at her. Like an avenging angel late to the party.

"You okay?" he asked gruffly.

She nodded. "I'm fine. I wasn't home." She cleared her throat. "How did you, ah . . ."

"Two police cars outside your place? Doesn't take long for word to spread. Your whole family will probably be here in a second."

"Oh."

"Can I have a look?"

Bryce looked at Jess, then back at Rick and nodded. "Yeah. Don't touch anything."

Rick headed for the loft stairs when Jess had a sudden thought. "Rick," she called out, standing up. He turned back and she knew she'd been wrong not to call him. "Um . . . the paint and stuff . . . it came from your supplies. Your, uh, projects you were working on. I'm sorry."

He didn't reply, just went to the door of the loft and then came back, his face drawn. "You looking into Greer?" he asked Bryce point-blank.

"Yeah. And you're going to stay out of it."

"Like hell."

"You are," Bryce emphasized. "You're going to let the police handle it. You can't go off half-cocked and get yourself into trouble, you hear? If Mike had anything to do with this, we'll find out and he'll be charged. Got it?"

"Dammit, Bryce!"

"You have to trust me to do my job. Promise me you won't go off half-cocked."

"Fine." Rick nodded, and Jess knew he got it but didn't like it. His whole posture screamed restrained fury. She knew it must be costing him a lot to hold his temper.

Bryce gave her a quick hug. "I'll go finish up in there and get out of your hair. I'll keep you posted. In the meantime, you might not want to stay alone, okay?"

Jess nodded, hating that the oh-so-familiar fear was once again a part of her life. Would it ever go away?

"Jess, about last night . . ." Rick stepped forward but she held up a hand.

"I can't. I'm not in a good head space to discuss it, okay?"

He nodded. "Okay."

She couldn't avoid him forever. At some point, and some point soon, she would have to tell him she was having his baby. But later, when she'd sorted through the mess that was their relationship and her feelings. When she could be clear-headed and logical.

"I should call Tessa and tell her not to come in."

"Why don't you call Abby or Sarah? You could use the company."

"I'll need to clean up, too, once I get the okay." Sadness began to seep in. "I'm not sure I'll ever feel the same here. This was my place, you know? My safe haven. If it was Mike . . ." She sighed. "Damn that man for coming back to town and stirring all this up."

"Jess . . ." Rick started to speak and then thought better of it and stepped back. "I'll come by later to check in on you, is that okay?"

And just as surely as her heart had broken last night, it broke again from his kindness and consideration even as he kept his distance. He was going through his own stuff but none of that was mentioned. His caring was only for her, and it only made it more difficult to do what she knew she needed to do.

"You don't need to check on me. Josh is around, and so are Mom and Sarah. I'll be fine, Rick. I'm just sorry about your stuff."

"I can replace it. Forget it."

He went to the back door, looked back and hesitated, but said nothing as he turned around and went out.

And now Jess was left alone in her workroom with police going through her private things.

Twenty-four hours ago she'd been sitting in church, content with her life. Now it had all blown up in her face.

She got up and went to the storeroom to grab a mop and bucket. Might as well get started on cleaning up the mess and starting over.

It took a few days for Rick to get his head in a decent enough place to make the drive to Augusta. Streetlamps were decorated with wreaths and storefronts advertised sales among bright holiday displays. He should have taken this step long ago, but better late than never. He just hoped it wasn't *too* late.

It had been difficult, but he'd stayed out of the way of Bryce's investigation. Mike was arrested, and Rick almost felt sorry for him. Karen Greer had died in her sleep the night before the break-in, and her death had pushed Mike over the edge. Bryce had found him passed out at the Greer cottage, paint from Rick's supplies all over his clothes and a good-sized dent in his car where he'd hit a stump in the driveway, spilling the better part of a bottle of rye over the interior.

Rick's compassion didn't extend too far, though. The man had terrorized Jess a long time, and he'd violated her space. Rick just thanked God Jess hadn't been home at the time. Who knew what might have happened if she hadn't been at Josh's? He couldn't help feeling guilty for that. If he hadn't messed up so badly, they would have been together. He would have protected her.

Watching her walk away, seeing her be that strong,

had been his breaking point. That had been the moment that he truly knew what it was to have lost everything.

He'd let her down. He had a history of letting down the people he cared about—Roberta, Kyle, even himself. And now Jess. If he hadn't been so angry, they might have talked their way through it. He would have been there for her. But he'd been so afraid. Afraid that she would ask more of him than he could give. That he'd fail her.

So he'd taken the first available opportunity to bug out, knowing that eventually she'd wise up and leave him behind. Her parting accusation had hurt so much because she'd hit the nail right on the head.

And then the phone had rang saying there were police cars at her home and he'd realized that he'd let her down anyway. Nothing he'd ever felt compared to the fear that something had happened to Jess. He'd hidden it well when he'd arrived, but he'd been frozen inside, running on autopilot. He didn't want to lose her. And if he was going to stand a hope in hell of being with her, it was time he got his shit together.

He'd made an appointment with a therapist. He stood outside the brick office building in Augusta and tilted his face up to the sun, letting the rays wash over him despite the bitter cold that seeped through his jacket. He'd thought he'd hit rock bottom before, but nothing was worse than losing her. That she'd stayed strong, that she hadn't fallen into his arms caused him to feel both consternation and admiration.

Her walking away had taught him one big lesson: he needed to learn how to deserve her.

Dr. Johnson wasn't what he'd expected at all. There was no touchy-feely woo-woo stuff in his office. They just talked for a while and Rick answered questions. Progress. One step at a time.

After the appointment, he stopped on the way back to Jewell Cove for supplies. Once at home, he busied himself by emptying his shopping bags of paint, brushes, and glass. Jess had gotten him some custom orders as a result of the Black Friday sale and he had lots to occupy his days. He'd work on those later, though. First he went to work on a door insert, painstakingly creating puffs of lilacs in dark purple, mauve, and white surrounded by rich green leaves. He was so engrossed that he forgot the time and only looked up when there was a knock on his door.

Jess, he thought, hope springing up in his chest. He stuck the brush in a can of water and hurried to leave the porch, careful to shut the door behind him. But it wasn't Jess on his front step at all. It was Mary Arseneault, big as a house in the last few weeks of her pregnancy, glowing and smiling as he opened the door and invited her in.

"Mary. What a surprise. Come on in."

"I brought you dinner." She held out a square pan covered in tin foil. "Lasagna. I made extra."

Rick didn't know what to say. He'd acted like an ass, and his friends rallied around even though he pushed them away. "Gosh, you didn't have to do that. But thanks. It smells awesome."

She laughed. "I must be getting close to my day, because I'm nesting like crazy. I made one for dinner and froze two more in addition to this one. We won't talk about the bread I baked either, okay? Or the fact that I vacuumed the entire house from top to bottom again when I just did it yesterday."

He was at a distinct disadvantage. He had no idea that women "nested," whatever that was, before giving birth. But Mary seemed happy so it didn't matter.

"Did Bryce send you over to check on me?" he asked.

"Not at all. I know you were spending a lot of time at Jess's, and that things have hit a rocky patch. Thought you could use a good meal, that's all."

He raised an eyebrow. Mary was looking a little too innocent. She was a great woman and generous to a fault, but she had a twinkle in her eye that she couldn't conceal.

"Okay, out with it. Why are you really here?"

He took the lasagna from her hands and put it on the kitchen counter as she moved farther inside and took off her coat. She hung it over a kitchen chair and then sat down, putting her hand on the table before lowering herself onto the seat. He sat down, too, and faced her.

"All right. I came here hoping to soften you up so that you'd say yes when I offered you a job."

He hadn't seen that coming. Not in the least. "A job?" What sort of work would Mary have for him?

"Rick, my baby's coming anytime in the next few weeks. The nursery is still pink, and we're having a boy. I want a mural and Bryce insists he can't paint it. . . . I want to hire you to do it. The stuff you've done for Tom and Abby is gorgeous, and everyone knows you're the one who's been painting the holiday glass for Treasures."

He looked up, shocked. "They do?"

She shrugged. "Hard to keep a secret in this town. And what people don't hear they guess at. I think you could be starting something great, you know?"

He was still absorbing the fact that his painting had become common knowledge when she reached into her handbag and pulled out a sheaf of papers. "I saw these ideas online. What do you think? Can you do it?"

He had a look. They were gorgeous. One had farm animals and a bright red barn, all in vibrant colors. Another had a tree with multicolored leaves surrounded by zoo animals, including a monkey sitting on a branch, eating a banana. There were puffy clouds on a blue background that met the ocean and had sailboats bobbing cheerfully on the surface. But Rick's favorite of them all was a tree that was painted in a corner, branches extending to each wall, and different leaves held different words like *love, family, fun, Mom, Dad* . . .

Right now the leaves on Rick's tree would be bare, but this little baby about to be born would know family and love and devotion. He was just about the luckiest baby in the world.

"I like this one," he answered, handing it back to Mary. "I know it's simple, but it's . . . personal."

"It's my favorite, too. Will you do it, Rick? I know it's a rush job . . ."

"And I've got some Christmas things on the go right now."

"Even if he's born before it's done, he'll be sleeping in a bassinette in our room for a few weeks anyway." She smiled at him. "Your work is so pretty. I know it's not glass like you're used to working on, but I'm sure you can do it."

How could he refuse? Bryce and Mary had always been so good to him, even when he made it difficult. Which was pretty damned often. And it was a job. Maybe for a friend, but it was a start. If he'd learned anything these last months, it was that a man had to start somewhere. It was time to stop spinning his wheels and get moving.

"Give me to the end of the week to finish up some stuff here, and we'll go sort out colors and what I need." He smiled at her and she smiled back. Her lips twisted a bit and she shifted in her chair and then beamed up at him again.

"I swear to God he's doing somersaults in there."

Rick looked over and his jaw dropped as Mary's tummy actually changed shape beneath her maternity top. "Wow. Does that hurt?"

She laughed. "Of course not, unless he sticks a toe in my ribs or kicks my bladder. Here."

Before Rick had time to resist, she'd grabbed his right hand and put his palm on her belly. Only a few seconds elapsed before the baby moved again, the sensation rippling beneath his touch.

"That's so cool." He stared at the shape of her stomach, amazed. Here he was, over thirty years old and the closest he'd ever been to babies was this moment, with his friend's wife. He felt a little awed and excited by it all. "How does it feel on the inside?"

She laughed. "Weird. When he was smaller, it was just flutters. But now? It's like everything inside is shifting even though it doesn't hurt. And in a way it's how we communicate. When he's moving and dancing around, I know he's happy and healthy. Sometimes I think he responds to my voice."

Rick swallowed thickly. There was such love in Mary's voice. "You're a good mom, Mary," he said quietly.

"Thanks." She leaned forward and kissed his cheek. "And you're a good man. Don't you forget it, okay? You're gonna get through this. A lot of people believe in you."

"Not Jess," he scoffed, wanting to believe her and unable to.

"Jess more than anyone," Mary argued, patting his hand. "Jess is just protecting herself, which we all understand. But if she didn't believe in you, she never would have let you this close. Are you just going to let her get away without a fight?"

He frowned. "It's not that simple."

Mary smiled softly at him. "It kind of is," she argued. "Hang tough and it'll come right. Now, go heat up that lasagna and have something to eat."

"Yes, Mom."

He wasn't prepared for the quick hug and the feel of her baby bump against his abdomen. She really was ready to pop.

After she was gone Rick ate and then went back to his painting, paying even closer attention to each flower and petal of the lilac blossoms. Everyone thought he was giving up when he wasn't. He was just waiting for the right moment to make his case.

To prove to Jess that he could be the man she needed. Because more than anything he wanted to be that man.

CHAPTER 22

He'd seen Dr. Johnson again and was halfway back to Jewell Cove when his cell phone rang. Abby's number popped up, so he pulled over to the shoulder and answered. "Abby," he said quickly. "Is anything wrong?"

Abby's voice sounded confused even through the staticky connection. "Wrong? Why would anything be wrong?"

He sighed. "Just worried about Jess is all. She's not exactly talking to me at the moment."

"Don't give up on her yet. She loves you, Rick."

The words sent something soaring through him. Jess had never said the words and neither had he. But Abby said it so easily that he figured it must be true. His elation faded though when he remembered how badly he'd let Jess down. What an ass he'd been. No matter how upset, he should have found a better way to deal with it than lashing out and pushing her away.

He loved Jess, too, but if he was going to finally say

the words it would be to her face and not to a friend. "So, did you need anything in particular, Abby?"

There was a slight hesitation. "Actually, I just wanted to make sure that, well, that we were okay. That you and Tom . . . well, you know. We're really sorry, Rick. I don't blame you for feeling betrayed."

He'd had time to think about all that had happened, and he knew deep down that Abby and Tom had meant well and tried to do what they thought was right. None of this was their fault. It wasn't really anyone's fault. It just was what it was.

"I'm getting over it," he responded. "It's not your fault. I know that. You were just trying to help."

"Thank you," she said, and she sounded very relieved. "And Rick? Please don't give up on Jess. She needs someone who will fight for her. To show her she's worth it."

"Thanks, Abby." His voice came out rough with emotion. He'd been such a jerk since he'd come home. He was sure he didn't deserve such good friends. It was time he stopped letting them all down. "It's just so overwhelming. All I wanted was to know where the necklace came from," he said, his voice breaking a little. "And I don't really know much more than when I started."

"I might be able to help with that." Abby's voice was cautious through the phone. "You left before we really finished, uh, talking. But it'll keep until you're ready. No pressure, okay?"

His chest constricted. Abby was being so careful, tiptoeing around him, and he felt terrible about going off on her before. "I'll call you, okay? I need to take care of a few things first." Right now Jess was his number one priority.

"Have you seen Jess at all since the break-in?" Abby asked, as if reading his thoughts.

"Not yet. But I will. I'm working on a few things before I make my case."

"As long as you make it."

Rick pinched the bridge of his nose. "She may not forgive me, and I don't blame her. It wasn't just what I did but what I said. How I treated her. She kicked me to the curb. She might not take me back, either."

"A mistake doesn't have to mean forever and you love each other—even if both of you are too stubborn to admit it. You're a good man, Rick, who's had to deal with a lot. Let Jess help you with that—the same way that you've helped her be strong again."

The backs of Rick's eyes stung a little. "I wish I could be as confident as you."

"You will be," she assured him, "when the time is right."

The conversation ended and he pulled back onto the road again. He started the downhill slope into Jewell Cove and his throat tightened up. This was his home. His memories were here. The people he cared about were here. He knew he was where he belonged. And he belonged with Jess, if she'd take him back.

It was five minutes to five on a Wednesday night. Jess had precisely two hours to close up, count her cash, grab some dinner, and prepare for tonight's class, which was wire and bead wreath ornaments. Easy concept, sometimes finicky on the execution. And she was not in the mood for it. She was tired and she was cranky.

Tessa closed out the cash register since the last customer had left. Jess made herself take a deep, cleansing breath and let it out slowly. She'd been irritable ever since the blowup with Rick. At first she told herself it was because of the break-in but the mess had been cleaned up, the insurance claim filed, and all she had to do was wait for the money to come through and she could order new furniture. She told herself that it was hormones, but that was just an excuse. No, it was Rick. She missed him. She loved him. And each morning, when her stomach didn't feel quite right, she was reminded that they still needed to talk.

The door opened, the tiny bell dinging merrily. "Sorry, we're closed," she said, turning around, but stopped short at the sight of Rick standing in the doorway, a flat cardboard box under his arm.

Her heart thudded against her ribs. She was glad to see him again. Her eyes drank in the sight of him, lean and rugged, dangerous dark eyes and black hair that she missed running her hands through. Every molecule in her body was happy to see him.

"See you Saturday, Jess." Tessa grabbed her backpack from under the counter. "Hi, Rick," she said shyly as she passed by him and out the door.

Rick turned around and locked the dead bolt. "Now you're closed," he said, smiling a little.

"I . . . I didn't expect to see you today," she managed, running her hand down her long sweater even though it didn't need smoothing. She wished now she'd dressed up a little or something, rather than wearing comfortable leggings and boots and the old sweater. She'd worn it because some of her waistbands were becoming a little snug as her figure began to change. The knowledge sent a little heat to her cheeks.

"The festival is this weekend. I did promise you I'd bring you more items."

"And you keep your promises?"

His gaze locked with hers. "I try, Jess. I really try. I'm not perfect, but I'm trying." He took a step forward and her pulse quickened. "You make me want to try."

Her breath caught in her chest. "I'm not much into taking emotional risks."

"I know. And I know I let you down." His throat bobbed as he swallowed. "God, I let you down, Jess. In so many ways. I was so afraid, and I let that keep me from you when you needed me most. I'm sorry, Jess. You have no idea how sorry."

She wanted to go to him. He was standing by the counter now and she was eight, maybe ten feet away. But she couldn't. Not yet. She had to get her thoughts together. Be ready for the logical and responsible conversation they needed to have. She folded her arms in front of her. "I'm sorry, too. For not trusting you. For not believing in you even though time and time again you proved yourself. Rick, both of us have baggage. I'd rather we be friends than end up hurting each other any more than we already have."

There was understanding in his gaze, understanding and tenderness and she wasn't sure how strong she could be. "Don't look at me that way," she said bluntly.

"I can't help it. I love you, Jess."

God, he didn't just say that. Tears sprang to her eyes and she blinked quickly, trying to clear them away. "Don't," she whispered, her voice wobbling. "You'll only make it worse."

He put the package down on the counter and took a step toward her. "It can't get any worse," he said, his voice quiet but firm. "I'm lost without you. Nothing is right anymore. There's so much going on inside me and all I want is to hold you in my arms at night and whisper my secrets in the dark. And you're not there and I'm dying a little inside. I need you, Jess. I love you."

Oh, how she wanted to believe him. He took another step closer and it would be so easy to launch herself into his arms, feel them tighten around her.

Another step forward and she could see the pain in his eyes.

"I was so wrong, Jess. I shut you out instead of letting you in. I should never have sent you away. I might have protected you that night, if not for my own stupid pride. Instead I was selfish, so selfish. I need to change that. I started seeing someone, Jess. A doctor in Augusta who's going to help me deal with everything. So I can be a better man." He was only a few feet away now. "A better man like you deserve."

He was saying all the right things and she was touched. More than that, he'd ignited a hope in her that had been extinguished for a long time. But there was too much to talk about, too much he didn't know for this to be a fresh start. Besides, she wasn't entirely blameless here either.

"You're not the only one who has issues to work through," she murmured, tucking her hands into the soft pockets of her sweater. "And there are things I need to tell you . . ."

"There are things I need to tell you, too. But first I need to know you're okay. That there hasn't been any more trouble with Mike."

"He'll go to court early next year," she confirmed. "And I have a restraining order now. He's an afraid little man, Rick. I don't think he expected I'd fight back this time."

"If you need me to testify about Thanksgiving, say the word."

"I will." She looked up at him and felt herself soften. He looked so sincere, so open. More open than she'd ever seen him before.

"Can we go somewhere more comfortable to talk?" he asked.

Her loft would be a bit too intimate yet and the only furniture was the bed, which thankfully had remained mostly untouched—only the bedding had been sliced. "I haven't bought furniture yet," she replied. "We could sit in the workshop."

"Wait here a minute," he said, and he went behind the counter and retrieved the two folding chairs there, gripping one in his right hand and looping his left arm through the hole between the seat and back of the second chair. He put them down and opened them up before the wide windows. An inch or two of snow had fallen and the town looked mystical as darkness began to creep over the harbor and Christmas lights began to come on.

She sat down and he sat across from her, close enough their knees nearly touched. He reached out and took her hands in his. She no longer minded the feel of his prosthetic. It was part of who he was, and that person was usually pretty great.

"You're really doing better? Getting counseling?"

"Yes," he answered honestly. "Jess, the reason I was so upset that night was because I felt so betrayed, like no one trusted me with my own life. Add into that my grief about my mom, my feelings of guilt about Kyle . . . it suddenly was too much for me to handle. It was like the people closest to me had gone behind my back because they were too afraid I couldn't deal with the truth. The truth is, it's going to take some time before I really sort out how it all fits together." He looked into her eyes, utterly honest. "But I'm going to do it. I need you to trust that I'll do it."

Jess left her fingers in his. This was the Rick she'd fallen for. Honest and open with her, showing his heart. Maybe there was hope for them after all.

"I also have a new job for a few weeks." He smiled at her. "I'm painting a mural for Bryce and Mary. She cornered me a few days ago and practically demanded. Stupid thing is I'm kind of excited about it. Painting a kid's room, for God's sake. After that, I'm thinking of spending the winter in my studio. Yeah, I was afraid at first of what people would say. And I was—and am— more afraid that if I make this my job, it won't be fun anymore. Fun probably isn't the right word. When I can't sleep at night or when the stress gets to me, it calms me. It's my therapy. If I make it my livelihood, will that part go away?"

She got that. She'd felt the same way before she'd opened Treasures. And yeah, there were times she missed the days when she could do things because she wanted to and not because bills had to be paid or commitments had been made or she was low on stock.

"It will be what you need it to be, I think," she answered, amazed by the calm strength she sensed in him now.

"I hope so," he replied, and he smiled at her, making her heart melt a little. "Anyway, Mary barged into my house with all these ideas and I found myself getting excited about it."

"That's great, Rick. Really great."

And it was wonderful to see him so happy, so animated, without the lines of stress that had marked his face in previous weeks. Still, it was his next words that really set her pulse galloping, simply because it hit so very close to what she needed to tell him.

"Guess what else?" he asked her. "She let me touch her belly when the baby was moving. It was pretty incredible. It's like a wave rolling underneath your hand. Coolest thing ever."

She bit down on her lip. Just because things were coming together for him didn't mean this could work . . . but it was a good sign, wasn't it? Dare she hope? "You like babies?"

"I never gave them much thought before. I mean, I was in the sandbox for so long, and then when I came back I was trying to get back a life that didn't exist anymore, dealing with the thing with Kyle and adjusting to my arm and stuff. But yeah, I think I like babies. Or will, sometime in the future." He tugged on her fingers. "What about you, Jess? Do you like babies?"

There were a lot of things that could upset her today,

but she hadn't expected that that particular question would be the one to set her off crying. But it did. The emotion came up on her so fast she couldn't guard against it. One moment she was looking in his eyes and the next she was weeping, because she wanted things to work so badly and she was scared to hope in case she got crushed again.

Before she could get her emotions under control, his arms were around her. He pulled her into his embrace and then somehow switched positions so he was sitting on the chair and she was in his lap. "God, Jess, what is it?" He kissed her hair and held her tightly. "I didn't mean to upset you."

She wanted to trust him so badly. He was doing all she might have asked of him and more. He'd even taken the step of getting professional help. Rick had dealt with one upheaval after another. She'd tested him time and time again and he'd passed with flying colors. And the one time things had gone wrong, he'd done everything possible to make amends. It was time to tell him the truth. She owed him that.

"Let me up for a minute," she whispered. "I promise I'll be right back."

His arms loosened but didn't let go completely. "You're sure?"

She wiped her face with her palms, clearing away the tears that had streaked down her cheeks. "I'm sure. There's something I need to show you."

She went to the counter, reached underneath, and took out the carefully folded knitted blanket. The yarn was soft against her hands, and nerves—both the excited and fearful kind—raced through her as she returned to the duet of chairs by the window. Only the low display lights were on now, leaving the shop in soft, muted light. She sat across from Rick, the blanket placed neatly on top of her knees.

"You finally finished it," he said softly. "It's beautiful."

"I did. And you remember how I said that when the time was right, I'd know who to give it to?"

"Yes. Is it for Mary?"

She shook her head, terrified to say the words. It would be real then. They'd be tied together forever no matter what happened. There would be no turning back. But there was no turning back for Jess anyway. It was unexpected, it was complicated, but she wanted this baby. He—or she—was already a part of her heart. The life inside her was a treasure to be cherished and nurtured—by both of them.

She picked up the blanket and put it on his lap. "It's for us, Rick. It's for our baby." As his gaze locked on hers, she finally said the words. "I'm having your baby."

"Ours . . ." His gaze snapped to her abdomen and back up. "Jess." He let out a breath and his shoulders slumped a little.

"That first night when we didn't use protection. I thought . . . the dates should have been fine . . . I didn't mean for this to happen."

"A baby," he repeated. His eyes met hers. "You're sure?"

"I'm sure. Josh and I did a test. The day we went to Abby's."

He put a hand to his mouth, swiped it over his chin. "You've known that long? And you didn't tell me?"

This was what she was afraid of. She knew how he

felt about secrets, about going behind his back, especially since that day at Abby and Tom's. She silently prayed to find the right words. "I was going to, but you had so much on your plate. And then everything fell apart—you were upset, and Mike's arrest . . ."

"The night you came over . . . you were going to tell me, weren't you?"

She nodded, the tears back again, and two rolled slowly down her cheeks. "I was worried about you and I wanted to see you, to see if I could help. I thought if you'd had time to cool off, we could just talk about it. And then I could tell you and we could decide what to do."

"And instead I sent you away. Oh, Jess. I'm so sorry. So, so sorry."

"You're not angry with me?"

"For keeping this from me? Considering how you found me that night, how could I possibly be upset? I've got no one to blame but myself."

She blinked and looked down, the yellow blanket on his knees blurry through her tears. "I know it's unexpected, but I want to keep the baby, Rick. You don't have to decide anything now and whatever role you want to take on is okay. I just know that I'm ready, and I'm not afraid of being a mom. Not now."

"Whatever role?" Rick pulled his chair closer and put his hands on her knees. "Father," he said plainly. "Look at me, Jess. Please."

She looked up.

"I told you earlier that I loved you. Do you think that changes because you're carrying my child?" He blew out a breath. "God, that's a huge thing, isn't it?

Life altering." And yet a smile started curving up the corners of his mouth. "You're having my baby," he said again, shaking his head. "It's a damned miracle, that's what it is."

Her throat was so tight with emotion she couldn't respond. Rick's smile faded and he reached out, placing a knuckle beneath her chin and lifting. "I guess the big question is whether or not you love me back. If you can forgive me for what I did. If you can trust me to put you first. I'm not perfect, Jess, but I'll do my best. I'll do what it takes, and that's a promise I can keep. Do you love me, Jess? Because I love the hell out of you, with or without a baby."

She nodded. She couldn't help it. This was the Rick she remembered, only better. Because he'd been through trials, walked through hell, and come through it a little worse for wear but stronger and with a greater appreciation of the good things in life. He'd lost everything he thought was true and still he was here pledging to be there for her and their child. He was, she realized, the miracle she'd often prayed for and never quite believed existed.

"I do love you, Rick. I think I always have, and I think that's what's always scared me so much."

"Don't be scared," he whispered, lifting his hand and cupping her jaw in his palm. "I have a theory. Want to know what it is?"

She waited, on the edge of something so huge she half-believed she must be imagining it.

"We are two wounded souls, you and me. But when we're together all the bad parts seem to melt away. And so you shouldn't be scared, because together we bring out the best in each other. We love harder, stand taller, feel stronger. We accept each other but know what else? We accept ourselves. And that's something I've never really had before."

She put her hand over his. "When I'm with you I almost believe anything is possible."

"It is. I promise you it is. And if you stumble a time or two, I'll be there to catch you."

Jess closed her eyes. This was the hardest part. After having so much taken from her—her independence, her *self*, it was terrifying to willingly give it away. But then she felt Rick's hand leave her face and the warmth of it pressed against her stomach and she had no choice. Her heart was no longer her own, and it was time she trusted it.

"And I'll be there to catch you, too. I promise."

Before she could say any more, Rick slid off his chair and onto his knees in front of her. He cupped her neck in his hand and she cradled his stubbled face in her hands as she kissed him at last. It was full-on, open-mouthed hunger with the taste of victory as they came together. The blanket dropped to the floor and Jess melted off her chair into his embrace until they were twined together on the floor of her shop, making up for lost time. He took little nips at her neck, molded her breasts in his hands until petting was no longer enough and clothes came off in a tangle of arms and legs and fabric.

Jess ignored the hard surface of the polished floor as she lifted her hips and welcomed him home once more. It was only then that their fevered actions slowed and Rick braced himself up on an elbow, utterly still inside her, his gloriously dark eyes delving into hers.

"I love you, Jess."

Moisture gathered at the corner of her eyelids. "I love you, too."

Making love with him had always been amazing but tonight was different. It didn't matter that they weren't on a plush mattress with candles and lacy lingerie and atmosphere. It was different because for the first time ever they'd given themselves completely to each other, heart, body, soul. When Jess cried out goose bumps rippled over her skin and Rick called out her name as he found his release.

Jess was sure she couldn't feel any more complete, but she was wrong. Rick tenderly put her back together, clipping her bra and pulling her sweater back over her head. He reached beneath the collar with both hands and pulled her hair out from beneath the fabric, spreading the curls out over her shoulders as a smile played over his lips.

"What?" she asked, tugging on a boot that had been tossed aside.

"I hope our daughter has your hair. And your eyes."

She melted.

"Well, chances are *he* will have your eyes. That's basic genetics. Brown is dominant."

"Healthy, happy, and with both of us works for me. He could have purple eyes for all I care." He put out his hand and helped her up. "I nearly forgot. I brought you something. I thought I might need an ace up my sleeve."

"You thought you might have to buy me off, is that it?" She grinned up at him, amazed at how an hour could bring such a change and take her from dismal to blissfully happy.

He led her over to the sales counter. "The night I sent you away, I don't think I've ever wanted a drink more. I just wanted to forget about all the pain, but I knew I couldn't, not after how far I'd come. So instead I started this." He opened the top of the shallow box. "I talked to Tom. He said he could fit this into your current door or put it in a new one, whatever you like. Merry early Christmas, Jess."

She stepped up and gasped at the beautiful sheet of glass on the counter. With trembling fingers she reached out and picked it up, the soft glow in the room backlighting the design. Lilacs, tons of them, in shades of purple and white, with delicate leaves surrounding them. It was the most beautiful piece of his she'd seen.

"For Treasures," he said quietly. "For your front door. I thought it would be appropriate for Treasures on Lilac Lane."

"Oh," she said softly, staring at the stunning creation. "It's amazing. You did this for me?"

He looked at her over the edge of the glass. "I did."

Reluctantly she put it back down so she could wrap her arms around his neck. "Who needs a treasure," she whispered in his ear, "when we have all this?"

He squeezed her close. "Will you marry me, Jess? Maybe I would have taken things slower if it weren't for the baby, and I know it seems rushed. But we would have gotten here eventually. I know that as sure as I know I love you. Will you do it? Will you be my wife?"

It was fast, he was right about that. But she'd known him all her life and loved him for probably half of it. "Yes," she whispered, surprising even herself. "Yes, I'll marry you."

He picked her up and spun her around, kissing her jubilantly until she started laughing and squirmed against his embrace.

"Rick, I have ten women coming here in less than an hour to make Christmas ornaments. You have to put me down."

"For now," he murmured softly. "But not for long."

CHAPTER 23

Rick and Jess kept the engagement under wraps for the first few days, but it was clear that they were back together as they stuck together like glue. Everyone seemed happy that they'd worked things out, and so Rick invited Abby to meet up with them at his house to clear up their unfinished business.

He was nervous. He couldn't quite explain why, but he sensed there was something important about that necklace that would change things somehow.

Jess grazed her hand over his back as she passed by him to put a pot of tea on the table. "Relax. It'll be fine," she soothed, and she'd barely said the words when there was a knock at the door.

Abby came in, a smile on her face and a foil-wrapped parcel in her hands. "I made fruitcake!" she announced proudly. "I thought I'd bring you some."

"Fruitcake?" Rick asked, a bit dubious.

"Don't knock it until you try it. It's Marian's recipe."

"Have a seat, Abby." Jess invited her in, taking the cake and Abby's coat. As Abby sat at the table, Jess sliced the cake and added it to the plate of cookies sitting next to the teapot.

They spent a precious few minutes pouring tea, but Abby only took a few sips before getting down to business. She reached into her purse and took out the velvet bag. "This is for you," she said, handing it to Rick. He held out his palm, too surprised to do anything else.

"It is?"

"It's rightfully yours."

He frowned. "I don't understand."

"Rick, you know that Tom and I know you were adopted. When we started digging around about the necklace, something extraordinary came to light. Something I could never have dreamed up in a million years."

Abby was smiling at him. What the hell?

"I need to go back a bit, you see. My great-aunt Marian never married. What most people don't know is that she bore a child out of wedlock. Elijah sent her away to have the baby. The thing is . . . she was told the baby died. But my investigator turned up some new information."

She paused and reached over to take his hands in hers. "The baby didn't die. Rick, Elijah *paid* to make the baby disappear. She was raised by a family by the name of Murdoch—Stephanie Murdoch was a nurse in the ward at the hospital where Marian had the child. The baby was christened Alicia. Elijah set the Murdochs up with enough money to be very comfortable. All the detective needed to do was follow the money trail."

"I still don't see what this has to do with how my mother came to have it," he said.

"The necklace was passed down through generations. Marian passed it on to her child . . . presumably to Stephanie, probably thinking it would be buried with her baby. That baby went on to have a son. In Camden. On June fourth . . ."

"That's impossible." He cut her off as his heart began to pound.

"Marian facilitated the adoption of her own grandchild," Abby said, nodding, "without even knowing it. And that child was you, Rick."

"I'm Marian's grandson?" His voice sounded stunned to his ears. Holy hell, what a thing to try to wrap his head around.

And how sad that Marian had been separated from her own child against her will, and had met her again without even knowing it.

She smiled. "Yeah. All we can figure is that the necklace was given to Roberta to keep for you. And that's why she put it in the safe deposit box."

He sat back in his chair, trying to make sense of it all. "Wouldn't Marian have recognized it?"

Abby shrugged. "Only if she actually saw it. But you know what this means, right? This makes us cousins. In fact, you have more of a claim to the mansion than I do. You're a direct Foster descendant. I'm from the black sheep side of the family." She gave a little chuckle.

"Go figure." Christ, a Foster. Who would have thought it? "Don't worry, I'm not about to serve any eviction notices or contest any wills. I've got my mom's place. That's all I need. Besides, you belong there."

"It does sort of feel like the house was waiting for me," she admitted. "And believe it or not, I'm excited about the news. I thought I didn't have any relatives left. It's kind of cool to realize that we're probably related. Which brings me to one last suggestion."

"Go on," he said, "you're on a roll."

"I thought we could ask Josh to do a DNA test and send it off to a lab. We'd know for sure if we were related then."

It wasn't a half-bad idea. He started to laugh a little and he shook his head. This was so hard to believe, and yet he knew Abby wouldn't ask unless she was sure.

"What's funny?" she asked.

"I was always the odd man out," he replied. "When we were all kids together, I was like a part of the Collins and Arseneault families but I wasn't really part of the family. And now it looks like I'm a Foster and a part of the family anyway—only through you and not the boys. Life sure is a kick in the pants sometimes."

"It's a lot to take in for one day," Abby acknowledged. "Why don't you take a while to think about it, come up with any questions you might have for the investigator. We can dig a little deeper for sure, or let it go, whatever you want. Either way, I want you to know that the necklace is yours, and I hope one day you'll give it to your firstborn, too."

Rick didn't answer, but he met Jess's eyes, saw the happy glow there. Just when he'd thought himself truly alone, he found himself with love. Family. History. Things had been taken away, but he was blessed, too. Blessings that he would never take for granted again.

*   *   *

The Saturday of the Evergreen Festival was chaotic to say the least. Jess was in the workroom, supervising a constant influx of children coming in to make their "Santa's List" holders. Tessa and Meggie were manning the store, which was overflowing with customers—each one carrying a greeting card and collecting stamps. Once all the spaces were stamped by local businesses, the cards could be dropped off for a chance to win a shopping spree at any of the participating stores. An extra stamp was handed out at the chicken à la king lunch at the church hall—and each year the lunch tickets sold out.

Rick was at Treasures, too, helping out. He fetched coffee, kept the hot cider going for the patrons, brought in sandwiches for lunch, and stocked store shelves. His hand-painted candle holders and ornaments were flying off the shelves and every time Jess looked up to see him nearby a warm glow filled her body.

Just for today she wore the ruby necklace beneath her hand-knit turtleneck featuring jolly snowmen. Rick had given it to her first thing that morning, before she'd left his place for the shop. She didn't want a traditional engagement ring—she wasn't really the flashy diamond type—so he'd given her the necklace instead with a promise that they'd have matching wedding bands custom-made.

He passed by her, carrying a box of peppermint soaps and pressed a kiss to her cheek. "You look good around all those kids," he said in her ear, the feel of his breath sending tingles along her neck. "Just be sure you don't overdo it."

"Get going and stop distracting me," she answered, smiling widely. Then Chase Brubaker started dripping glue and she dashed off to divert the emergency.

When the day was over, Tessa went home, carrying her Christmas bonus, and Jess asked Meggie to hang back for a minute. They were sitting with a cup of tea in the workroom, chatting about the success of the day when Jess finally got up the nerve to break the news. "Mom, we wanted you to be the first to know. Rick and I . . . we're getting married."

She'd expected shock. She hadn't expected her mother to grin from ear to ear and clap her hands together.

"It's about damn time!"

"Mom!"

Rick burst out laughing. "She was pretty worried about telling you. I know it's kind of sudden."

"Oh, honey, it's not sudden at all. You two had eyes for each other before either of you hit puberty. Then you just got . . . caught up in troubles and forgot for a while. Those troubles are over, though, right?" She looked sternly at both of them.

"Meggie, troubles are never completely over. But I started seeing someone to help me deal with stuff rather than trying to drink it away. And Jess . . . well, she's the strongest woman I've ever known. We just take it a day at a time and get through it together."

Meggie reached over and took his good hand. "And that's the only way to go through life. I'm happy for you both. I was starting to worry Jess would never get married!"

Jess raised an eyebrow. "Well then, the next news should totally freak you out."

Rick started to laugh and then bit it back. Jess gave him an elbow, but the both of them were smiling like fools when they faced Meggie again.

"We're having a baby. Hope you don't mind being a grandma again."

"Mind? Are you kidding? I'm thrilled! Even though you kind of did things out of order." She waggled a finger at them. "You're feeling okay?"

Rick put his arm around Jess's shoulders and she nodded at her mother. "A little sick in the mornings, but otherwise fine. And Rick's taking good care of me. He's going to make me go home and put my feet up now."

"Darn right."

Meggie's eyes watered. "I wish your dad were here to see this. And your mom, too, Rick. Roberta would have been so happy for you both."

Jess reached out for her mother's hand. The rest of the news—about Rick, about Marian, all of it—could wait for another time. "Now you just have to worry about Josh."

"Don't get me started. He's buried himself in work lately. You'd think he was chief of surgery at some big hospital rather than a small-town GP . . ."

Jess smiled to herself. It would be nice to have Josh be the focus of everyone's concern rather than her. "We decided that we're going to live in Rick's house. It's made for families. Maybe a dog. A little craziness. And Rick's going to use my loft as his studio. The space and lighting are perfect."

"And have you set a date?"

Rick nodded. "Next week, at Abby and Tom's in the drawing room. Just family."

"Next week?" Meggie's mouth dropped open.

Jess looked into Rick's eyes.

"Well," he said softly, his loving gaze locked on hers, "when you find the person you're going to spend forever with, you want forever to start as soon as possible."

Read on for an excerpt from Donna Alward's next book

Summer on Lovers' Island

Coming soon from St. Martin's Paperbacks

CHAPTER ONE

As punishments went, Lizzie Howard could have done a lot worse.

The "recommendation" was for her to get out of town for a few days, and so she'd chosen to visit her best friend, Charlie, in Jewell Cove. Charlie and Dave's home was a few miles from town limits, nestled along a curve in the road and with a cedar deck overlooking the shimmering waters of Penobscot Bay. Gray shingle siding and white-trimmed dormer windows gave the cottage a cozy, worn-in look. The trees and lilacs were budding, unfurling their new spring-green leaves to the sun. At a small, white picket gate was a quaint little sign that read, *Seashell Cottage*.

Lizzie loved it immediately. It was like something off a postcard.

As she got out of her car, she realized that the walkway to the door was lined with shells. She let out a soft laugh. Her best friend was living in an idyllic world far away from the high-class suburb of Boston where she'd been brought up. Charlie's future was looking brilliant, while Lizzie's "charmed" life had fallen spectacularly apart.

But Lizzie pushed the thoughts out of her mind. They had no place there today and she was happy for her best friend. She breathed in the sweet-scented air and smiled to herself, thinking of the shell-studded candles she had in her bag as a delayed housewarming present. Her only regret was that she hadn't come sooner.

Lizzie shouldered her travel bag and blew out a breath, determined that she wouldn't be dragged down again. She'd make the most of the days ahead and recharge her batteries. This was only a weekend, after all. Didn't she deserve that much of a break?

When Lizzie returned to Springfield, it would be time enough to fight to get her job back. This forced leave from the hospital was utter nonsense. If there was a lawsuit, it would be settled, just as they always were. She was a good doctor. Everyone would move on . . .

She was halfway up the shell-lined path when the screen door slammed open and Charlie was there, bouncing on her toes and with one hand on her slightly rounded belly. "You're here! You're finally here! At my house!"

"Yes, I'm here." Lizzie laughed, her dark thoughts banished by Charlie's enthusiastic greeting. "I promised, and here I am."

Charlie came down the stone steps and drew Lizzie into a hug. "Gosh, it's good to see you."

Lizzie felt Charlie's strong arms around her and closed her eyes. It wasn't one of those polite, restrained hugs full of pretension that Lizzie was used to—hugs out of social obligation rather than a real sense of intimacy. This was big, hearty, and full of affection. She could feel the firm baby bump against her own tummy and laughed, drawing back and framing the gentle roundness with her hands.

"My God, look at you. You're beautiful." Tears pricked her eyelids and she laughed self-consciously. "And showing already."

Charlie laughed too, wiping her eyes, then tucked her dark hair behind her ears. "Dave says future linebacker in the making. I'm not due until September."

"He could be right." Lizzie straightened, looked at her best friend, and couldn't stop smiling. "You're glowing, Charlie. God, I'm so happy for you."

Charlie sniffled and beamed even as she flapped her hands at her tears, dragging Lizzie into the house. The inside was as charming as the outside, filled with sunstrewn windows whose light bounced off walls the color of the sand on the beach below. The flooring was wide plank hardwood, stained a gorgeous shade of oak. White country cupboards filled the walls in the kitchen and a stunning butcher block held a bowl of lilacs, bringing the fragrance in from outside.

Lizzie put down her bag and went to the windows. The kitchen overlooked the ocean, the sun glinting almost painfully off the constantly shifting surface. She knew why she was here and it had little to do with birthdays. She was running. Running from her grief and running from her problems, pure and simple. Running to escape truth and inevitability and the terrifying fact that her life felt utterly out of her control.

A lone sail bobbed on the water, skimming parallel

with the shoreline. She squared her shoulders. Not running. Regrouping. There was a difference.

She found Charlie in the kitchen heating the kettle. "Tea," Lizzie said with a smile. A plate held several cookies. "And shortbread. Did you read my mind?"

"Orange spice. Told you. Jewell Cove has all sorts of treasures and I'm going to show you them all tomorrow. We're going to hit all the shops along the waterfront."

"You wouldn't still happen to be trying to sell me on covering your maternity leave, would you?"

Two weeks ago, just before Lizzie'd had news of her "break," Charlie had called asking if she wanted to do a locum. Leaving Springfield right now wasn't an option, not when what Lizzie really needed to do was get her act together. She had a job, a reputation at stake. Responsibilities. Like proving to Ian and the rest of the administration that she was worthy of the faith they'd placed in her. Proving to herself that she hadn't lost her edge. Physicians lost patients; it came with the job. They had to deal with it.

Besides, family medicine in a small town would bore her to death, even for a few months.

Charlie handed over the mug, a saucy grin lighting her lips. "Shamelessly. Is it working?"

Lizzie's gaze caught on a small sailboat slowly making its way around the point, heading out of the bay towards open water. The words on the side were still clear: *Jewell's Constant.* How could she be anything but cheerful when faced with such a scenic picture?

"I don't know where I'd live," Lizzie said softly. "And don't say with you and Dave. No way. I refuse to impose on you two that way. And then there's my mom . . ."

"Not that it would be an imposition, but I already thought of that," Charlie replied smugly. "And as far as your mom goes, it's not that long of a drive. With your schedule, it won't be difficult to visit often."

Lizzie let out a deep breath, really considering the situation. She should have known. Charlie always had a contingency plan, always had her bases covered. Lizzie suspected she'd never stood a chance. Not that she'd truly put up much of a fight. God, she was weaker than she thought.

"Does this mean you want the job?"

"Are you really going to make me ask?"

Charlie's smile was so big Lizzie thought her cheeks might crack. "You're really thinking about it?"

Charlie looked so excited it was impossible to remain immune to her enthusiasm. The idea of going back home right now filled her with dread. There were memories back there too, memories she'd rather not face. Why not give herself a break?

Lizzie threw caution to the wind for the first time in her life. "I can't believe I'm going to say this. I'm not just thinking. I'm offering."

Charlie let out a squeal. "Hot damn, Dave owes me ten bucks. I told him I could do it!"